"I'm not in the market for a dog."

"I'm not trying to sell you anything. Honestly, Mara. Yes, my guide dog is about to finish her training and I am looking to place her. Yes, I think she'd be perfect for you, but she'd be perfect for some other person, too. Is there any way we can make this thing work?"

She moved her hand to the door latch. "I don't think so. Griffin only tolerates me when you're around."

"How about I come along?"

Her blue eyes widened. "I didn't mean—that is, I didn't mean to involve you."

"Listen, you're doing me the favor. Hopefully it'll just be for a few times until he gets used to the situation."

He held his breath. And why was he doing that? He wasn't asking her out on a date. Except they'd be alone together, doing something that would look very much like a date. And he liked that...

Dear Reader,

This story couldn't have happened without help. I relied on the experiences and wisdom of those in the visually impaired community to inform Mara's struggles and victories. My thanks to Derek Ness with the Canadian Institute for the Blind, who spoke to the societal challenges. Special thanks to Victoria Nolan. A powerhouse in her own right, she has retinitis pigmentosa, RP, like Mara, is the mother of two children and has a guide dog. She was a storehouse of emotional and practical knowledge. I also turned to vlogger Molly Burke. Her candid documentaries lent insight into the unique relationship between a guide dog and the handler. It is because of her that Mara too sees "fireworks." Any errors are mine alone.

This completes The Montgomerys of Spirit Lake miniseries. See what's coming at mkstelmack.com. You can also find me on Goodreads, Facebook and Instagram.

Best!

M. K.

HEARTWARMING

Their Together Promise

—

M. K. Stelmack

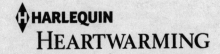

HARLEQUIN

HEARTWARMING

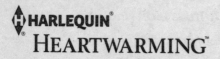

ISBN-13: 978-1-335-42669-7

Recycling programs
for this product may
not exist in your area.

Their Together Promise

Copyright © 2022 by S. M. Stelmack

For questions and comments about the quality of this book,
please contact us at CustomerService@Harlequin.com.

Harlequin Enterprises ULC
22 Adelaide St. West, 41st Floor
Toronto, Ontario M5H 4E3, Canada
www.Harlequin.com

Printed in U.S.A.

M. K. Stelmack writes historical and contemporary fiction. She is the author of A True North Hero series—the third book of which was made into a movie—and The Montgomerys of Spirit Lake series with Harlequin Heartwarming. She lives in Alberta, Canada, close to a town the fictional Spirit Lake of her stories is patterned after.

Books by M. K. Stelmack

Harlequin Heartwarming

A True North Hero

A Roof Over Their Heads
Building a Family
Coming Home to You

The Montgomerys of Spirit Lake

All They Want for Christmas
Her Rodeo Rancher

Visit the Author Profile page
at Harlequin.com for more titles.

To those who struggle with disabilities—and, every single day, triumph

CHAPTER ONE

MARA MONTGOMERY FEIGNED interest as her two sisters stood like performers in front of the fireplace directly across from Mara on the sofa. She hadn't the heart to tell Bridget and Krista that at ten feet away they were still blurry, their matching gray sweatshirts melding them into a cloud. If they were indeed gray, and not brown or blue or orange or whatever other color that her brain now registered as that dull, dull hue.

At the periphery of her vision sat their respective husbands, Jack and Will, on either side of their wives. Sometimes she couldn't tell the difference between them and had to wait for their voices or a little cue. Will, whether he knew it or not, always cleared his throat before speaking to her. Jack opened with a gesture.

Beside Mara, her mother gusted out her breath. "Just get on with it, will you?" She sounded impatient and bored. Did she know what her daughters were about to announce, too?

The seat cushions dipped and jiggled as Bridget and Jack's daughters, Sofia and Isabella, bounced into the room in their pajamas, their hair perfumed strawberry and vanilla. Mara protected her full wineglass with her hand.

Krista-cloud said to Bridget-cloud, "Are you ready?"

They stripped off their sweatshirts to reveal white shirts with dark lettering and pictures. Mara couldn't make out the words, but her mother read them.

"Bridget's says 'Cinna-bun in the oven.' And Krista's says 'Farm help on the way.'"

Just as she thought. In the lead-up to tonight's dinner at Bridget and Jack's house, both Bridget and Krista had laid on the hints. *I'm so tired! So weird, I crave pickled onions! I've decided to give up alcohol.* Their mother must've gotten the same treatment because her surprise sounded forced. "Oh, who would've thought? Congratulations, girls."

The shirt messages were too subtle for Isabella and Sofia. "What? What!" They tugged on Mara's sleeve. She slid her glass onto the relative safety of the coffee table. She would need every drop to get through this happy ordeal. "Bridgie-ma and Jack-pa are having a baby," she said. These were the names the girls had chosen for their parents since their adoption last year. "Auntie Krista and Uncle Will, too."

Sofia squealed and hugged Bridget. She cupped her mouth and shouted at Bridget's belly. "*Hola!* Can you hear me? This is your sister, Sofia. I am six and I will share my things with you." She turned to Isabella. "Your turn. Say something." Instead, her nine-year-old sister kissed the cinnamon bun on Bridget's shirt.

"Congratulations." Mara forced herself to smile. Her facial muscles quivered. She never knew a smile could hurt so much. "When?"

"November!" They said simultaneously. Seven months from now.

"Our due dates are two weeks apart," Bridget said. "Mine is—"

"—on the second and mine is on the sixteenth which means we could have them on the same day."

Her mother rose and wrapped her pregnant daughters in a hug. Wearing a shawl, she was a great gray cloud enveloping white cloud puffs. "I could be a twin grandma." Her grumpiness had given way to teary excitement. Their mother was family-renowned for her emotional swings. Mara, for her lack of them.

"And me a twin auntie," Mara said, trying to make it sound as if it was all she ever wanted. She lifted the wine to her lips, smelled the faint nutty, sun-and-leaf aromas, let the stream flood her tongue, sluicing over her taste buds and trailing, warm and healing, down her throat. That was the thing with wine—you didn't have to be sighted to understand it.

In the middle of distributing her gift of "Big Cousin" shirts to Isabella and Sofia, Krista gasped and spun to Will. "Speaking of twins—you want to tell or me?"

Will waved her on, and Krista bounced as bad as her nieces. "Keith and Dana are expecting twins! In September. I'm going to be a twin auntie, too!"

"Triple," Will said. "Don't forget Laura."

"Right, she's up first in May. A month away! Weeks! Days, if she hurries up."

Will folded his hands across his stomach. "Claverleys littering the place." He spoke as if he'd pulled off the feat single-handedly.

"And there's a shirt for it!" Krista reached into her bag. "'Double Auntie' T-shirt." Soft cotton brushed Mara's empty hand and she took the shirt. In yellow letters the size of a traffic sign, Mara read "Double Auntie premiering November." "I ordered the same one in red for myself," Krista said.

Mara tucked the shirt by her side. "Thank you," she managed to choke out. "I think it's time I topped up my wine."

Once in the kitchen, Mara brushed her hand along the wall and found the light switch. A jumble of shapes. Pots and pans and dirty platters, points of light radiating away. Jack and Bridget insisted that no one help with cleanup because they liked to do it together as their nightly wind-down routine. Sweet, except that the clutter was a potential trap for Mara.

She had no intention of drinking more. Two glasses was her cutoff, especially since her volunteering started in less than an hour at the youth center, but to keep up appearances, she navigated the corners and counters toward the wine rack, depending on her muscle memory from when she'd lived in the house for a few months. That had been more than a year ago. How things had changed. Both sisters now married and pregnant, with good husbands. As for her, no husband, not even a boyfriend, certainly not pregnant. Her world had grown darker and narrower like the aperture on an unfocused telescope.

She leaned against the counter beside the wine rack, the one spot that couldn't be seen from the living room. She'd pull herself together before reentering the fray.

"If you're not having one, I will," her mother said, coming into the kitchen.

Mara tipped the bottle over her mother's empty glass and listened to the glug of the wine, lifting it up in time. She tilted her head to the chatter in the living room. "Did you know?"

"I suspected," Deidre said. "I thought you were in on the secret, too."

"No," Mara said. "I wasn't." She usually was privy to her sisters' secrets. Krista's, especially. But motherhood had changed all that. The oldest and youngest sister formed their own little club of two now. They'd exchange their experiences and stories. Tips about teething and diaper rashes and nursing and sleep schedules. Nothing for her to add. And probably after these babies were born, there'd be more. She'd be an auntie again. Always an auntie, never a mother.

Her own mother leaned close, her shoulder touching Mara's. "This is hard, isn't it?"

No, it wasn't hard. Hard was learning when you were thirteen that you had degenerative vision loss, hard was watching (notice the pun, ha ha) her vision deteriorate year after year, the world closing into a narrow tunnel and then that tunnel losing its contrasts, its depth and brilliance. Even as sounds and smells and textures sprang up to make up for her crumbling vision, like wild plants over an abandoned house.

That was hard. But hard was still doable. She had graduated with her master's and, during the past year, moved from British Columbia to Alberta and built her business as a psychologist. She couldn't drive but she could get around the smallish town of Spirit Lake easily enough, especially in daylight hours. She could have groceries—and wine—delivered. All manner of listening and decoding devices smoothed out obstacles.

Family birth announcements were…fine. If she could process them in her own time and place. If she could curl up on her living room sofa or meditate or play Solitaire Chess.

Or watch her fireworks. Shortly after her father's unexpected death from a stroke six years ago, her vision had worsened. Lights—blue, purple and green—appeared constantly. They spiraled, exploded, rained down…exactly like fireworks. Her specialist had said it wasn't unusual, that she might as well enjoy the show. Their constant activity had distracted and annoyed her at first, but they'd become their own kind of mandala, a focal point when grief threatened to immobilize her. A place of beauty to travel to at any time and from where she could return calm and detached.

She could do none of that yet. But she could go for a walk. "I'm delighted that our little family is growing. Unfortunately, I've got to be on my way. The youth group is tonight."

"You're going to that?"

"I go every Wednesday." She loved the kids. She soaked up their energy, their plans for the future, their playing at adulthood. She could live through them.

And because Connor Flanagan would be there. The other group leader. The guy that made her heart beat as if she were a lovestruck teenager. A stupid, futile crush she couldn't stop, no more than she could stop her blindness.

"Let me drive you."

"Mom, that's your third glass of wine. No."

"Let someone else take you, then."

She most certainly did not want to be confined for any amount of time with either of her sisters or brothers-in-law, pretending to be over the moon. "I prefer to walk. The exercise will do me good."

"Why do you need exercise? You're skinny. And soon enough, you'll be skinnier than all us Montgomerys for a good long while."

Meaning no chance Mara would get pregnant, not being in a relationship. She'd never told her family that relationship or not, she'd never have children. It seemed irrelevant, obvious. Like announcing that rain was wet. But it grated that her own mother assigned her the role of family spinster, because mothers tend to reflect societal perceptions.

To hide her annoyance, Mara corked her bottle and edged into the living room to say her goodbyes. "But it's getting dark," her mother called after her.

Of all the things to say on this day. "It's been getting dark for most of my life!"

Voices died away. She could feel the heat of

her family's gazes concentrate on her. Lovely. She'd ruined her sisters' joy. She could think of nothing to say or do to repair the damage. Except to leave.

She held aloft the bottle. "Since you two won't need this," she said to her sisters. "I'm off." The room remained quiet.

Her coat. Where was it? "Isabella, can you get my jacket, please?"

Jack stood. "I'll give you a ride."

Would they all just stop? "I've got the youth group tonight. I'll walk."

"You sure?"

"Yes. I'm sure." Isabella pressed Mara's sheepskin-lined coat into her hands. "Thank you. Congratulations, everyone."

She fumbled with her coat. Something was stuck in the left sleeve. The double-auntie shirt. "I put it there," Isabella whispered, "so you wouldn't lose it."

Protective, thoughtful Isabella. Mara felt a shot of resentment toward the niece who every other day she adored. She shoved the detestable shirt and the bottle into her bag and hustled for the door, not trusting herself to say something that wasn't petty or self-pitying.

Outside in the cool air of late April, she snapped together her extendable white cane.

Tap, tap, tap to the top of the stairs. She bet every single one of her family was staring through the front windows. Let them look. At least they could.

It was animal floor hockey. The dozen or so kids were divided into two teams, Bears versus Penguins. Half were on all fours, trying to use a stick with their front foreleg, while the birds waddled about with bands around their ankles to restrict their motions. All wore helmets with face guards at Mara's strict insistence.

Judging from the shouts and raps of sticks and squeaks from runners on the gym floor, along with the occasional play-by-play called out by the kids, Mara had scored big with this activity. The teenagers could cut loose for the evening, released from the usual pressures at home, school and, for a few, work. They were misfits one way or another. They didn't participate in Spirit Lake's massive sports programs. They weren't academic achievers. No musicians or inventors or artists here. She'd been the same when she was their age.

A figure broke from the fray and walked over to where Mara sat on the lowest bleacher. Talia Shirazi. One of the oldest at sixteen, she was usually in the thick of whatever was happening, sorting out conflicts, organizing, strategizing. She'd shown leadership, a true talent, but tonight she dropped to the bench beside Mara.

"Taking a break?" Mara said.

The metal seating shook as Talia gave a quick one-two stamp to dispense with her ankle band. "I'm not feeling well."

"Where is it hurting?"

Talia gusted out a sharp breath. "Everywhere. And nowhere."

"My mother calls that being 'out of sorts.' Would you like to go home?"

"Not really."

Was everything okay with her parents? Mara had met them a few times—busy, professional types who doted on their only child. Perhaps too much. Mara suspected Talia was a regular here because she was free to squirt whipped cream, get mummy-wrapped in toilet paper, sing opera off-key. One night a week where she could be less than perfect.

Mara could relate. But no. At the doors to the youth center she'd promised herself not to surrender to any more self-indulgent thoughts or behaviors. She pressed her fingers to her temple and focused on Talia. "Any plans for spring break?"

"We're going to Mexico."

Mexico. That brought back memories of brightness and color. Mara had traveled there with her parents and Krista when she was a kid. Back when she could see almost as well as everyone else. When she'd run and not worried about crashing into things and people.

No. Stop with the boohoo, poor you. This was not her.

"That'll be nice. Loads of sun and beach and water."

"I guess. But it's practically spring now. We have sun and beach and water here."

Talia sounded cranky. Mara dived to the heart of the matter. "You'll miss Dane."

"I don't know. I guess." Yes, something was amiss between them. They'd been dating for nearly a year, their relationship growing steadily more serious. A breakup now wouldn't be fixed with a good cry into a pillow.

Beside them, the double doors rattled, the metal handle snapped down. A ripple of energy passed through the kids. "It's Dog Man!"

Connor Flanagan. The gym floor thundered as the kids moved as one to him and his three dogs. The board on the bench vibrated as Talia, too, joined them.

"Whoa, guys. Thanks for the big welcome. Oh wait, it's the dogs you want to see." His laughing words in his easy tenor rolled across the room and right into her heart. Every single time this happened. Mara made out a jumble of dogs and kids, and the tall, solid shape of Connor. She assembled the sounds. The faint drop of knees on floor as some kids got eye level with the dogs, the jangle of collars as canine necks were rubbed, a yip. That would be the year-old pups. These were therapy dogs-in-training, and this was their downtime. To come and mix it up with the kids and give the kids opportunities to touch and cuddle with warm beings when the humans in their lives were harder to access.

Mara was navigating her way over, when her cane encountered something narrow and long. A hockey stick, abandoned in the rush to meet Connor and his dogs. She picked it up and straightened. Connor had appeared in front of her. When she'd explained the nature of her vision loss to him, he'd immediately adjusted to center himself in front of her pinhole vision.

"You found the stick before I could get over," he said. Had his voice dropped, become more intimate? No. She had a crush on him, not the other way around, as much as her heart might manipulate her into thinking so.

"Dogs trump safety," Mara said.

"They shouldn't," he said, annoyance clipping his words. "Hey," he said in a louder voice. "Who turned their stick into a tripping hazard?"

Three pairs of feet suddenly broke away and pounded to different points of the gym floor, followed by the scrape of lifted sticks.

Another pair of feet ran to her. "Sorry, Miss M." That was Bryson.

She handed him the stick. "Next time be more careful. You don't want Mr. C falling flat on his face." She refused to call him Dog Man. The kids had nicknamed him after a fictional canine detective popular in upper elementary grades. Even after Isabella had explained the reference, Mara couldn't bring herself to pin him with that flat descriptor. He was so much more than a man with dogs.

"I don't think that—" Bryson broke off. "Are you making a joke?"

Bryson had difficulties figuring out the subtleties of jokes. Or even why people would bother to make them in the first place. Normally, she would assure him, but tonight, double auntie-hood made her a little unhinged. "Not a bit. I have my cane, but Mr. C is on his own. You need to put yourself in his shoes."

"He's not wearing any."

So that was how he'd sneaked up on her. "And the dogs?" Mara said to Bryson. "Are they wearing any shoes? Or did they take them off, too?" She injected a light tone into her voice, a clue to Bryson that humor was… afoot.

"Uh. I can tell you that none of them have shoes on now." He tapped his stick on the floor, quick and nervous. "I'm going to put away the stick."

Connor reappeared in her vision. Close. His wide mouth with its perpetual upturn at the corners. The blue eyes radiating warmth and good humor. That was Connor Flanagan. A force of energy and lightness. But right now, a frown had appeared. "Are you all right?"

During the year she'd known him, mostly chatting at the youth group, he'd never asked her that. The conventional "How's it going?" and "Life treating you okay?" but not this intimate concern. "Of course."

"It's just that you sounded a bit off with Bryson."

"I was showing him different ways to look at the same thing."

"Except he comes here not to have to deal with those challenges," Connor said.

He was criticizing her. She must not take it personally that the man her irresponsible heart bounded after should question her logic. "Perspective gets us through the challenges."

"So does alcohol," he murmured.

Did he smell wine on her breath? Had Talia? She hadn't drunk anything in nearly two hours. The bottle was stowed under her coat in the kitchen off the gym.

She better come clean. "I had two glasses earlier. Our family was celebrating."

"Yeah?"

Here was her chance to declare how absolutely thrilled she was with her freshly updated status. She raised her eyebrows and her voice, to exude excitement. "I'm going to be an auntie. Again. Twice over. My sisters are both expecting in November."

Connor's eyebrows shot up as high as hers. Was he faking it, too? "Whoa. Congratulations." No, he did sound genuine. From the way he mixed it up with the kids, he had a clear affinity with the young.

He touched her elbow and a zing shot up her arm. "We'd better move off to the side, or between the dogs and kids we'll take a header."

Once on the lower bleacher, Connor stretched out his legs in front of him and leaned against the row behind him. "The day I heard I was going to be an uncle was the second-best day of my life. The best day was when he was born, of course." There it was. Connor Flanagan, family man-in-waiting and the reason she'd never act on her crush.

Mara forced herself down a more useful line of thought. Dane was Talia's boyfriend and Connor's nephew. Connor lived with his sister and Dane a few miles out of Spirit Lake. He might know if the two were going through a rough patch. She leaned toward him, an excuse really, since no kids were close enough to hear their conversation. She breathed in Connor's shower soap, the cool flavors of the outdoors, the muskiness of his dogs. "Are there—" Her voice sounded too high, as if drawing in Connor was like sucking on helium. She cleared her throat and tried again.

"Are you aware of any problems between Dane and Talia?"

"No. Why?"

"I talked to Talia earlier. She's upset about something, and I think it involves Dane."

"I can talk to him."

"Don't, please. Because if he's the problem but doesn't know it, then he will ask her and I'm sensing she needs some space."

"One of the dogs is in her space right now," Connor noted. "Resting her head on Talia's lap over at the other end of the bleachers."

He made a low tongue click to the roof of his mouth. It signaled he was thinking to himself. She stayed quiet. Let him have his space, too.

"Griffin!" Kids were calling one of Connor's dogs. She felt his soft, thick body suddenly wedge between them.

Mara touched Griffin's head with its mixed hair, short and long, soft and coarse. He allowed her touch but she felt his subtle shift toward Connor.

"What's with you, Griffin?" Connor said. "You like to play. Now's your chance." To Mara, he said, "He loves people but he doesn't always know how to deal with them."

Mara leaned forward until she was on

level with Griffin's long snout and brown eyes. Connor had once described Griffin as mostly German shepherd, black with brown and with the occasional lick of white. Right now, all she saw was gray brown and gray black. "Hello," she said softly. "What's the matter? You want a piece of Connor, too?"

Too. That made it sound as if she also wanted Connor. "Everybody does," she added quickly. She didn't dare look up, worried she wore her emotions on her face. Griffin allowed her to scratch behind his ears and pet his head, tolerated the long strokes down his spine, but he kept his body angled to Connor.

When she felt confident her heart was shoved back into place, she remarked, "He's a one-man dog."

"Unfortunately, that's a problem," Connor said.

She stroked Griffin behind his whiskers. "Why? Have you given your heart to another dog?"

His gaze beat down on her. "Many dogs."

Wasn't that the truth? She'd visited his website. Excessively so. *Flanagan Dog Academy. We repurpose dogs.* His site described how he trained dogs for therapy and search-and-rescue, ran obedience classes, and as his "pet" project took in strays and unleashed their potential before matching them to forever owners and releasing them back into the world. A canine heaven on earth.

It also mentioned the launch of his guide dog program, a subject neither of them had broached. The guide dog was their white elephant in the room.

Her phone chimed to let her know it was the end of the evening, and she allowed the alarm to escalate in pitch to penetrate the squeaks and shouts and dog barks. The dogs obeyed first, gathering around Connor. The kids were next, Talia arriving last. On Connor's command, they all heeled, including the dogs.

Sensing more than seeing the curve of kids in front of her, Mara instructed them to put away equipment and to come next week when, weather permitting, they'd play Frisbee baseball outside. Once Mara and Connor had closed the door on the last of them, he asked, "How about I drive you home?"

Every week he asked her the same question as if it were the first time—with a bit of uncertainty, almost shyness. It always made her heart do a little flip. And every week, she pretended to inject surprise as if she hadn't come to expect his offer. "I'd love a ride home. Thanks."

She detected his smile in the easy sway of his next words. "Griffin still needs to learn to give up shotgun if I've got passengers." Passengers. A girlfriend, perhaps? He'd never mentioned one, but why would he? And what did it matter if he was seeing someone? She and Connor had no future together.

CONNOR PARKED HIS long-box SUV outside Mara's town house and spoke before he lost his nerve. "I have a favor to ask."

Griffin stuck his head between the front seats and panted like he'd run a mile in the sun, effectively blocking Connor's view of Mara.

"Go back with the others," Connor ordered. Griffin looked away, as if he hadn't heard. The brat. Connor stiffened his voice. "Back." Griffin retreated.

Griffin would've obeyed immediately if Mara wasn't there, but he seemed to consider her a rival. No, not quite that. As someone he needed to keep an eye on. As if Mara might cause trouble.

As if.

When she'd told him in her quiet, steady

voice about her vision loss, he'd sat in this same cab seat after dropping her off and looked up retinitis pigmentosa. Hereditary. Often diagnosed in childhood. Degenerative. Can lead to total blindness. He'd learned enough to have more questions. Did she have the recessive or dominant gene? What was her prognosis? What were her plans? Was she scared? How could he help?

He'd dwelled on this last question the most. He wanted to help her because, well, that was what he did. He might've walked away from his police career but he couldn't suppress his innate drive to serve and protect. He was like the dogs he trained.

But to be truthful, he also couldn't suppress how he felt about what she was doing right now.

She tilted her ear to him, presenting the curve of her cheek, as if priming for a kiss. She often did this around him, and more than once he fought the urge to give her one. He'd held back because she'd never indicated interest. Until tonight. *You want a piece of Connor, too?*

He pivoted his attention back to Griffin. "It's our buddy here. I'm convinced that he would make someone a great companion, but he's stuck on me."

"Why not keep him, then?"

"Because dogs are my business. Kind of like how cattle are a rancher's business. He deserves a home, not a business."

"If you're suggesting I take Griffin, I can't. I don't want a dog."

Griffin inserted his head between them again. Connor ordered him back. "He's hypersensitive to his name. He expects to be included in the conversation."

"I think if he could be," Mara said, "he'd take my side."

Her reaction didn't surprise him. She clung to her independence like a burr to a dog. "It wouldn't be a permanent move. That would be too much for Griffin. I was thinking an afternoon here or there. Maybe you two go for walks."

"I don't trust us on walks, Connor. Or the backyard. I only moved here last month, and I don't even trust myself alone in the place, much less Griffin who doesn't really want to be with me."

"You live by yourself?"

Not that her home status was any of his business, and she let him know that by a stiffening in her posture. She touched her bag and her pocket. Checking that she had everything. "Yes."

Her fingers slid down the sides of the wine bottle between her thighs. Would she finish that off tonight? He knew all too well where that led. It'd taken him a good year of his life to dig out of that hole before he'd switched to the dog training division of the RCMP and then struck out on his own. Dogs had saved his life, and they'd save Mara's, if she let them.

"Look, Connor. I know where you're going with this. You want me to get used to Griffin, we become buddies, and then you graduate me to a guide dog. Isn't that what you're driving at?"

He'd never mentioned the guide dog side of his operation to her, because he didn't want to mix business with how he'd come to see his time with Mara—pleasure. She must've discovered it for herself, which meant she was interested in him. Or at least, and more importantly, his dogs. "I'm not in the market for a dog," she went on. "I don't want to be responsible for any living creature. Not a fish, not a cat and especially not a dog."

That didn't make sense. Reaching out to

the hurt and lonely, those trying to get their heads together, was her life. She wasn't made to be alone. His eyes slid to the half-empty bottle, her hands still around it.

"I'm not trying to sell you anything. Honestly, Mara. Yes, I have a guide dog about to finish her training and I am looking to place her. Yes, I think she'd be perfect for you, but she'd be perfect for some other person, too." Empty words, a lie even. While training Daisy he'd thought of Mara often. A single drop of an idea about how suitable the two were for each other had swelled into what was now a steady current in his mind.

"Look, I'm not so blind—" Mara gave a short bark of laughter "—as to think that I won't need to consider other options someday. But not now."

She'd slapped him down. In his peripheral vision, he saw the liquid shine of Griffin's eyes fixed on him. A one-man dog, Mara had said. Griffin had come to him as a rescue pup a year ago, when he was six months old. A brilliant animal, he'd resisted training. Stubborn like Mara. "Is there any way we can make this thing work?"

She crawled her hand to the door latch. "I

don't think so. He only tolerates me when you're around."

"How about I come along?"

Her blue eyes widened. "I didn't mean— that is, I didn't mean to involve you."

"Remember, I'm the one asking for the favor. Hopefully after a few times you two will be best buddies."

He held his breath, as if he was asking her out. They would be alone together, doing something that would look very much like a date.

Mara's hand caught the door latch. "Sure, that sounds fine. Text me and we'll set something up."

He waited, as he always did, while she unlocked the door to her town house, the process complicated by her hold on the bottle. The door opened and she turned to wave at him—as she always did. A wedge of light spilled onto her pink cheeks and light brown hair.

Griffin repossessed the shotgun seat, and panted a grin at Connor. "Don't get too comfortable, boy. You're taking a back seat the next while."

CHAPTER TWO

"YOU READY FOR the stairs, Daisy?" Connor had a firm hold on the Lab's guide harness as they stood at the bottom of the flight of stairs in the house he shared with his sister and nephew.

A ribbon of tension traveled up the harness into his hands. He would have to explain to Mara how to detect that when she took over. Because she would soon enough. Once he and Griffin showed her the advantages of dog ownership.

He placed his foot on the bottom step, and Daisy followed suit with her paws. She'd learned to watch Connor's feet as her signal to proceed forward. He continued upward, deliberately slowing his step. Sure enough, by the fifth step, Daisy was tugging on the harness, eager to gallop up the stairs, following the instinct of all healthy dogs to take an incline as fast as possible. Connor felt the same way himself. He stopped, tightening his hold. "Slow."

She obeyed, but her attention had shifted to the top of the stairs. It should be on his feet. He switched commands. "Ready."

Only when they reached the top did he discover the source of Daisy's disobedience. His sister was observing their progress from the upstairs railing.

Again Daisy tugged, this time for a pet from Kate. "Sorry, girl," she said, "you know the rules. No pets from anyone except the one holding your harness."

The tension in the harness remained. "Don't address her," Connor said. "That's giving her mixed messages."

"But that's realistic. People are going to address her, and depending on where she ends up, she might have a whole family talking to her even if they don't touch her."

"True." Mara would have a family of all ages to deal with. "You know of any babies I could borrow?"

Kate lifted a brow. "I suppose I could make off with a great-grandbaby." She worked as a nurse at seniors' living. "Why do you ask?"

"It would round out training is all," Connor said. He hadn't told Kate about his long-term plans for Daisy. He was unsure himself why he was fixated on placing Daisy with Mara.

"I'll let you know if anything comes up," Kate said. She scraped her bottom lip with her teeth. "Hey, I've been meaning to ask. Has Dane talked to you lately?"

"No, I missed seeing him before he left for school." They lived seven miles out of town and rather than taking the bus, Dane drove Connor's old truck.

"I met him on the road back from my shift." Kate was working nights this week. "I usually get to have a bit of breakfast with him before he heads out. But today, he barely had time to stop. He said he was meeting Talia for breakfast at Tim Horton's."

"That's good."

"You sound relieved."

How much could he tell without betraying Mara's confidences? Or was there anything to tell? He was a foreigner in the territory of romance. None of his relationships had lasted as long as the yearlong one between Dane and Talia. At some point he'd bring up the subject of family and the women would be off like a shot. His rotten luck to always get involved with women who viewed a kid as a ball and chain. "Because you brought it up as if there's a problem."

"I don't know if there is or not. I've caught him staring at his phone as if waiting for a message, and when a call comes, he races off to his room. Usually he takes calls from her when I'm around. Now he's become all secretive. Do you think he's found someone else? Do you think he's—" Kate broke off, looked away.

Cheating. Kate's thoughts would go there. Five years ago, she'd discovered her husband was having an affair. She'd confronted him and left, but not before the jerk had drained their joint bank account. Connor, six months dry and about to launch his business, had moved in with her to help out with expenses and to have the space for his kennels on the acreage. They'd fallen into a comfortable enough arrangement, neither of them having taken on a serious relationship that might've crowded the place.

"I think," Connor said softly, "you know your son better than that."

Dane was nothing like his father, couldn't abide the man who accounted for half his DNA. Kate straightened. "You're right, but something's up. Would you—would you mind talking to him?"

Exactly what Mara had asked him not to do. But maybe if he came at it from the angle of Dane's strange behavior rather than Talia's, his nephew might open up. "I'll try."

"All right then. I'd better get ready for work. I plan to stop at the grocery store after my shift. Anything you want?"

"I'm going in later. I can do the shopping then if you want."

"You're going in?"

Connor kept his voice casual as he said, "In a bit. I'm meeting up with Mara. From the youth center. She offered to help me socialize Griffin."

Humor sparked Kate's eyes. "Griffin needs counseling?"

"He's a mess. Obsessive, stubborn, demanding. I only hope it's not too late for him. We'll begin with walks. I'm there to translate."

Kate leaned against the railing and Daisy rose to try her luck again with inducing a pet. "You like Mara and you are using Griffin as a way to get close to her."

"Sit," Connor said to Daisy and then turned to Kate. "I like Mara. It's more like I'm using her for Griffin. I want Griffin to start bonding with other people instead of me."

"Or do you want Mara bonding with you instead of other people?"

There was that, but he wasn't about to tell his sister. "We're just friends."

"Uh-huh. Tell that to Mara."

"What do you mean?"

"Remember when I came by that one night to give Talia a lift home?"

Connor held a vague memory of the time and shrugged.

"You were chatting with Talia, and Mara was staring at you as if you walked on water."

He dipped his head, petted Daisy's fur, the color of ripe wheat. "You're just saying that. She's made it clear that she likes her independence. And I can't say I blame her."

"I'm only saying that she likes you, too." Kate pushed off the railing and headed to the top of the stairs.

Daisy made to follow her, and Connor pulled back. "First, doors. We need to practice opening and closing them."

And he'd have to decide how far he wanted to open a door with gentle, wise Mara. She'd cracked one already with her comment on wanting a piece of him and now with Kate's little story—maybe he'd kick it wide-open on their walk today.

THE LAKESIDE WALK with Connor and Griffin in the late afternoon should've felt natural and pleasant, but Mara could barely contain her frustration, the sense that the world around her jogged along while she stumbled about, as if in clown shoes.

She usually kept to a slower pace, her cane sweeping in front of her, allowing for the fraction of a second to adjust her footing for a bulge in the sidewalk or the skateboarder cutting close in front. Griffin had dragged on the leash, stretching Mara's shoulder to the max. Connor had repeatedly commanded Griffin to heel but in the end had taken over, which defeated the entire purpose of the walk.

It didn't help that this was also the busiest time of day on the popular walkway as couples and families absorbed the last hours of daylight before hurrying home. With Griffin and Connor on the grass side of the sidewalk, Mara took the center, which meant that whenever anyone approached she had to step behind Connor quickly because she didn't sense them until the last possible moment.

Conversation consisted of Connor's commands to Griffin and her distracted comments.

"Who knew a walk could be so stressful?" Connor said. He must mean her edginess, because he didn't sound stressed. Like with the kids at the youth center, he acted as if there was no place he'd rather be.

"I usually come at lunchtime," Mara said, "when everyone is at school, or eating or shopping. Only joggers and seagulls then."

"The fewer the people, the happier you are?"

"The fewer the people, the lower the risk of collisions. The light is the brightest then, fewer shadows."

"Are you really worried about that? You seem so good with the cane, and most everyone I've seen today makes an extra effort to give you space when they come close."

People always did, but they weren't the problem. She was. "It's a sensory thing. It's hard to explain but I pick up on the air around me. If I feel the wind and every sound spins away, then I know I'm in an open space. If I hear leaves or trees creaking or even feel a change in temperature, I know I'm closed in. And if I concentrate, I can pick up on where people are, how crowded things are. A bit like echolocation. But if I'm talking and walking, things get trickier."

A weight slammed into Mara's legs. She froze. It was a toddler, flat on her bum at Mara's feet. Her giant hair bow had slipped over one eye. With the other eye, she stared up at Mara, her eyes wide, her face scrunched into the prelude to crying.

The mom swooped in, set the toddler on her feet. "You're fine. Next time watch where you're going." She turned to Mara. "Sorry about that."

The mother stood with the sun behind her, a fuzzy blob in a diffused halo. "It's all right," Mara said. That didn't seem like enough to say. "I'm sorry, too."

The blob seemed to wave and pass on in pursuit of her toddler but Mara couldn't move. She'd always taken such care around kids, ever since the episode last winter. A week, two weeks could go by without her thinking about what she'd done. What she hadn't done. But one little setback, and she was thrown right back into the same state of stunned helplessness. This was why she couldn't have children. She was a menace around young kids. How could she ever take care of her own?

Connor filled her vision. "Shins bruised? Would you like to sit? There's a bench up ahead."

She knew the bench. She often sat there to think, to feel, to deep breathe, to watch the fireworks in her vision play out against the reflected light of the water. She preferred to do it alone.

"Griffin is already champing at the bit. I don't think he would approve of us coming to a full stop."

"He might not approve, but it does him no good to get his way all the time."

Which Connor seemed to be used to getting, for in no time, they were all parked on the bench with Mara in the middle, Connor on one side and Griffin on the ground at her right knee, the leash chafing lightly across her legs. Griffin attempted to cross over to Connor, but Connor ordered him back. The two faced off, and Griffin unexpectedly yawned.

"He doesn't care what you think," Mara surmised.

"He does. That's him submitting."

In an act of sideways defiance, Griffin jumped up on the seat beside Mara, the leash now abraded across Mara's middle. His slobbery jaw was at her eye level, his curvy tongue flapping from his pants. His breath smelled like grass and kibble. "I'd like to see when he misbehaves."

"If you want him to get down, tell him," Connor said. Compared to Griffin's, his profile was far more pleasant to look upon. He smelled much better, too. His usual shower soap and something woodsy. She could breathe him in all day long.

She gave herself a mental shake. "Griffin, down."

Griffin looked in the direction of squawking seagulls and stayed put. It was exactly what Sofia did when bedtime was announced. "Is that dog for 'I hear you but I don't hear you'?"

"You can't let him get away with it."

"I thought the point was for Griffin to bond with me. He won't if I'm always bossing him around."

Connor dug into his jeans pocket and squeezed a hard, small block against her palm. A doggie biscuit. "Bribery?" she asked.

"A reward. Try again."

She held up the treat and Griffin pivoted to her hand. "Griffin. Down."

He jumped to the ground and sat, snout in line with her hand. She held out the treat and felt the graze of his lips and teeth as he took it.

"Honey and flies and all that," Connor said.

"I thought you said that it does him no good to get what he wants," Mara said.

"To get what he wants *all* the time," Connor said. "He still has to sit until we're ready to go."

Which was when? She had spent far too long preparing for this outing that wasn't a date. She'd tried on half a dozen different outfits, redone her makeup twice and performed more hairstyles on herself than Krista did on her clients in a month. They sat with their arms brushing against each other, looking to all the world as if they were an item. Or was that wishful thinking? She could edge away, now that Griffin had vacated the spot.

Or she could pretend it was no big deal and sit tight. "What got you into the business of repurposing dogs?"

Connor scrummed his foot on the gravel. "Trained with dogs on the force. After I left, I worked with them at a rescue place. Socializing them enough so people would take them. I got into all aspects, took extra training myself, and seven years later, here I am."

"There's the police dog training center south of here. Are you connected with them?"

"Not anymore."

Mara had found in her work that the shorter the answers, the deeper the issue. But Connor Flanagan's psychological health was not her business.

"Do you like dogs?" he said. "I never asked. I assumed."

This would be the perfect lie. She could say they were tolerable, she preferred cats and geckos, and that would stop him from pursuing his attempt to warm her up to guide dogs. But perhaps she shouldn't do her own kind of assuming.

"I do, except for guide dogs. Why are you so intent on getting me one?"

He laughed. Not his usual rollout of genuine amusement, but a short, embarrassed one. "My sister wondered the same thing."

Mara understood that people talked about her blindness. She just wished that wasn't the only thing that they came up with. Had he also told his sister that she ran her own business and had traveled on four continents? "And what did you tell her?"

"I couldn't give her much of an answer." He cleared his throat. "I guess I don't want you to be alone."

Heat crawled up her throat and across her

face. She must have turned brighter than her rosy scarf and matching capris. It hurt that he foresaw a solitary existence and that the best she could hope for was a guide dog to ease the loneliness. Never mind that he was likely correct; it wasn't his place to make those assumptions. She opened a gap along the bench between them. "How about we agree that you can repurpose dogs but not me?"

Connor sighed. Griffin circled past Mara and tucked close to his favorite person. "I'm sorry, Mara. That came out wrong. It's the way I think. It's the business I'm in. I crossed a line and I'm sorry."

He was trying to make her life better. Their lives intersected at the youth center, and it wouldn't do for any awkwardness to hang between them. Now that he'd made it clear that he wasn't romantically interested in her, she could set her own record straight.

"This is the thing," she said. "It's not that I aspire for lifelong solitude, but neither will I pursue relationships at all costs. I'm not opposed to a roommate or…a…life partner, for that matter. But the dynamic therein typically evolves into the expectation for the standard family unit—" Connor was frowning in concentration. Krista once said that something was up with Mara when you couldn't understand a word she said. "I'm not ever having children."

"You don't like kids?"

"I prefer other people's kids, rather than my own."

"Fair enough."

She couldn't tell if he was buying it, but she already dealt with too many gray areas so she expanded. "I don't want kids because I'm blind, okay? And don't tell me how lots of blind women have had kids. I know that for some it's an option. It's just not one for me."

"Are you worried about them having RP?"

"No. It isn't generally inheritable that way. I could take a test to determine that probability, at any rate."

Connor shifted in his seat, about to press the point. She cut him off. "I lost my niece."

He stilled, and she pressed on. "She didn't die. But I physically lost her. This was a year and a half ago before my sight took this latest decline. I was babysitting for just a few hours and she disappeared on me. My sister found her on the roof. It all ended well. But I didn't even know that she'd disappeared. She'd walked right past me and I didn't see her."

"Kids do that to even the sighted," he said.

"But you can see to find them. You can climb a ladder to get to them."

"You could climb a ladder."

"I lost depth perception years ago. I could climb a ladder but if I'm putting myself in danger, then I'm not really of much help to anyone I'm rescuing. That whole idea of putting on the oxygen mask first on the plane, right?

"The point is, that was a close call that I don't want to experience on a daily level. A dog is no different. Its life depends on me, and I can't guarantee its safety. In fact, quite the opposite. I refuse to take on that responsibility. I appreciate that you've thought of me, but that's where I stand."

Connor didn't answer right away. The tags on Griffin's collar jingled as Connor scratched his neck. So much for making Griffin bond with her.

"You said 'before this latest decline.' Can I ask what this means?"

"RP is different for everyone. Some lose their sight entirely by age eighteen, most feel it dribble away. With me, I lost a lot in the past two years…and I don't know when or if it'll stabilize. I'm already legally blind in my left eye and my right isn't far behind."

"And there's nothing you can do? No operation or anything?"

"Supplements. Vitamin A, mostly. I pop them every day for what it's worth."

"Oh." He cleared his throat. "Tough news."

"I hear worse on YouTube," she said lightly, to make him feel better and because it was the truth. "But can we agree that you give up on this whole guide dog thing for me?"

He hesitated and then said, "Agreed."

Good. Things were settled now between them. Except that she didn't feel the least bit better, and their largely silent walk back to her town house didn't improve the situation.

Connor opened the passenger door to his truck and Griffin jumped in as if it were the last seat on a lifeboat off a sinking ship. "Whoa," Connor said. "Don't get used to it. We'll be doing this all again in a few days."

"We will?" Mara expected that she'd only ever see Connor at the youth center.

"Aren't we?" Connor countered. "Now that we got the rules of engagement in place, it'll go easier. Plus, Griffin had fun."

Hadn't Connor heard a word she'd said? He wasn't giving up. She'd fallen for his sunny, easygoing ways, but he had a stubborn streak a mile wide.

She could flatly refuse him. But where was the fun in that? After a couple more outings, she'd prove her point and he would admit defeat.

"Sure. We'll do this until Griffin falls in love with me."

So long as she didn't make the mistake of falling even more for Griffin's owner.

CHAPTER THREE

"HAVE A SEAT," Mara said to Talia, indicating any of three mismatched pieces of furniture in one corner of her office. There were two beanbags—a wide red leather one that crinkled and squeaked every time the occupant so much as twitched and a lumpy blue cloth-covered one straight from a college dorm. There was also a stool with an uneven leg. Nobody stayed on that one for long.

Abigail Shirazi had contacted Mara to book a counseling session for Talia. She and her husband had noticed their daughter's recent withdrawal. "Our goal is to identify the source of her anxiety. She has become uncommunicative, which is uncharacteristic, and although both my husband and I, separately and together, have attempted to open dialogue with her on various occasions, we have…have failed."

Mara wasn't alone in hiding emotions with fancy language. "I should make you aware of my policy," Mara said. "I won't share any discoveries with you unless I believe that there's a personal safety issue for her or for those she's in contact with."

"But are we not paying you for information?" the mother had asked.

"You are paying me to counsel your daughter."

"And how are my husband and I to counsel her if you refuse to share your discoveries?" Sarcasm laced the word *discoveries*.

"I would request that you maintain confidence in the process. Your passive participation at this juncture will hasten a successful outcome for everyone concerned."

There was silence on the other end of the line and then, "Talia herself requested this session with you. Future sessions will be determined as required."

Mara appreciated for the first time just how annoying the habit of overstating was.

Talking should go easier with Abigail Shirazi's daughter, who was gazing around Mara's large open office. "This looks like a furniture showroom." Her attention drifted to the corner where the treadmill and exercise ball and box of sports equipment were. "Crossed with a gym."

It did, in a way. Mara had inherited the space above the restaurant belonging to Jack and Bridget from Aunt Penny a year and a half ago. It was many times larger than a conventional office space, and so Mara had unleashed her imagination on the place, creating "rooms" to accommodate the different ages and needs of prospective clients. A round mahogany dining table with chairs before the bank of windows. Armchairs and a couch before a fake fireplace. The rec room area with the beanbags.

Mara pointed at the bar fridge in the adjacent gym area. "Please help yourself to a drink."

As Talia dropped into Lumpy Blue with a can of carbonated water, Mara sneaked a close look at her. The girl wore the same baggy hoodie as she had the two previous weeks at the youth center, and shadows ringed her eyes that hadn't been there last week. Whatever was wrong had robbed her of sleep. Mara sat on a wheelie chair Krista had found online for her. It was checkered black and white, good contrasts, she'd said. She subtly rolled closer to Talia.

Talia cracked open her water and downed several gulps before breaking off. "You talked to my mom."

If that exchange worthy of an aristocratic parlor could be labeled talk. "Yes, your parents feel you're troubled by something. But I understand that you requested the meeting?"

"Yes. Yesterday. Yesterday was Mother's Day, you know?"

It had been a rambunctious affair at Jack and Bridget's house featuring her mother and Bridget receiving flowers and chocolate. Even Krista had. Mara had privately thought she should deliver the goods first, so to speak, but saying so would only make her appear sour.

"I guess I'm going to have to talk to somebody about it." Talia crackled the can. "You can't tell anyone what I say here, right?"

"There are limits to our confidentiality. If you tell me something that will likely cause harm to you or someone else, then I am required to pass it along."

"Physical harm?"

"Typically yes. Are you concerned that

what you're going through falls into that category?"

Talia shook her head, shrank further into her hoodie, then blurted, "I'm pregnant."

"Oh."

Talia frowned. "You don't sound surprised."

Mara was surprised. Not at Talia's sexual relations. Given that she and Dane were teenagers and the length of their relationship, it was almost expected. But Talia and Dane seemed to be responsible. Hadn't they taken precautions? "It is unexpected, and the unexpected happens in life."

"Okay." Talia sounded deflated at Mara's response. Perhaps she was looking for...a little more warmth.

Mara tried again. "How are you feeling?"

Talia buried her face in her hands. "I don't know what to do."

Mara had meant physically, but it was telling that Talia cared more about her mental distress. "There's a lot to think about," Mara agreed.

Talia dropped her hands to her lap, only to start picking at a frayed cuff. "I only found out for sure fifteen days ago. I've looked at options online. I know what they are."

"Oh?"

"I go to an abortion clinic, I give the baby up for adoption, I keep the baby."

That covered the bases.

Talia looked at Mara with pleading eyes. "What do you think I should do?"

Oh no, not going there. "I am here to discuss your choices, not make them for you."

"Yeah, I got myself into this mess. I need to get myself out."

"I don't know that it's a solo journey. Have you talked to Dane?" At the youth meeting last night, Connor quietly told her that he'd had a chat with Dane at his sister's behest but Dane had only said that Talia was acting "weird."

Talia wormed deeper into Lumpy Blue. "I can't. It's my fault. We were so careful, but one time he didn't have a condom and I said it was okay because I was on the pill, but I must've slipped up. Not taken them on schedule."

"You're afraid he will be angry with you."

"He thinks I'm angry with him, and that's why I'm not talking to him. Only he's the one who'll be angry."

"That will be his decision."

"And a good one. I'm angry with myself, so I'm sure he will be with me." She sucked in her breath and said in a rush, "He'll break up with me, I know that for sure."

So there it was. Pregnancy as loss.

Talia wasn't the first teenager Mara had given pregnancy counseling to. There were already good community services elsewhere in place for Talia, but right now she could be the familiar adult figure with no skin in the game.

"A part of me thinks I should go to the clinic, get it done, and he won't ever have to know. I could, I'm only nine weeks in."

Two months. Like her sisters. "You're due in November."

"Yes. But then I think to myself that it might be my decision but Dane has a right to know, doesn't he?"

"Would you feel personally safe telling him?"

Talia's eyes widened. "Do you mean do I think that he would hit me?"

"That's one possibility. Or harass you. You mentioned anger. How far do you think he would take it?"

"He might yell at me, I don't know. I'm not sure he would even do that. Once he got in a fender bender, and it was the other guy's fault. Dane asks me if I'm okay, which I am. Then he gets out and the other guy starts shouting at Dane, but Dane doesn't even blink. Takes down the license plate, takes a few pictures. Agrees with the guy and pretty soon the guy is apologizing. He could do your job," Talia said.

Dane must've inherited Connor's equanimity. "I've let him down." Talia drew her knees up to her chest and dipped her head so all Mara could see was the girl's black hair, black leggings, black socks with her hoodie clouding around her. "Mom, Dad. I've disappointed everybody."

The dutiful daughter had strayed from the path. "Again, that's up to them," Mara said. "You have your own feelings to deal with right now. Your own decisions to make. Have you told your friends?"

"No." Talia's voice was muffled. "I only have two friends I'd even consider telling because they might be able to keep a secret. Neither of them has a boyfriend. They wouldn't understand." She lifted her head. "But you think I should tell Dane."

"If Dane is as calm as you describe—and

from what I've experienced with him, I would tend to agree with you—then you could consider bringing Dane into your circle of two."

Talia uncurled from her ball, taking the form of a young woman again. She pulled out her phone. "I'll call him."

Mara started. "I didn't mean now."

"But then you're here, so all three of us can talk."

"I think that Dane and you should have your own private discussion. Though it can be in a public place. On a walk or even at a playground. You two are the parents and that relationship is very special."

Talia jumped to her feet. "I'll talk to Dane tonight."

And once Dane knew, Connor wouldn't be far behind. And if she knew Connor at all, he'd want her to keep the baby. And that would only complicate matters for Talia. Mara rose with her. "I suggest you give it twenty-four hours. Let your decision feel whole and solid within you. Nothing will have changed."

"Okay." Talia bit her lip. "You won't tell Dog Man, will you?"

Mara cringed inwardly at the moniker. "Confidentiality applies to everyone." She could've left it there, but silence as much as gossip fed rumor mills. "He and I are casual friends only."

Talia frowned. "Really?"

"Really."

Talia gave herself a shake. "All right then. What do I know about relationships, anyway?" She gave Mara an unexpected hug. "Thanks. Talking to you was like talking to an older sister."

Mara could relate. If she'd ended up in Talia's predicament, she would've wanted to go to her sisters. Or would she have? It would've only made things more painful when there was no option of keeping the child.

Mara gave Talia the best professional advice she could. "Take care."

Her sisters would've said the same.

CONNOR SCHEDULED THE next Griffin walk with Mara at the dog park during the quiet of mid-afternoon. This way, Mara wouldn't have to negotiate any obstacles and Griffin could have the free run of the park. He'd also brought along Griffin's favorite squeak toy for Mara to play fetch with. He hadn't taken into account that Mara threw like a four-year-old. It also didn't help that he'd forgotten she wouldn't see where the ball landed. His learning curve for her blindness had its own curveballs. He and Griffin wouldn't win her over if he couldn't put himself in her shoes.

"I left my throwing arm at home," Mara said as Griffin trotted off to retrieve the ball she'd thrown maybe twice the length of his truck. Griffin brought it back to Connor. "I don't blame him. He's trying to improve the quality of his experience."

Connor wiped Griffin's spit on his jeans and handed the ball to Mara. "He needs to see that he can get twice as many throws this way."

Connor tried to suppress his disbelief at where Mara's next lob landed. "It's gone underneath the garbage can," Connor said. "I'll go get it. It's not far."

Mara touched his arm. "That's not your problem. It's Griffin's."

She was right. Griffin was on it. Driving his snout into the space between the bin and the ground, he was gnashing his teeth to grip the ball.

"He just might do it," Connor said.

"He strikes me as very persistent," Mara

said. Her voice was muffled behind a scarf. The downside to having chosen the dog park was that on the far westerly side of Spirit Lake, the winds blew straight across the open field, cold enough to scour skin even now in early May.

"We'll give him a couple of minutes and then we can head back. I didn't expect it to be this cold." He couldn't expect her to continue these dates—these training sessions with Griffin—if wind or toddlers roughed her up.

"I don't mind waiting, and I can stay warm," Mara said, and broke into jumping jacks. Automatically, he began counting aloud. It gave him a reason to watch her. She had a smooth grace, her motions more of a sweep and touch, no slapping of hands and thighs. She stopped at fifty.

Griffin returned to Connor and barked. "What's up? Go get your ball."

Griffin ran to the bin and sat. "He's sitting by the garbage," Connor reported for Mara's benefit.

"Looks as if you're his solution to the problem."

Connor thought of a twist. "How about you go get it for him?"

He expected resistance, but Mara walked the thirty or so feet in the direction of the bin, sweeping her approach with her white cane. If she had Daisy, she could trust that she'd get there the safest way possible. Although he'd agreed not to raise the subject again with Mara, he hadn't given up on finding a way to change her mind.

At her destination, Mara retracted her cane and bent to the task. The ball was on the other side. He was about to call out but stopped. This was Mara's problem. Like with Griffin, she could find it or call on him to help.

Even if he was nearly vibrating with his need to help her. Griffin was, too, and began whining softly.

"Where's your ball, Griffin? Where is it?" Mara asked. Griffin circled the bin to where it was. He began scraping at the ground. No ball would be left behind. Still crouched, Mara followed his whines, her hands patting where Griffin had dug. Connor held his breath.

"Here? Is it here?" Griffin sat and Mara reached underneath. Then she held it in her palm for Griffin. Did she see his single tail wag of thanks? He took it nicely from her and then trotted over to Connor.

"Did he go to you?" Mara said. "He totally deserves a real throw."

Connor was about to let fly a long throw when he caught sight of Mara's small smile of triumph. She knew that the ball search would frustrate Griffin, proving she was right that Connor should be the one throwing the ball. A trick of her trade, to let the person discover their mistakes. Except mistakes were opportunities to become better.

He hucked the ball as far as he could. It disappeared over a small hill, Griffin in full pursuit, his paws skimming the ground. Hopefully there wasn't another garbage bin.

"You made Griffin one happy dog," Mara said.

"The object was for you to connect with him, but you knew it wouldn't work out, right?"

She tipped her cheek toward him, and as irritated as he was, he still thought the exposed bit of skin above the scarf was very kissable. "Could I have said anything to convince you?"

A blast of wind speared Connor's back. He hunched his shoulders. "I suppose not. I admit I have a hard time taking no for an answer."

Griffin surfaced onto the hill, ball in mouth. He took them in but sat. He'd often do that. Sit at a high point and sniff the air. "Griffin's hanging out on the hill ahead," Connor filled Mara in.

"He likes to know where you're at, but keeps his distance," Mara said.

"The job of a psychologist."

"Or a police officer."

"It's why I made such a poor cop."

"I doubt that," she said softly.

Maybe it was her vision impairment that allowed her to stare at him without blinking, but coupled with her tone, Connor found himself unloading on her. "At first it was easy enough to do the right thing. But I realized later it was death by a thousand cuts. It was the kids that got to me the most. That's not unusual, you know. I'd see the same ones over and over again, and each time they had fallen a little bit more."

"Drugs?"

"Yeah. Some kids, they smoke pot at age eleven and just keeping doing it. Others move on to the heavier stuff. Every kid in high school knows who to go to for drugs. I wasn't there to practice politics, but it was tough."

"I've had my own experiences working with kids," Mara said. "It is tough."

Connor felt a surge of sorrow, of missed chances. "I wish I could've connected you with one of them. A teenager. A little younger than Talia.

"She was a dealer, and she had our respect on the force in a way. She kept herself clean, polite. She carried nothing on herself. Smart.

"Smart but not strong enough to overpower males. After a while we could see that she was pregnant. I tried asking her about it, but she closed down on me. She denied she was pregnant. We brought along a female officer, thinking she might relate better to her, but that backfired. It was the only time she blew up at us, at her specifically. Said that just because she was female didn't make her a mother. I should've clued in at that point. But I didn't. She kept dealing, and she threw our pamphlets about the pregnancy center into the dumpster. Told us to save them for someone who actually was pregnant.

"One night in February, I'd been checking on her. I'm back from Family Day. The holiday a former premier instituted, when his own son tried to traffic cocaine. She was in her usual place. Dealing. But she'd had her baby.

"I asked her where the baby was. She said she didn't know what I was talking about. That there was no baby. She said it with her old politeness but it had another quality. Vacant. I threatened to take her in. I had nothing on her and she knew it. I asked her if she had medical help. She kept on telling me, 'I am sure I don't know what you're talking about.' Extra polite, like a servant in a historical drama or something. She looked past me, past the rec center arenas where she dealt, out to where there were bushes. I finally gave up and was halfway back to the station when it hit me. My partner and I turned back, and I followed her line of sight right back into the bushes.

"I found the baby wrapped in a T-shirt, in a plastic bag from a convenience store. Frozen solid."

Beside him, Mara took his hand. "There was nothing I could do. I couldn't arrest her, because there was no proof it was hers. She'd always denied the baby. Remember me telling you she was smart.

"There was an investigation, of course. But

she disappeared. That's what I heard, anyway. I left the force. I took stress leave, but it wasn't good enough." He didn't want to tell her everything. What happened afterward was not as important as the reason behind where he ended up. "I kind of went into a bad place for a while, too. I had to accept there was no going back. And that took me a long time. Even now, I have a hard time letting go of things, people I care about."

He was as much as confessing he cared about Mara. He glanced at her, but she didn't seem to have heard him. She looked out across the park to the field beyond. Like Griffin. What could she see exactly? If he could see the world through her limited vision, he could help her so much more.

"So you would advocate for a teenager to keep her child?" she said at last.

"I would not advocate for her to give birth and leave the baby to freeze to death."

"Yes, killing a child…is especially horrendous," Mara said. She sounded distracted.

"I don't get how she could deny even being a mother."

"She was right about what she told the police officer. She proved that giving birth didn't make you a mother, either. She made an awful choice, but she probably had her reasons."

"You sound as if you're on her side."

Her distant gaze pivoted to him. "Who knows what she was thinking? Maybe she intended to keep the baby or drop it off at the pregnancy center. Maybe she gave birth and changed her mind. Maybe she honestly didn't think she was pregnant—the mind is an incredible storyteller—and somebody else took her baby to the bushes."

"I guess we'll never know."

"No. We won't. The only thing we can do is try to be there for others."

"That's why I'm at the youth center. I can't help them, but the dogs seem to work a certain magic."

Her eyes flashed above her pink scarf. "Perhaps it's because the dogs don't judge the kids."

Her hint for him to let go of that terrible memory. He had, for the most part. But he had held on to the important lesson of not giving up on someone in need. He wouldn't press the point now. He'd already unloaded enough on her. "Why do you go?"

"Because I find that on occasion they'll talk to me when they'll talk to no one else."

The soft hope in her voice had him suddenly taking her hand. "I wish you'd been there for that girl. I bet she would've talked to you."

"I wish I'd been there for her." She paused. "And for you, too."

He squeezed her hand before letting go. "It was enough that you were here for me today." And it was. He had a handle on his issues. He knew when to let go and when to hang on. He wouldn't let Mara down.

CHAPTER FOUR

DANE BROKE THE news of Talia's pregnancy to Kate and Connor over breakfast. Kate had been all smiles that Dane had lingered at the table instead of rushing to school, but Connor had to rescue the coffeepot from her loosening grip at his blunt announcement.

"It's due in November."

"The baby," Connor said automatically. "The baby's due in November."

Kate took her seat gingerly, as if she feared the chair might break. "Is this why you haven't been yourself lately?"

"I wasn't myself because Talia wasn't herself," Dane said. He stared at his eggs, twirled the fork and pushed his plate back. "I can't believe it. She showed me the pregnancy stick to prove it."

Connor poured a tall black coffee and set it down in front of his nephew. "Drink up."

"But I don't like coffee."

"You will come November when you've

been up all night with the baby. Might as well get used to it now."

Kate glared at him, and Dane looked away. What had he missed? "Talia's not sure if she's going to keep it—the baby."

Connor gripped the coffeepot handle. "What kind of garbage talk is that? Of course she's going to keep the baby. Don't you get a say?"

"Connor!" Kate said sharply.

Connor couldn't back down. Silence, avoidance, regard for boundaries were not options. "You have a right to tell her how you feel. You can't stay quiet and let her make the decisions."

"I don't know how to feel, okay?"

"You don't know how to feel? How about you wait until November and hold your baby in your arms. Then you will know how to feel. I remember exactly how I felt when I held you."

And the other baby he'd held years later. Stone-cold.

Kate slammed her hands on the table, jolting Dane's plate of eggs. "Connor, you need to back down. Nothing is going to change in the next few days." She knew where he was coming from. Drunk one night, he'd spilled what had happened, why he'd left his RCMP career. Kate had told him that night that he was not responsible for what had happened, made him repeat it until a tiny part of him accepted it as true. She said it again now. "You're not responsible. This is not your decision to make."

That was the frustrating part. He could never make things better if no one listened. "Could you at least tell her that we—" he waved his hand between Kate and himself "—would welcome the baby?"

Kate bowed her head. "That comes off as us pressuring her to keep the baby. And that again is not our call to make."

"But you kept me," Dane said to his mom.

"Yes. Your father and I also got married. The decision was easier."

"Are you saying I should marry her?"

Connor had minded his business for nearly a minute. Long enough. "Yes."

Kate pinned Connor with another glare hard enough to leave burn marks. Griffin must feel the same when Connor nailed him with a look for his misbehavior. Except unlike Griffin, Connor was right. An image of Mara eyeing him above her scarf rose from his half-filled coffee cup. *Don't judge, let it go.*

Not in this case. Connor topped up his coffee. "What do Talia's parents think?" He'd met the mother a couple of times when she'd picked Talia up from the youth center. Well-dressed. She and her husband owned a real estate company. Talia was their only child, their princess. Connor suspected they thought Talia could do better than Dane. In the year of dating, not once had they invited Dane to their place for dinner, a movie, anything. Like Dane might wander out of Talia's life if they ignored him long enough.

"She hasn't told them yet. She told me first. Well, actually she told Ms. M first. Talia's parents arranged for her to have a session with her."

Mara knew and hadn't told him at the dog park yesterday. For confidentiality reasons, which was fair enough.

"Ms. M's advice to Talia was to tell me."

Good advice, but if Talia hadn't wanted to tell Dane, he doubted Mara would've pressed her. She would've given in to Talia, just as she had respected the girl's choice that ultimately led to the death of a baby. He could accept Mara's stance about the girl from long ago, but they were on a collision course in this case, because there was no way on earth he was giving up on his own flesh and blood.

"What was Mara's—Ms. M's advice to Talia about keeping the baby?"

Dane picked up his phone as if the answer would appear. When he was Dane's age, he looked to his dad. Connor never felt his role as a father figure for Dane more than he did now. "I don't know. Talia didn't say. I don't know that Ms. M said anything. She went over options is all."

Would Mara's personal stance about not having children mean she'd advise Talia to give the baby up for adoption or—the other? Yes, Mara was a professional, and would work to keep her own feelings separate, but he'd registered her quiet look of terror at the thought of being a mother.

Mara might influence Talia to give up her baby. He'd have to make sure that Talia explored all her options. He owed the little body in the snow that much.

"Is now a good time?" It was Jack Holdstrom, Mara's brother-in-law. He was unfolding himself from his SUV, the Penny's Restaurant logo on the door. Griffin had started barking as soon as the vehicle turned in, sending four other dogs inside the kennels into a backup chorus. When Connor recognized the visitor, he ordered Griffin to heel, the others falling quiet as well. Griffin was a natural leader.

"Anytime is good," Connor said, crossing the open yard to meet him. He meant it. He and Jack had graduated from the Spirit Lake high school the same year, though the closest they'd been was when their headshots had appeared in the same row among the one hundred and forty-two graduates in the annual local newspaper. Jack had been far more popular than Connor—in high school and after. They'd both lost a parent when they were young, and then their second when they were adults. Not exactly the strongest of connections, and their lives had branched even further. Jack was married and an expectant father.

"I hear congratulations are in order," Connor said. "Mara tells me you're due to be a father and an uncle come November."

"She told you?"

"The day you announced it, about how she was going to become a double auntie."

"Really? Well, that's good." Jack sounded wary, and a little surprised. Had Mara reacted differently with her brother-in-law than she had with him? Mara had proven herself quite capable of disguising her feelings. He'd planned to talk to Mara during their volunteering last Wednesday but she'd ducked out early to keep an evening appointment with a client. He'd get a straight answer tomorrow at the youth center.

"That's sort of why I'm here," Jack said. "Bridge and I had talked about getting a dog, and then with the baby coming, we decided to move the date up a bit. I was wondering if you had a dog that might work for us."

Jack glanced down at Griffin where he was pressed against Connor's leg. "I take it he's off the table."

"You wouldn't want him," Connor said. "I'm trying to get him more socialized." He stopped, realizing. "I guess Mara might've mentioned him to you."

Jack shrugged in confusion.

So Mara hadn't told Jack about their walks with Griffin. She who shared all kinds of stories about her family with him. Did that mean she thought their time together too special to share with her family? Or not special enough?

"She's helping me with Griffin. To make him more of a people person." Despite their dismal outing last week, Mara had agreed to try again, though he suspected she was humoring him.

"I can't think of anyone better suited to the task," Jack said. "She has a talent for keeping us civil. There's a family joke. Whenever any of us have to make a decision we think, 'What would Mara do?'"

"I know what you mean," Connor said. He thought he'd spoken neutrally enough, but Jack shot him a quick assessing look.

"I take it you've undergone her treatment?"

Connor thought of her probing questions about his police days, about how she'd guessed he was trying to force a bond between her and Griffin. "In which she asks uncomfortable questions and then waits for you to bumble out an answer?"

Jack laughed. "Exactly. She was all over us with the dog. Maybe because she'd been out with you and Griffin. Asking us if now was a good time. Was it fair to the baby? Was it fair to the dog? Would we have time for the dog after the baby was born?"

"Those are good questions. Do you have answers for them?"

"We told her that we have a nine-year-old going on fifteen who's willing to help, we've got the summer coming up to help us all adjust, and we're planning to get a dog, not a puppy."

Connor liked the answers. They were thinking of the dog as a family member and not a toy. But he couldn't resist asking, "What did Mara say?"

Jack laughed. "She told me to come see you."

"Really?"

"She's probably hoping you'll talk us out of it."

Connor would, if necessary. He prided himself on matching the right dog to the right people. When he didn't sense compatibility, he refused to release his dog. He'd made disgruntled customers, but just as many understood where he was coming from, and had happily put their names on a waiting list. And his list was long enough to cover all the dogs-in-training.

To let Jack jump the queue wasn't best business practices, but there was no harm in letting him look. "I feel as if I already know your family through Mara. Come on, there's someone I'd like you to meet."

Jack fell into step beside Connor as they walked to the kennels. Griffin nosed the ground ahead, searching for who knows what. "I'm surprised. She talks about nobody to us.

I understand about her clients, but she doesn't talk about her personal life, either. Bridge and I kind of wondered if she had one." He grinned at Connor. "Apparently, she does."

Was he insinuating that they were dating? Connor didn't mind the misconception, but Mara might. "We're not dating, if that's what you're getting at. What I know about you guys is mostly through our chats at the Wednesday youth meetup. And the couple of times we've gone on walks with Griffin. Here we are."

The kennels were housed inside the giant tractor and large equipment shed that used to belong to Connor's father. When Connor moved out to the acreage, he'd renovated it into a boarding and training center for his dogs. He opened the side door for Jack, though Griffin was the first to push in. There were whines, barks and claws scraping steel gates as dogs pressed to be let out.

"Oh wow, this is a nice setup here," Jack said, looking around. Connor copied him, trying to see the place through his eyes. A bank of metal kennels and pens, a rubberized gymnasium with hurdles, steps and platforms. He spotted a stray dog toy, and his mind shot back to the hockey stick Mara had nearly tripped on. He'd have to be more diligent when he invited her out.

When?

"Thanks," Connor said. "I'm a little late opening the kennels. Here, I'll let out the one I'm thinking of for you. The Claverleys from up the road brought him over when he showed up at their place about a month ago. A nice little dog, but I already have three with the same personality."

The instant Connor opened the gate, out shot a black-and-white bundle in an ecstasy of tail wagging, darting to greet Connor and then Griffin and back again. "He's got a streak of border collie and something else that keeps him on the smaller size. But as you can see, he craves contact."

Jack crouched and he promptly came to him, his head lowered in submission. "Hey, boy," he said. "What's your name?"

"I've avoided giving him one," Connor said. "I let the new family decide."

"The Claverleys brought him over, you say? Will and Krista never mentioned anything, but then again, a month ago we weren't looking for a dog."

"It was Will's dad who brought him. I think

he might've kept him, if they hadn't already just gotten another one."

While Jack roughhoused with the adoptee, Connor opened the rest of the kennels, the dogs falling over one another, Jack and Connor. Griffin remained aloof. A few of the more gregarious ones came over and he sniffed necks and rears with one or two, but he didn't engage in their games, his attention solely on Connor. His attitude might change if Daisy were about, but Connor had left her in the house to get her used to being home alone. Her training would continue, even if Mara had refused to adopt her.

"There are a couple of others," Connor said, returning to Jack. He gave them their due when Connor introduced them, but his attention quickly drifted back to the Claverley donation. "I'm kinda stuck on him."

"Don't blame you."

"Where do we go from here?"

This was where he should tell Jack about the waiting list. But his gut told him that the Holdstroms were the stray's forever family. He also liked the idea that Mara would get a dog in her life, even if it wasn't hers. "Bring out the family to make sure everyone is on side. If it's a match, he's yours."

Jack kissed the dog smack in the middle of the forehead. "Whoa. Did I just kiss a dog?" He shook his head. "Funny how things change. A couple of years ago, my only goal was to get back to Canada. Now I've got my wife, the girls, a baby on the way, a dog soon enough."

"Things can change on a dime," Connor said.

Jack quieted. "You'd know it," he said softly. He knew that Connor's father had died suddenly. A heart attack while driving a bulldozer. Connor had been three weeks away from graduating.

Connor said. "You'd know it, too."

Jack shifted on his feet. "I have another dad. Biological. You heard that Penny was my biological mother?"

Mara had explained the connection. "He from around here?" Connor asked.

"I don't know. I have no idea who he is. The birth certificate says 'unknown' under father, but my gut says he is. I intend to find out. He's the missing piece to my family."

It could also cause all kinds of problems. "What did Mara say?"

If Jack noticed that Connor sounded like one of the Montgomerys, he didn't let on. "Bridge and I haven't told her. If getting a dog triggered an hour-long interrogation, imagine what a search for my dad will do. I just feel a part of me is missing. And it's for the baby, too. Bridget has no biological family. Maybe cousins she doesn't want to know. She's happy with the family she's got, but I'm not. I want to know, and I want to give the baby as much family as I can."

"Not a bad goal," Connor said. "If you can't forget what happened, then best to work on remembering it."

Jack raised his eyes to Connor's. "Yeah, that's it."

Connor experienced the same kind of satisfaction he'd once felt during his early days in the force when he'd made somebody's life a little easier. Cleared up the wrongs and confirmed what had gone right. He had done it, and for a relative stranger. But unlike in his old job, this was for a stranger he had a connection with. Through their dads, a dog... and Mara.

CHAPTER FIVE

"I GUESS WE know why Talia hasn't been herself the last while," Connor said to Mara as he took a seat beside her on the gym bleachers. Connor's dogs were mixing it up with the kids, with Griffin barely tolerating the masses, a stiff brownish shape sitting a ways off. She didn't blame him. It was mayhem out there—rolling, wrestling kids, jumping dogs, barks from dogs and humans alike. "Looks as if November is going to be a busy month for both of us."

Had Talia decided to keep the baby, then? They had scheduled a session next week to discuss the options. Nothing, so far as Mara knew, had been settled. "I realize that it was me who brought up Talia's off behavior but since she is a client now, I can't talk about the situation."

"So I heard." His response was uncharacteristically cool.

"Are you annoyed I didn't tell you?"

"I don't have a problem with why you didn't tell me. You've done nothing wrong, Mara."

Now she experienced a flash of coolness. "Glad to know you approve. I was worried." She aimed for bland sarcasm to cover up that it was the truth. She had been worried, which wasn't healthy. Mara represented Talia's interests. That she cared what Connor thought was not professional or relevant.

And then he nailed it on the head. "But my opinion shouldn't matter, right?"

"I was being sarcastic."

"Don't be, Mara. It's not you."

As if he knew who she was. They'd known each other for a school year of weekly evenings minus holidays. Yet he presumed to know her. Just as he presumed to know what was best for Talia and her baby. Connor had said that it took him a long time before he could accept what had happened to the dead infant. She seriously doubted he ever had fully. Talia was case in point.

"Excuse me," he said. "I'm going to check in with Talia."

"Don't," Mara said. "You don't have the right to pressure her into your way of thinking."

"Hey, I'm a volunteer here. And I've made

her and Dane spaghetti and meatballs at my house. I think I have the right to talk to her."

He moved off across the gym, transforming into a grayish fog. He crouched beside another figure next to the fuzzy form of Griffin. Talia, likely. Connor had absolutely no business, no business at all luring Talia down a path that was hers alone to take. Mara was tempted to tap her way over and intrude on their conversation.

Well, why couldn't she? Talia had likened her to a sister and while she was far from that, neither did she have to stand idly by. And Talia remained her client, in and out of the office.

Talia looked up first at Mara's approach. "Hey, Ms. M," she said. "Dog Man says we should do a field trip out to his place."

It was a good idea. She'd thought of wrapping up the program next month with a barbecue at the lake, but at Connor's kennels would be more fitting.

And that was all Talia and Connor would talk about tonight. She lifted her whistle to her lips and let off a long, ear-piercing blast, all her growing irritation channeled through the tiny metal slot. "Let's clean up, everyone, and then into a circle. Time to talk about our year-end party."

The kids shouted their approval and began charging about, Talia included. Connor straightened. "Well played," he said quietly before moving off to gather his dogs.

But any victory fell to the wayside when he approached Mara as the last kid left, Talia getting picked up by her mother. "How about we take Griffin on an outing now? Since we're all here."

"What about your other dogs?"

"They can come with. I'll take them, you take Griffin."

"That didn't go so well last time, if you remember."

"The sidewalks will be quiet."

"You'll have to walk them all back."

"I'm not called Dog Man for nothing."

"I hate that name," she blurted. "Aren't you more than your dogs?"

Connor handed Griffin's leash to her. "Walk with me and find out."

She was on the point of begging off but then Griffin gave a soft whine of anticipation. He'd heard talk of a walk, and as usual was eager to make it happen. She couldn't disappoint him.

And Connor knew it. She took the leash. "Well played."

The dogs on new territory contentedly sniffed at signposts and patches of grass, slowing their progress, which suited Mara as she used her cane to detect tripping hazards. Tension hung between them, broken when Connor said, "I am not going to stay silent on the subject, Mara."

If he couldn't, then neither would she. "Past events compel you to speak, Connor. But you can't project what happened to you and another girl under different circumstances onto Talia. It's not fair."

"It's not fair for Talia to know that Dane's family would welcome her baby? How do you figure that? You will enjoy being an auntie twice over. Why can't I enjoy being an uncle? Especially if I'm willing to take on more responsibility than you will."

Mara's phone rang. She peered at the screen. Talia's mother. She indicated to Connor that she had to take the call and handed him Griffin's leash.

Abigail Shirazi lost no time getting to the point. "Talia has come home quite upset. It would seem that Dane's uncle spoke to her and is pressuring her into taking a specific course of action. Talia had wanted to come to the center to escape for a while, but from what she says, he approached her and began hounding her."

There was an eruption from Talia but Mara couldn't make out what was said. Still, the girl's distress was clear.

"I'm genuinely sorry that happened," Mara said. "I will speak to Connor about the situation." Indeed, she would.

"I don't appreciate his influence over my daughter. Please convey to him that he's not to contact her in any way."

Mara bristled. Connor might have overstepped his bounds, but Talia's mother was reacting as if he were a predator. Which would only open a schism between Talia and Dane.

"Might I make a suggestion about Connor, Mrs. Shirazi?"

Connor, who'd stepped discreetly away when she took the call, returned into her focus at the mention of his name. As she'd hoped. She wanted him to hear what she had to say next. "How about we have a family meeting with everyone involved? You, your husband, Dane's mom and Connor. And of course, Talia and Dane. There, everyone can present their views without Talia feeling ambushed, and I will moderate."

Connor nodded his agreement with the plan. Mrs. Shirazi told Mara to hold. It was Talia who came on the line. "When can we meet?"

Connor was smiling when Mara got off the phone. "There," she said, "did you get what you wanted?"

"A chance to say how I feel," he said. "Thank you." He leaned forward and for a bizarre moment he seemed about to kiss her cheek. Then he righted and reached around her to untangle a leash.

Of course he hadn't meant to kiss her. "How about we set all talk of Talia aside, and enjoy the rest of our walk."

He handed her Griffin's leash. "I'm all yours."

His voice had dropped into soft intimacy. Their fingers brushed as she took the leash. Inconsequential contact, but her hand tingled, as it had when they'd briefly held hands at the dog park. The almost kiss, the soft voice, the touch…was he proposing more than friendship?

Except this family-loving man never could be hers. Griffin had a greater claim than she ever would. She was the peacemaker in his family, and given the chaos he'd created, that was enough.

MARA USHERED DANE'S AND TALIA'S families into the "living room" area of her office, the tension among them all suddenly constricting the usually roomy space.

Talia's parents sat together on a hard cushioned sofa, dressed in sharp creases and stylish patterns. Sparks of light glinted from Mrs. Shirazi's jewelry and from Mr. Shirazi's large gold ring. Opposite them, Kate Anheim sat in an accent armchair that had one leg a smidgen shorter than the others. If she came forward too hard, it would thump down. Mara debated warning her but she looked comfy there, still in her scrubs after coming off shift. Connor had forgone her range of other comfy chairs to take up a beige stool that Mara had meant only as overflow seating. Well, let him be uncomfortable. He had no trouble making others feel that way.

Talia and Dane sat together on a love seat, the worn cushions tilting them toward each other. Mara herself often chose it when she wanted to relax between sessions. She brought her fold-up chair adjacent to their couch, close enough to hear Talia's every breath, every swallow, every fidget.

The room quieted and Mara began. "I'm sure we've all come here with our separate agendas. That being said, I represent Talia's interests, as I'm sure we all do in our way. My way is to create a safe environment for her to hear from everyone involved. There will be no decision about the future made here today. It has only been a couple of weeks since Talia's announcement and I'm sure everyone is still processing the information. If I ask anyone to leave, I expect to be listened to. If I close down the session, it will be in the interests of Talia. Is that understood?"

General murmurs of agreement all the way around, and Talia released a breath. "Right then, let's start. Perhaps with you, Talia. How are you feeling today?"

"I'm better. I'm glad I told Dane." She nudged his shoulder with her own. "That went way better than I thought. But I still don't know what to do about—" she placed her hand on her lower belly "—this."

"So you're glad of Dane's support, and you're still uncertain about the future. What would you like from the rest in this room?"

"I guess I'm confused about that, too. I appreciate that nobody is angry with me—us, and I know that Dane's mom and uncle have been really good about it and my mom and dad—" she bit her lip "—want what's best. And everyone has an idea and I don't disagree with any of them entirely... I guess I want to hear from everybody."

The girl who didn't want to disappoint anyone. "You can certainly hear from everyone today," Mara said, "but if you hear three or four views and they contradict each other, you will logically disappoint somebody. Your responsibility is to yourself. All right?"

Talia nodded at the same Connor said, "And to the baby. She has a responsibility there as well."

Mara fastened onto his blurry green shape. "That is understood. She would not have called this session if she wasn't acutely aware of that responsibility. And please don't speak out of turn."

"But I want to hear what he has to say," Talia said. "He's been like a dad to Dane. I can guess what he'll say, but I want everyone to hear it, anyway. I want everyone to hear what everyone else has to say. It will make it...easier."

Talia still strove to please those she loved,

and Connor's interjection only knotted Talia's anxiety tighter. Mara strained to keep her voice level and light as she turned to Connor. "Well then, Mr. Flanagan. Why don't you go ahead?"

He lost no time. "Talia, you don't have to go through this by yourself. Yeah, I want you to keep the baby. But that's because I believe that everyone in this room is the baby's best choice, and that includes you, Talia. You've made Dane really happy. He's better because of you, and I can't help but think that you bringing us this baby will make everyone here better."

From her chair beside her brother, Kate said, "You going to help Talia and Dane change diapers in the middle of the night?"

"I changed Dane's a few times, if you remember."

"True," Kate mumbled. "You were more of a help than his father." She gave an irritated growl. "Sorry, Dane. I shouldn't have taken shots at your father."

Dane shrugged. "It's all right. I talk smack about your ex, too."

Talia slipped her hand into Dane's and said nothing. Dane must've shared his anger at his father with Talia. Connor was right about how the two were good for each other. Still, good for each other didn't always translate into good for a baby. Or vice versa. "Was that all you wanted to say?" she asked Connor.

"I guess I just want to add that it's not right for me to speak for my sister but I am willing to commit to helping you with the baby going forward. The baby won't lack for a thing."

Kate gave a little squawk. "That's easy for you to say, Connor. What will you do when you get married and have your own kids? You won't have time then."

"I have no plans on getting married soon."

"Soon? Are you saying you have plans, then?"

Mara didn't want to know the answer to that question, and protocol saved her from having to. "I must interrupt. We are going off on a tangent here. Let's go to one of Talia's parents. Talia, who would you like to hear from?"

Mara expected Talia to name her mother, but she lifted her chin and said, "Dad. What do you think I should do?"

"Abort."

Talia paled and cupped her belly. Dane squeezed her other hand.

"What kind of boneheaded advice is that?" Connor was on his feet, glaring at Talia's father.

Mara pointed to the green-gray blur. "Sit."

Connor hesitated, then obeyed.

"I'm afraid this is the second time I've had to redirect you, Mr. Flanagan. If I have to do it again, I will be asking you to leave. Understood?"

She couldn't see his expression fifteen feet away, but he'd see hers. She hoped he saw her resoluteness and not her annoyance or—heaven forbid—her sympathy.

"Understood," he said flatly.

Mara turned to Talia. "Are you ready for your father to justify his reasoning? Or would you like us to move on for now?"

Talia's hand clenched over her lower belly. "No. Let him speak. I'm…not surprised."

"Mr. Shirazi. Could you explain your position, bearing in mind that you are here to help your daughter make the best possible decision?"

He tugged at each of his long sleeves and cupped a hand over his knee. "Your mother and I have sacrificed much to bring you what we didn't have at your age. Much. I wished you'd known my parents. If you had known them, you would know what to do now. There would be no hesitation. No need for this meeting. The matter would have stayed within *your* family.

"You are intelligent, very intelligent. Top of your class, but your spirit is lazy. That is why you gave yourself to this boy. He is not bad. But he is unproven. He has done nothing yet in his life. He has not even graduated from this mediocre high school, and has no plans yet to advance his career. He is not yet a man, much less a father."

Connor made a grumbling noise but held his tongue.

"You have made a mistake. Take responsibility and correct it. Do not ask this boy or his family to take it on."

Talia nodded, head down. She was slouched forward so much her spine curved like a shell. Dane's posture wasn't much better.

"That is all I have to say," Mr. Shirazi said.

All he had to say had crushed his daughter.

The leg of Kate's chair thudded to the floor. "May I speak?" Kate said. Her tone was sharp, her question bordering on a demand.

Mara asked Talia, "Would you like to hear from Dane's mom now?"

Talia nodded, still in her ball.

Mara directed her attention to Kate's white

shape. "I realize that Mr. Shirazi may have made remarks that as Dane's mom you might take personally. Now is not the time to comment on them, unless they have direct bearing on helping Talia make her decision."

"They do. Talia, your father says my son is 'unproven.' He doesn't know the father of your baby is all I can say. I don't think he has even bothered to have a conversation with him. If he had, he would've known that there is no better son. Your dad doesn't know that when Dane's father called me names, told me I was useless, that my son stepped between me and his father and told him he couldn't speak to me that way. He more than proved himself. He made meals when I was away on my shift work, did his homework without a word from me. He has always, always been responsible. Look at him. Talia, my son is good. And good sons make good fathers."

Kate's words uncurled Talia from her slouch and she looked across to her mother. "Mama?"

Her mother had not moved during her husband's speech or Kate's. At her daughter's soft question, her bracelets clunked together. "I agree with your father. We, too…at one point, made a similar sacrifice. The time was…not right. An opportunity would arise again, your father said. And he did much to make that opportunity happen and you were the result."

"You mean—" Talia faltered.

"She means we made a hard choice. Which you need to do now."

The atmosphere held enough heat and friction to light a match. Well, if no one else was going to bring up the obvious…

"There is also another possibility that hasn't been discussed," Mara said. "Adoption."

"We don't give away our children," Talia's father flung back. "We don't ask others to take on our responsibility."

Mara fought to keep her posture relaxed, her voice balanced and inviting. "There are those who want that responsibility. Whose biology has denied them that, as your wife worded it, opportunity. Talia could be seen as fulfilling their needs, and the baby receives financial and emotional comfort in return."

"No. It is an admission of failure."

Talia's despair rolled into Mara. The man was impossible. The purple and blue lights she always saw seemed to spiral and spark a little faster. No, she must not tread into the personal.

"I agree." Connor.

Her vexation with him and Mr. Shirazi flamed into anger. "That is an interesting comment, given that you are in the adoption business, for all intents and purposes."

"I take on dogs that owners have discarded, and do my best by them. But don't think that I haven't judged those people for abandoning their responsibility. For not even having the courage to show their faces as they do it. I get there are circumstances where keeping a pet becomes impossible, but this is not the case in this room right now. We all agree Talia has a responsibility. With Dane's help. We differ on how it'll be managed."

He was wrong. Fundamentally wrong. He was dragging his own personal views into the equation, but then she had never said that he couldn't. That any one of them couldn't. It was she who needed to control herself, and the situation.

"Then I will speak directly to Talia. Your parents and Dane's caregivers have clearly stated their position, but those are not your only choices. Because adoption can accommodate any number of situations, I think it is only fair that you take it into consideration. Adoption doesn't always mean giving up responsibility. It can also mean sharing responsibility with people who want to take that on."

"That's exactly my point," Connor burst out. "We—the baby's family—are willing to share in that responsibility. The baby doesn't have to go to strangers, doesn't ever have to feel rejected. Why are you being so stubborn, Mara?"

Mara snapped. "Third strike. Please leave."

There was the slightest hesitation, but then he rose. "Fair enough. This is your show."

He left and she listened to his feet pound down the back stairs that led to the exit. Kate stood. "There goes my ride," she said. "I think we're done here, anyway." She stopped in front of Dane. "I'll see you later. Take care." Unexpectedly, she bent down and hugged Talia. Mara caught a whiff of her soap. "You take care, too."

"Thanks for arranging this," she said to Mara, the warmth she'd extended to Talia cooling. "And for paying for it," she said to Talia's parents, the coolness dipping to iciness. "You've proven your worth."

She left and once her steps could no longer be heard on the stairs, Mr. Shirazi stood without a word and left. His wife crossed to the door, too. Mara detected a hesitation in

Abigail's sharp heels, as if she were about to speak. Was she looking back at her daughter? But then she clipped down the stairs after her husband.

There was one last person left to speak, one she'd almost forgotten about. Because she assumed that she knew his position.

"Talia? Would you like to hear from Dane?"

"She knows what I think."

"Perhaps then for my benefit would you mind repeating it?"

"I will stand by whatever Talia decides."

"I can tell you what I'm not going to do," Talia said with sudden vehemence. "I'm not aborting."

"Because your father wants you to," Mara confirmed.

"Because as soon as he said it, I knew in my gut that's not what I want."

Connor would rejoice at her decision. Mara would have to trust that it was indeed hers.

"As for what I will do," Talia added, her vim fading away, "it's my responsibility to figure that out."

That was far from the takeaway message Mara had hoped for. As the moderator of the meeting, she'd utterly failed to provide a safe environment for Talia. On top of that, she'd lost her cool under Connor's provocations. As much as she hated to admit it, Connor was right about her. She'd withdrawn into herself so much that if anyone rocked her cemented life, she literally gave them the boot.

Mara touched Talia's knee. "We are all responsible for what happened here today."

Herself the most.

CHAPTER SIX

ONE LOOK AT Mara's closed expression and Connor knew he had his work cut out for him if he hoped to repair the damage from the family meeting. She looked ready to slam the door in his face, so he quickly pointed over his shoulder to where Griffin waited. "Time for Griffin's regular Tuesday therapy session."

It was hardly regular, but after yesterday's interfamily wrangle he hadn't rested easy with himself. He'd been a disrespectful twit as Kate had lost no time in telling him on the ride home.

Mara leaned against the door. Her feet were bare and she wore yoga pants and a worn T-shirt, the kind of stuff Kate pulled on when she intended to park herself in front of Netflix with a family-sized bag of chips. "I assumed it wasn't happening."

"Because you're angry with me?"

Her toes with shiny red polish curled, like bright claws retracting. "Yes."

"I'm not backing down from what I said. I'm not giving up on what I think is best for everyone involved. But I do sincerely apologize for upsetting you and everybody there. I was rude and undermined your authority." True, but it still came off stiff. As if he didn't care, which wasn't the case at all. Caring was what had driven him to her place this evening. He got the impression that Mara leaned toward the adoption route, and he wanted to convince her otherwise. But more than that. He also wanted to make things right with her. During the hours he'd lain awake last night with Griffin getting heaved about with the tossing and turning, he'd come to realize that he couldn't stand to be on the outs with her. It felt as if they'd had their first fight as a couple. Even though they weren't.

She regarded him. Could she see him in the falling light? "I accept your apology. But I'm not up for a walk. Perhaps another time."

She'd accepted his apology but not him. He tried again. "Griffin thought you might not be. He wondered if you'd like to come out to his place. See where he hangs out."

Her lips twitched. "Griffin's quite the

charmer. Just a moment." She left him with the door still slightly open. Was that an invitation to enter? He was curious about how her place was set up to accommodate her vision loss. Was everything stripped to the bone? Did she bother with pictures? He guessed she liked comforts, beauty. He could see her curled on the couch with a cup of something warm and fragrant, reading. Braille, or an audiobook, or maybe she called one of her sisters or played a podcast or—

From inside the cab, Griffin barked. He detested waiting. Connor sat on the top step and pulled a video up on YouTube, trying to ignore Griffin's occasional impatient bark.

The door behind him widened. Mara appeared in jeans and runners, holding up a plastic bag of doggy treats. "I brought Griffin a hospitality gift."

"I thought," Connor said, "you were opposed to the reward system."

"It's not a reward," she said. "It's a gift. He doesn't need to prove his worth."

Prove. Mr. Shirazi had described Dane as unproven. Connor had enjoyed Kate's takedown of the man but doubted Talia's father had changed his mind. Oh well. This evening was for him to prove his worth to Mara. "Fair enough, let's hang at Griffin's casa."

When they arrived, Connor and Griffin got out of the truck quickly, Griffin to make the rounds and Connor to hold the passenger door for Mara. But she'd already hopped out, turning this way and that, her body tense and alert like when the dogs sniffed the air.

Which, as he rounded the hood to join her, appeared to be exactly what she was doing. "If you were a dog, your ears would be perked up."

She lifted her face to the wind. "The air feels different here than at the lake. There, it comes sweeping across the surface. You can almost feel the water. Or at least, I can. And only from one direction. Here, it's from everywhere." She frowned. "The noise, too. Do they do this every time you come home?"

He'd grown so accustomed to the cacophony of barks that he didn't realize what she meant at first. "I guess so, though they do it with everybody."

And the barking didn't ease as they approached the center. "They are all outside playing," he explained. He'd purposely arranged to have the dogs in the open space to avoid taking Mara indoors with its tripping hazards and unconventional layout. He took her to the back of the building with its half-acre enclosure. "I'm not sure what you can see, but it's like their own private dog park. Come on, I'll show you."

Griffin led the way through the gate, dogs crowding around. "I was given a couple of old fire hydrants and I fenced around bushes and trees to make it more livable for them. Gopher holes come free for the diggers in the bunch."

The two from the youth center bounded over to her. Mara's face relaxed into a smile and she tucked her cane away. "Hello, there. Thanks for having me." Their noses zeroed in on her pocket with the treats. "If I give some to them, what about the others?"

"Yeah, best not to cause a ruckus. Go on with you," he ordered the dogs. They did, and Connor was more or less left alone with Mara. She had dropped to her knees for a pair of spaniel crosses, one-year-olds with a whole lot of floppy, gangly puppy still in them. They were ready for adoption and seemed to think she was a prospective buyer, and plied her with doggy kisses. Leave it to the dogs to get what he had no idea how to go after. Because well, if it felt as if they'd had their first couple fight, then their first make-up should follow.

The gate rattled behind him. Daisy had jumped up onto her hind legs, forepaws on the metal pipes.

"How did you break out of the house?" Connor said. "Did Kate let you out?"

He opened the gate for Daisy, and she joined the dogs mobbing Mara. She shoved her snout into Mara's ear, and Mara fell back against the tickles, laughing, her hands rubbing first this dog and then the other. "This one's Daisy. The guide dog I'm training."

Mara sat up, her legs sticking straight out in front of her and her hair mussed. She looked…like another Mara. Relaxed, playful, at home. It was working. The dogs were opening her up, and man, she wore happy really well. He sat on a tractor tire nearby, a faint rubbery scent from the day's heat rising off it.

"Isn't she supposed to be better trained than this?" Mara said.

"She's perfectly trained," Connor said. "Off harness, she gets to be just like every other dog. Because she knows the difference, it makes her better."

"So she can draw a line between the professional and personal?"

"Even a dog can."

"Are you implying I can't?"

He frowned. Had he missed something? When had she not been professional? She dug into her jeans pocket and slipped Daisy a doggy treat when the other dogs had run off. "That's for having to put up with mean old Dog Man."

He had brought Mara here to bond with Griffin—okay, himself—but if she took to Daisy, that would be even better. "You like her."

She tilted her cheek to him, that signature move. One day, he would follow through and kiss her there, right under her cheekbone. "I do, but I don't want her."

"How about Griffin, then?"

"Did you not already agree to leaving this alone?"

"That was before Talia."

"And how has that changed anything?"

How to honestly answer that without getting his head bitten off? Griffin came over not to him, but Mara. The reason became obvious as he sniffed around her pocket, his attention soon taken up by Daisy herself.

"Hey, go easy, Griffin." He explained to Mara, "Neither one of them is fixed. Daisy I will spay, if I can't find her a match soon. But Griffin I might breed."

Again her cheek presented to him. "You plan on developing an antisocial pedigree?"

"I get your point, but there's a spark in Griffin I want to see more of. I can't explain it."

"Can you explain then why you're pushing Daisy on me?"

"I'm not pushing her on you. I honestly thought she was in the house. Still, even you said you weren't ruling out anything."

"Doesn't mean I'm actively seeking a dog."

"Are you seeing someone?"

He had less impulse control than a puppy. He was about to withdraw his question, then stopped. Now that he was considering something more with her, he'd better check to see if he stood a chance. He half expected her to tell him to once again stay out of her business. Instead, she said, "No." And then, "You?"

"No. Are you not dating because men are idiots or because you knock them back?"

"Those aren't exclusive to each other, you know."

"Ha, point taken."

"I'm looking for a special man. One who can accept my visual disability. There've been a couple like that. And someone who doesn't want a family. None like that. So far."

"Tall order."

"Yes, I foresee a future of quick, shallow relationships."

"But that's not your style."

"No. And what's your style?"

Wordy types with kissable cheeks. "Someone who likes dogs."

She glanced away. "That's not a tall order."

"And someone I want to have a family with," he added. "That's a tall order with the women I've met. I need someone who doesn't scare easily."

"Ah well. Then you might have your work cut out for you." Mara rubbed Griffin's ruff. They looked good together. That gave him an idea for how he might get her used to dogs. And him.

"Take him for a month," Connor said, and before she could once again turn him down, he rushed on. "You already said that you might have to consider a guide dog in the future. A buddy dog is a good way to start, and Griffin has the makings of one. I'm not saying forever. I'm saying for one month. And I'll come by. Every day, if you like."

"The only buddy he wants is you."

"Call it a thirty-day challenge. There's one

for everything else. Diet, exercise, subscriptions, pots and pans."

"It's not fair to Griffin. He won't understand."

"Neither is it good for him to be so attached to me. He worries every time I'm out of sight. He's got to see that he'll be okay with or without me. And it's not as if I'm dropping out of his life. I'll stay on the couch the first night, so he'll feel more comfortable." He'd stay every night if she asked.

"Face it, Connor. You're worried about me. I'm the one you think needs a dog because nobody will want me," she said.

"What?"

"Remember on our first walk? You said that you didn't want me to be alone. That's why I should get a dog."

"I mean... I didn't..." Except he more or less had said that. "I'm sorry if I gave you that impression."

She looked away. "It's the truth."

"No, it isn't."

"You yourself said it would be a tall order."

"Tall, but not insurmountable." Her lips pursed into a mock whistle, and he affected a drawl. "That's right, pretty lady. I got me all kinds of big words."

She ducked her head, smiling softly. "You

know what? You're right. Griffin and I both need to deal with change. Let's do this."

He'd gotten exactly what he wanted. Not a month away from Griffin, but a month with Mara. He caught Griffin's steady brown gaze on him, and Connor felt a shot of guilt—and envy. What he wouldn't give to hang out with Mara for thirty straight days.

Oh right. For the excuse to possibly see her, he'd given his favorite dog.

DRIVING BY THE dog park on his way out of town, Connor spotted a white husky cross streak across the field. Slowing, Connor saw the dog brake to a stop and mouth a throw toy. Yep, it was Docker all right. Which meant that Greg was probably there. Greg was a retired dentist and more to the point, Talia's grandfather. Connor and he had met because of their dating relations, and it turned out that Greg was a natural with dogs. He watched the kennels whenever Connor was away.

What did Greg think of Talia's news? If he knew. On impulse, Connor pulled into the parking lot.

"Connor," Greg said as Connor approached, and then shouted across the park, "Docker. Look who's here."

Sniffing around on the same hill Griffin had scouted from, Docker raised his head. He didn't need to be told twice. He tore down the hill to Greg as best he could on three legs. Connor and Greg made twin grunts of sympathy when the downward momentum tipped him over and he skidded along on the new green grass. He pushed himself up, a wide grin on his face, and kept going.

Connor rewarded him with a biscuit he'd earmarked for Griffin. "Good to see you, boy," he said, kneeling. "You keeping Greg honest?"

"As the livelong day," Greg said. "How are the dogs?"

"Good. Keeping me busy. I was just making a run to pick up dog food, and then back for more training this afternoon."

Greg looked to his truck, narrowed his eyes. "No Griffin?"

"He's boarding for the next month to help with his socialization." Twenty-two more days, Mara reminded him yesterday at the youth center. Griffin had nearly flattened Connor in his excitement to see him. Connor had bunked at Mara's the first night, and Mara reported that every night after that Griffin had slept on the couch with Connor's scent. Things were not going well. He offered to take Griffin back, but oddly she'd refused. "With Mara Montgomery. I know her through the youth center. She wanted to see what it was like to have a dog." True, as far as it goes.

"Not another of your thirty-day challenges," Greg said. "You know it doesn't work for everyone."

"I haven't had one failure yet. I'm sure she's up to it," Connor said with more confidence than he felt.

Greg let fly another long throw and Docker was off. Greg stared after his dog and seemed to ignore Connor. Taking the hint, Connor began to edge away when Greg said, "I hear we might end up related."

So he knew. "It's unexpected," Connor said.

"It is," Greg said. "Abigail told me. It's thrown her for a loop."

Connor wasn't sure if Greg was referring to Talia or her mother. "The kids are in a bit of shock, but Dane's behind Talia all the way." In case Greg had any doubts.

"She's going to—keep it?" Greg said. He spoke neutrally, a lifetime of keeping his opinions to himself when that close to people's gnashers.

"She hasn't said otherwise," Connor said,

hedging the question. He hurried on. "Kate and I are okay with her moving in with Dane at our place. We've got lots of room." Well, room enough.

"Big decision," Greg said.

"I suppose," Connor said. The consequences were life changing but so would be the rewards. "She's not having to make it on her own."

"There is that," Greg said. "Good that she has family. Dane, too. Good that he can be there for her."

Connor picked up that Greg was carefully skirting his own daughter's disapproval. It might help if he knew that she wasn't entirely unsupportive. "Talia's parents have retained a psychologist for Talia to meet with. Mara."

Greg jerked, his eyes widening. Then recovering from his obvious surprise, he looked away and commented, "That's nice."

What was that all about? Greg clearly had an opinion about Mara, and Connor couldn't resist prodding. "She's there to help Talia talk through the problems. Probably for the best. There was a meeting of both families. Things got heated on both sides. Me included. Mara handled it really well."

"Good to hear," Greg said. The very model of discretion.

"Her advice is to put the baby up for adoption."

Greg spun to Connor. "She said that?"

There, a reaction. "She implied that."

"And you don't like the idea, I take it."

"No. Not when there are other options."

Docker reappeared over the crest of the hill and then, like Griffin, sat, his lone foreleg thrust out at an awkward angle to support himself. Greg twirled the ball thrower in his hand. "You don't like her ideas, but you trust her with Griffin."

Trust. He hadn't looked at it that way. "Yes. I do trust her with him. And with Talia. She's definitely got Talia's interests at heart."

"That's good Talia has her. She's not alone. She came to me but I'm not the best person to talk to about…these matters."

Greg sounded like a man defeated. Reconciled to staying on the outside. Connor couldn't help himself. "If Talia came to you, it was because she values your opinion. You know what it's like to be a parent, take care of a family. Nothing wrong with passing on your wisdom."

Greg gave a snort, then whistled for Docker. "I'd hardly call it wisdom."

Connor waited for an explanation but all he got as they watched Docker gamely hop-jog across the field was Greg repeating, "I'm glad Talia has family."

"COME ON, GRIFFIN." Mara patted her thighs from outside the passenger side of the truck, the door open. "Let's go." Connor heard the begging in her voice.

Griffin sat in the passenger seat beside Connor, shifting uneasily on his paws and staring out the windshield. Connor nudged Griffin in the ribs. "Go on. Be a good dog." Now he could hear the begging in his voice.

Mara was patting her thighs so hard she had to be leaving marks. "Let's go inside. Treat." So much for standing strong against the reward system. "Do you want a treat, Griffin-boy?"

The stubborn mutt dipped his head in polite refusal and held his seat. He must've plotted this standoff from the time they left the dog park on their regular Tuesday outing.

"Well, that's that," Mara said. "I believe that Griffin has officially terminated our little challenge."

Her voice was light and even, but he picked up on a hint of glumness.

He opened his door and went around to Mara. "If he sees me with you, he'll come."

"And what happens when you have to get back in the truck?"

"I guess we'll see who runs faster."

Mara sighed. "We're hooped."

"You could always invite me inside." He tipped his head to Griffin, who had his ears cocked to their conversation.

Mara caught his meaning, but… "Back to the same problem. What happens when you have to leave?"

He had no idea. His only thought right now was getting inside Mara's place. Day fifteen into the challenge and he still hadn't gained access to her place, much less her lips. Yes, he'd slept overnight there, but a late-night run to the vet and an early-morning intake meant that he'd spent a bare six hours there, all of it in the dark and most of it sleeping. "They don't call me Dog Man for nothing."

Mara gave him a sour look. "You'll prove tonight if you deserve that ridiculous moniker."

Connor entered Mara's home and resisted the goofy urge to thrust his arms in the air as if scoring a winning goal. Instead he surveyed the place with pretended nonchalance. Far from minimalist, Mara had decorated with plenty of eye-catching decor from pillows to knickknacks to a great steel-and-glass installation above her gas fireplace. It looked like a homier version of her office.

A home Griffin wanted no part of. A quarter hour passed with both truck doors open, and Mara's door closed to confirm that Connor was not exiting Mara's territory anytime soon.

"Has he budged from the seat?"

Connor turned from the living room window to Mara carrying in a tray with tea and coffee, and were those chocolate chip oatmeal cookies?

"He's pacing about the cab, a good sign. Either that or he's under attack from mosquitoes."

"Or he's about to run off?"

"He knows where I am. He's not going anywhere."

"Do you want to give it a try then, before we sit down?"

There was something to how she phrased that, as if they were about to have a little ceremony, a little daily ritual, that settled nicely inside his gut.

Connor called from the front door. "Griffin. Come."

Griffin scrambled from the cab and into Mara's narrow entryway, his tail wagging so hard it slapped both walls.

Connor rubbed the dog's head. "Sorry, boy. You took a gamble and lost."

Mara joined them. "What about your truck doors?"

Connor looked down at Griffin plastered to his side. "Option one. I leave the doors the way they are. Option two. I make a run for it, while you hold on to Griffin's collar."

"Or option three," Mara said, "I go out and close them."

That made the most sense. Connor watched as she tapped her way down the steps to the sidewalk where she pushed one door shut, carefully rounded the hood and shut that door, too.

"I could've done all that in a tenth of the time," he told Griffin. What else in her life took her that much longer? Changing a light bulb. Matching socks. Or shoes. Chopping onions. Some things even the best of guide dogs couldn't do.

He could come around more, if she'd let him. But her independent spirit would kick and scream at the idea.

Back inside, she knelt down and Griffin obligingly came for a pet. "Miss me?" she said, and smiled up at Connor. An ironic smile but one that included him in the joke.

Connor grinned. "You have no idea," he said, deliberately misinterpreting the subject of her question.

Mara kissed Griffin's temple. Griffin reciprocated by licking Connor's hand.

"Griffin," Connor reproved.

"Never mind," Mara said, rising. "As long as he has someone to be loyal to. Let's have tea."

Connor decided on an armchair adjacent to the sofa, which seemed to be Mara's domain with its bottle of lotion and a basket of yarn on the adjoining coffee table. Could she knit or crochet or whatever one did with yarn? Did she do it by feel or could she still see well enough?

"Are you okay with me sitting in your spot?" Connor said.

"I'm sure Griffin can share his sofa with me for one evening."

Griffin took up one end of the sofa and

Mara curled up on the other, stripping off her socks and wiggling her bare toes. Griffin's ears perked up, his eyes fixed on the wiggling toes.

"Uh, Mara," Connor whispered. She hadn't seen Griffin's reaction.

Mara turned in his direction, adjusted her ear to him.

"Griffin has this…fetish I forgot to tell you about."

"Oh?" Mara snuggled further, her hand cupping her tea. Absolutely cozy, and wasn't it human nature that when cozy—she stretched and gave her pink-painted toes a full happy wriggle.

Griffin launched. He landed on all fours on Mara's feet like a coyote pouncing on a mouse.

Mara jerked, her tea sloshing.

"Griffin!" Connor reprimanded.

Griffin looked about but didn't release his prey. Mara faced him. "What is this all about?"

Griffin sniffed her toes and Connor's own toes curled at the memory of how that damp snuffling felt. Sure enough, Mara burst into giggles. "Griffin, you brat."

"Yeah, he has this thing about bare feet. He sees them as toys attached to legs."

Mara shifted into a cross-legged position, her feet tucked underneath her. Griffin flattened himself on the cushions and lined his nose up to where her toes were buried under her knees.

Mara turned laughing eyes to Connor. "I've gone around in bare feet for days and he's done nothing."

"You can walk in bare feet, but you can't wiggle them or else this happens." He pointed to his feet. "It's why I always wear socks. You okay?"

Mara patted the damp spot on her sweatshirt where the tea had spilled. "I'm good."

She scratched behind Griffin's ear and his head sank to his paws, his eyes still trained on the gap where her toes had retreated. She laid her head back on the couch. "I think he's playing because he feels relaxed now that you're here."

She looked relaxed, too. And he—well, he discreetly wiggled his toes. "If you want," he said as casually as possible, "we could do this more often. Since Griffin is still having problems."

"Sure," Mara said, also casually. "It might

be a good idea, make him feel as if both of us belong to his pack."

Griffin's pack of three. He and Mara belonged to each other in a small, important way.

"What do you usually do on Wednesday nights after youth group?" he said.

"I play chess."

"Against yourself?"

"It…gets me out of myself. The board is modified. The contrasts stand out for me still. It's hard to explain. I neither win nor lose, but my perspective always changes."

Connor had taught Dane chess but brooding over a game board with his uncle ranked a far second to hanging with his girlfriend.

Now Connor had the chance to have both a girl and a game. Not that Mara was his girl, but she saw them as part of the same pack. And that was a good start.

He leaned forward. "I'll play black."

CHAPTER SEVEN

"GRIFFIN DOESN'T SEEM depressed to me," Jack said to Mara, looking up from where he'd just drilled screws into the planking for the covered deck in his backyard. She'd brought Griffin over to the house so he could have a playdate with their newest member of the family and Griffin's former mate at Flanagan Dog Academy, Amigo. Mara had nearly tipped over in her folding camp chair, trying to track the two energized bundles of blurry fur torpedoing around the backyard. It was the most she'd ever seen Griffin mix it up with any dog. He was probably so tired of her quiet, granny-like company.

"It's the happiest he's been in the two and a half weeks I've had him," Mara said. Well, except for when Connor was present. "I took him to the dog park yesterday, thinking that on Sunday he could do a canine meet and greet. But he moped. He couldn't be bothered to play fetch. And I bought a special thrower, too."

"Ungrateful beast," Jack said, lowering a plank alongside the row of others already screwed in.

"And the ball is still there. I couldn't begin to find a green tennis ball in a green field."

"You made some other dog happy."

"Connor offered to take him back, but…"

"But what?"

"But we have sort of a bet going on. He thinks that I can keep Griffin for thirty days, and I have serious doubts, but I want to prove him right."

Jack zipped his measuring tape shut. "So if you lose the bet, you'll be right, but if he wins, you'll both get what you want."

"Something like that."

"But he's not a guide dog, right? That kind of puts you at a disadvantage. Having to take care of a dog that doesn't particularly like you or other dogs."

"I guess if I can win over Griffin, then a guide dog will be a breeze."

Reaching for his cordless drill, Jack stopped. "What are you saying, exactly?"

"I…I might require one in the future."

It was the first time she'd voiced that possibility aloud to any of her family. It felt like an admission of defeat, of relinquishing yet another piece of her independence. But if she had to spill the beans, better that it was to Jack. She loved her sisters dearly, but Jack was the easiest to talk to about her visual disability. She suspected that he'd seen enough in his former career as an international humanitarian worker not to be overly concerned about the setbacks of blindness in a sighted first world. For a little while, she had him all to herself, Bridge having taken the girls to the library.

"Let's just say that Griffin is a launching point."

"In that case, I hate to see what Connor has planned for the finish line."

"But I'm failing with Griffin. He's too attached to Connor."

"Connor's easy to like." Jack gave her a sidelong look. Time to squelch that idea.

How to explain that relations between her and Connor weren't exactly those of dog trainer and client? Nor were they exactly that of a couple. "That he is," she said. "He'll make someone very happy, I'm sure."

"But not you?"

He most certainly would. The other night,

Connor had eventually won their chess game, but she blamed the distraction of his presence. For the better part of an hour, he'd sat close enough for her to study his face even as he studied the board. She noticed the downward slant of his eyebrows, that he brushed the bridge of his nose just before he moved his piece, that he did the telltale click of tongue to roof of mouth as he considered his next move. She could study him every day of her life.

Except she would make him miserable. Maybe not now, but eventually. She and Connor both knew that, and she might as well pass that understanding on to the people she cared about the most.

She consciously lounged back in her deck chair, a casual pose she'd struck earlier that day with a client determined to gaslight her. "We actually talked about dating."

"Oh?"

"We both agreed that while we enjoyed each other's company, we weren't suited for a life together."

"That's very mature of you two." Jack's voice contained an edge of amused disbelief.

"It is quite possible for a single man and a single woman to be friends, providing they've addressed the issue through open and honest communication."

"Back in high school, Bridge and I decided to be friends." The drill screamed as Jack drove in a screw. "That lasted five days."

"Perhaps you two weren't being honest."

"I know I wasn't. But so long as you and Connor are doing the open and honest thing, you shouldn't run into problems."

"Problems? What problems?" It was Bridget on the higher deck. Mara looked up, cursing herself for not bringing sunglasses. The spiraling light diffusion made her sister almost impossible to discern. She came a little more into focus as she descended the stairs to the unmade deck, the light intensity dimming to the usual spray of blue and purple. Amigo broke away from Griffin to greet her. Panting, Griffin sat and observed. "I saw Amigo and Griffin were engaged in parallel play." Mara could make out that the dogs were walking, nose to the ground.

"Parallel play? That's a fancy term," Jack said, lowering another plank into place.

"I read about it in a baby book. It's a stage."

"How about we deal with the stage of getting the baby into the world of play first?"

"I'm all over that," she said, patting her

belly. "I picked up a couple of books on fetal development and the girls filled three grocery bins with theirs. They're getting into jammies now." She glanced between her husband and sister. "So…everything okay?"

"Why wouldn't it be?" Mara said, willing her face to go blank. Bridge was a high-tech radar when it came to detecting distress in her younger sisters. Bridge turned to look squarely at Jack. "You haven't told her?"

Jack had wanted to talk to her, and here she prattled on about her boring relationships with Connor and with his dog. He dipped his head. "I hadn't gotten around to it yet."

"My fault," Mara said. "How can I help?"

"I don't need help, exactly. We just thought you should know Bridge and I have decided to move on something that I've been thinking about since a couple of Christmases ago."

That jingled bells for Mara. Jack had returned from his assignment in Venezuela two years ago with surprising news. Bridge's high school sweetheart turned out to be their Auntie Penny's biological son. It had been a shocker at first, especially for Bridget. Adopted and so not blood-related to Jack or Auntie Penny, she'd been closer to both of them than either Krista or Mara, and the news had rocked her world. They'd all drawn together as a family, one made even closer when Jack and Bridget married.

"Okay," Mara said. The less she said, the more clients opened up. Family worked much the same.

"We decided—"

"Jack has. I'm going along for the ride," Bridge modified.

"I want to find out who my biological father is," Jack said in a rush. "And I know what you are going to say, that I already had a father and there are reasons I was put up for adoption, and that it won't be easy given Penny didn't leave us a clue about his identity and there are no records naming him. I understand the difficulties, but it's like Connor says, if I can't forget it, I might as well remember it."

Mara had followed Jack's tumbling explanation well enough, but at the mention of Connor, she braked. "Connor knows?"

Jack looked sheepish. "I might've mentioned it when I went out to look at his dogs."

Connor was privy to Montgomery matters ahead of her. An acquaintance to Jack at most. Why him and not her? "Does Krista know?"

Bridget set to tossing loose screws back into a metal can. The plinking grated on Mara's nerves. "Yes."

"So I'm the last one to know." Mara swallowed. "Why did you put off telling me?"

Jack and Bridget gave each other sidelong looks, and then he set down his drill. "I was afraid you'd try to talk me out of it."

Both her family and Connor thought she tried to get her people to do her will. She didn't. She prided herself on her professionalism, her rational approach to highly charged situations. Yes, she'd lost her cool at the family meeting, but that had been an exception. Wasn't she allowed to make a mistake? Mara took a deep breath and with the greatest calm, interlaced her fingers on her lap. "I might've alerted you to challenges. I've been clinically involved in these types of searches before, and counseled through the fallout, but I wouldn't have stopped you."

"Only because you couldn't," Jack said. "Tell me straight up, do you think my search is a good idea?"

Her fingers tightened compulsively. "That's for you to figure out."

Jack and Bridget groaned. "That's always your go-to response."

"Because it's always the right one," Mara said. "I would tend to point out the difficulties. I would throw up caution signs. Is that so wrong?"

"No, it isn't," Jack said. "And the thing is that you are right. Only—"

"Only you tend to throw cold water on new plans," Bridget said bluntly. "Anytime anybody sets out to do something, you put up roadblocks. And that's fine in your life, you have your reasons, but it gets hard when you do it to everyone else in your life."

"I never tried to talk either of you out of having a baby, and that defines life changing, I'd say. Especially when—" No, she wouldn't make them feel bad for her own private grief.

"—when you have decided not to have children," Bridget said softly. "Isn't that what you were going to say?"

No dodging Bridget. "Yes."

"You could," Bridget said. "If you weren't so cautious."

"I don't want to bring a child into this world I can't see and—what if I carry the gene, too?"

"You don't know yet?"

"No. There seems no point." She opened her hands and flattened them on her lap. They still shook. "But maybe I should. If by a slim chance I do carry it, then you and Co—everybody else can stop nagging me about having children when I'm most definitely not having them."

Jack laughed. "Sensible choice, given you're having a hard enough time with a dog."

Bridge glared at Jack. Sure, it sounded cruel, but he was being honest. She'd chosen to believe that Griffin's disinterest in her stemmed from his over-attachment to Connor, but it didn't. It was about her. She was the withdrawn, timid one, and her attempt to undergo a personality makeover with this silly thirty-day challenge proved only how circumscribed her life had become. Griffin came right up to her knee and stared up. He'd learned that he had to come close if he stood a chance of getting her to respond. As soon as she made eye contact, he nosed his leash. She had her excuse to leave.

"I'd better head out while the experience is still good for him."

"Look, Mar," Jack said. "We're not trying—"

"I know you mean well," she said hurriedly. She felt for Griffin's collar to hook on the leash. "I'm not here to tell either of you how to run your lives." She unsnapped her walking cane and stood. "Just as you're not here to tell me how to run mine."

She tightened her hold on Griffin's leash and left, eager to go, even if it was with a dog who didn't much like her.

MARA'S NEWEST CLIENT sat in the dining room area of her office, Griffin's head in his lap. She might've experienced a pang of jealousy, except she couldn't blame Griffin. Her client was Greg Rasmussen, retired dentist and on-call help at Flanagan Dog Academy. Griffin had met Greg there, and in these desperate times away from Connor, likely saw her former dentist as a fond reminder of a better place.

But it was in Dr. Greg's capacity as Talia's grandfather that Mara suspected he'd booked an appointment. He hadn't explained his reasoning, citing "complications" that had recently arisen he'd hoped to sort through. That was her specialty, so long as the complications weren't her own.

"He likes to have his eyebrows smoothed," Dr. Greg said, adjusting his straight-backed chair outward so Mara, sitting at the diagonal corner, could better see as he demonstrated on Griffin. "I discovered it when I was pulling thistle burrs off his eyebrows. Next thing I know, he's flat on his side, half asleep."

Griffin's entire body had softened, his tail wags slowing to intermittent swipes, his head sagging deeper between Dr. Greg's legs. "I'll have to try that," Mara said. "He's taken a while to warm up to me."

"Try that and he's yours," Dr. Greg said. He'd invited her to call him Greg, but she still had the amalgam on her molars as a reminder of how their former relationship still cast its shadow. Tilted back in his dental chair, she had seen his face clearly in the bright lights, one of the few times when her vision problems, cropping up even then, didn't apply.

"He's back with Connor next week," she said. "I'm sure that whatever mojo I perform, it'll be nothing compared to being back with him."

"I completely relate," Dr. Greg said. "I learned that trick with Griffin, and the next day when Connor returns, Griffin lies down at Connor's feet, belly-up, in complete surrender. He has a knack with dogs. People, too."

She wasn't the only one to see Connor's people skills, then. Probably because Dr. Greg was like her. Something of his professionalism still clung to him, a discreetness in the way he took in her office upon entering that made her choose to guide him to the dining table where he could experience the casualness of the nicked wooden table balanced by the austerity of the wood chairs.

"Take my granddaughter. Talia. You know her, right?" At Mara's nod, Dr. Greg continued. "She's the one who introduced me to Dog Man." Dr. Greg grimaced at the moniker. Mara liked Talia's grandfather even more. "At the youth center one night. I was there to pick her up, and she made him out to be the coolest guy alive. Above Dane even and he's a great kid, don't get me wrong. But she seemed softer and also stronger alongside Connor. He brings out the best in the kids, I guess."

And if Mara would let him, Connor was trying to bring out the best in her. Or at least to turn her into someone who could look after a dog.

Dr. Greg laid his long, limber fingers, useful for his trade, on Griffin's head. As if Dr. Greg's touch were a sedative, Griffin folded at Dr. Greg's feet, head on paws.

Mara opened the recording app on her phone. "I think Griffin will now permit us to talk."

Dr. Greg leaned back in his chair. "I understand from Connor that you're seeing Talia about her pregnancy."

Mara stiffened. Connor hadn't exactly broken confidentiality, but it smacked of indiscretion. She must've betrayed her annoyance because Dr. Greg rushed to add, "Never mind, I don't want to pry. But I am going to work on that assumption."

"If you would like to speak to her with me present," Mara said, "that can be arranged."

"No," Dr. Greg said quickly. "I don't wish to speak to her on the subject, but when Connor said that you were the one helping Talia, well, that got me thinking again."

"Okay."

He cleared his throat, swallowed water from the glass she'd provided. "A couple of years ago, I read that appeal Jack Holdstrom made in the paper. He was asking for donations for the Christmas campaign. He, uh, confessed that his mother had embezzled the funds so he and his daughters could make it back from Venezuela."

"Yes, I remember," Mara said.

Another round of throat clearing. "He said that he'd learned that Penny was his biological mother. I was wondering if Jack ever asked about his biological father."

Mara felt her skull prickle at what Dr. Greg was implying. Not two full days after Jack had confided his intent to identify his father, here he sat.

"I think," she said slowly, "I understand what you are trying to tell me. Please let me point out that I am in a potential conflict of interest, though I would like you to verbally confirm my suspicions."

Dr. Greg squared himself to her. "I am certain beyond a doubt that I am Jack Holdstrom's biological father." He paused. "And I suppose, by extension, your uncle, since Jack's mother was your aunt."

Even though Mara had braced for his confession, it still left her winded. Greg Rasmussen had collapsed her professional and personal life together in a way she wasn't sure how to resolve.

"I'm willing to take a paternity test to prove it," Dr. Greg said. "But I have no doubt in my mind."

It was at times like these Mara wished she was fully sighted, so she could examine reactions after such monumental statements. Instead, she had to gauge his feelings by the hitch in his breathing and the lifting and setting down of his glass, the water untouched. He looked ready for an interrogation.

"You have lived with this information for a long time," she said.

He reached again for the glass of water and, from the long gulp, had more success this time around. "A lifetime. Jack's lifetime. There were reasons. And I was married. Unhappily so, but married nonetheless, and a father, too. My business was in its early years, and money was tight. Suffice it to say, I already had obligations. Penny said she'd take on the responsibility. And I—I let her. When she put the baby—Jack—up for adoption, I was relieved.

"We never saw each other after she told me of her decision. We were both terrified of the consequences. I failed her, so the best I could do was not fail the family I already had. Penny and I led separate lives, and on the rare occasion we'd meet, we avoided each other."

He stopped, and Mara waited a moment to make sure that he was finished. Just as well, since she needed time to formulate a response. But Dr. Greg had turned on the tap to his suppressed memories, and out they poured.

"Once she was right ahead of me at the grocery till. I was with my wife, and she pulled in behind Penny. There was no avoiding it. My wife left to dash back for some spice she'd forgotten, and I was left to load the groceries onto the conveyor belt. Penny was close enough to touch. Eighteen years on and I still wanted her. I realized I always would. It took everything in my power not to touch her. I remember wrapping my hand over a cabbage, smooth and cold like skin, holding it so I wouldn't do something inappropriate. After the first look, Penny ignored me, chatted with the checkout clerk about how all her nieces were visiting for the week and tonight was their favorite, grilled steak bites with homemade fries and cheesecake. 'Nothing,' she said, 'makes me happier than cooking for my family.' I wonder now if she intended for me to hear that. To make me feel better about my choice. To say that even if I hadn't chosen her, I'd still chosen family and that was enough." He reached down and gave Griffin a scratch. "The day I heard of her death…that broke my heart. Made worse, because I could tell no one of my grief. Until now."

"You never spoke about your…affair to anyone?"

"Not a single person. Not my wife. I stayed with her, you know. Our marriage got better, but it was never what Penny and I felt for each other. She passed a year ago. I definitely didn't tell my children. It was not their business. Now…I'm not so sure. Three girls. They might like to know they have a brother."

"Is that why you're coming to me now?"

"Partly. I can't hurt my wife now. I guess you would know if Jack ever expressed an interest in the identity of his biological father. If he has, I'm willing for him to know."

"You want me to pass along the message?"

Dr. Greg shifted in his seat, the leather rubbing and squeaking. "If you think that's best. I just want him to have that option. If he wants."

Jack most certainly would want. "I am reluctant to act as messenger. I'm willing to facilitate a meeting between you two, though."

"Except I don't want to tell him if he doesn't want to know. I can understand his anger, his disappointment. His adoptive father was a patient of mine. He was a good and decent man, prized Jack. I can understand if Jack thinks he was father enough. I guess

I'm saying I want to do what's best. To not mess up again."

She could approach Jack, say she was contacted by a man claiming to be his biological father. But her mind had already shot ahead to another complication. She and Jack were blood cousins, which meant that she was also some kind of blood cousin to Talia, Greg's granddaughter. The relationship was remote, but the professional was now personal on two counts.

Could she continue to advise Talia in a professional capacity? Time enough to deal with that.

"I will speak to Jack. Learn his feelings." Of which she was fairly certain. "I will promise not to reveal your identity, even if you give me permission now. If he indicates a willingness to proceed, I would suggest a meeting."

"Here?"

She made a quick decision. "I could host at my home. This is a family matter now, and I'd rather not use my office."

Dr. Greg's hands gripped his knees. "Then let's do this."

Another meeting that would pull her and Connor together to the extent that he might become a distant member of her family through Talia.

She'd end up like Greg with Penny. Connor would exist in the orbit of her life always out of reach.

CHAPTER EIGHT

SOMETHING WAS UP with Mara. At the windup party for the youth center out at his center, she'd been distracted, her responses to Connor and the kids slow, and she'd sat on a straw bale, petting the dogs only if they approached her and nibbling on cookies and sipping on juice like an emo teenager. She'd invited him in for tea and chess but had then sat on the sofa and stared up at her metal-and-glass installation as if entranced. When he'd called her back, she'd jumped up and nearly tripped over Griffin and had bumped into Daisy, who'd come with him.

The dogs were now stretched out together in the living room back-to-back, dozing like a married couple.

Mara took her turn on the chessboard, and Connor realized she was about to throw the game. "Did you mean to move your queen there?"

She skimmed her hand over the pieces. His

black pieces had notches on the top to differentiate them from her white counterparts. "Yes," she said.

"My rook is clear to take your queen."

"Isn't your pawn between?"

"No. Your knight took it way back."

"It did?" She peered at the board. Her hand fluttered down, nearing but not touching his rook, like a skittish bird. He took her hand. He'd expected the contact to approximate the last time they'd held hands—a special moment that triggered a craving for more. Except intense heat rushed through him. Of course, of course. Dogs, families, secrets…the round of life had drawn them together, fired them up like two lit logs. Now, one spark, one hand touch was enough to set them ablaze.

He guided her hand to her queen, and then across the recessed and raised squares to his rook.

"Oh," she said. "I see."

It made sense to release her hand. Instead, he stroked his thumb across her knuckles. "Mara, what's wrong?"

Her hand jerked in his, but didn't pull completely away. "I'm sorry. Nothing. Just…work. I had a…difficult client earlier today."

Old instincts from his enforcement career reared up. "Difficult? As in…violent?"

"What? No, no, nothing like that. My client presented a scenario that complicates my life. That is all."

He couldn't shake his mind from the threat her clients could pose. "You should bring Griffin to your office. He would intervene if any of your clients tried anything."

"If you must know he was there, and he worked his own kind of magic. That's all I'll say. Look, I'm sorry. Take my queen and let's finish this off."

Not yet was he letting go of her hand. "Don't you have your own therapist? Can you talk to her?"

"I would, except that she's away on sabbatical this summer."

"And you can't talk to me?"

She looked at where their hands were joined. Had she experienced the same jolt at his touch? Did she still want a piece of him? "If I could," she said softly, "you'd be my go-to when I need someone to talk to."

She was choosing him above all others. He kept his hold on her hand light, not wanting to push his luck. "I'm flattered. I usually get along better with dogs than people."

She laid her other hand on his. "You can be pushy and opinionated—to the point of recklessness. But people are still drawn to you."

With his hand captured between both of hers, he definitely felt the urge to do something reckless. Something that would take their newfound friendship into unexplored territory. Or smash what they had.

He kept his captured hand still. "I've given up before on…others and for a while, myself. It didn't get me anywhere. But coming on strong…well, that gets me kicked out of places."

"A fine line. One you walk wonderfully with the kids at the youth center."

"They want me for the dogs, that's it."

"It's not the dogs that no less than five kids came up to talk to about their adventures tonight."

And here he'd thought her too distracted to notice him. "Bryson wanted my opinion on Latin American presidents. I couldn't name one, much less have an opinion."

"Except now you do."

"He gave me almost too much information."

She pressed his hand between hers hard enough for the knuckle bones to bunch. He wasn't complaining. "Bryson was looking to share, and not just with anybody. Remember I was there a full hour before you showed. He could have just as easily talked to me. I even know the name of the Guatemalan president. But he chose you. Not me and not your dogs."

This was torture. He desperately wanted to capsize the chessboard and drag her into his arms. "Dogs make it easier. I wouldn't be here right now after all, if it weren't for the dogs."

"It could be argued that life is a chain of events. Where would either of us be without the kids at the youth center? Besides—" her hands stilled on his "—besides, no dog made you take my hand and not let it go."

Their heads were almost touching. "You noticed, eh?" He took a chance and skimmed his fingers along her inner arm. He could almost see sparks flying off. "Sometimes I wish we were more than friends." If sometimes meant several times a day.

"Yes." Was her simple admission an invitation? He took mental command of his traveling hand and brought it back to stroke her fingers. He'd memorized them during their chess games. Her thumb had a curious perky upturn, while her pinky on her left hand had a slight inward crook.

He was afraid of breaking their connection, this fragile, newborn thing they were breathing life into. What they had mattered, more than anything had in a long while. *Don't push.*

He touched a white scar on her forefinger. "How did that happen?"

"I cut myself while cooking."

"Ouch."

"I was preparing a roast. I didn't feel it at first. And I didn't see the blood pour into the meat. Krista screaming her head off was my first clue."

"Stitches?"

"A butterfly Band-Aid. Krista could barely down her meat, convinced that she was consuming human blood, even though she'd watched Bridget cut away the portion."

"And then you told her about your hepatitis results?"

Mara laughed. "I should've pretended that. She's our drama queen."

"And you are?"

Mara's hand balled. "The cautious one. Or so I've been told."

He had told her that, though not in so many words. "I don't want you to miss out on life, Mara."

"I'm wishing the same for you, too, Connor."

They stared at their entwined hands. Connor had no idea what to do next. It was Mara who slowly, slowly slipped her hands from his. "Go ahead. Claim your win."

He had her king in checkmate five moves later. But he left her place feeling only loss for what else he might've won.

THE BIG REVEAL, as Mara privately billed the meeting between Jack and Dr. Greg, was held two weeks later, delayed by Dr. Greg's previously scheduled travel plans and by Jack and Bridget's relentless restaurant hours. Jack and Bridget were pressed together on Mara's couch as if huddling for warmth, Mara in the armchair Connor usually took during their weekly game of chess.

Mara had restored her winner's title last week, but their bit of intimacy had charged their time together, like animals before a storm, like Griffin right now. He had picked up on the tension in the room and was pacing about.

"Griff," she called. "Come."

His low bulk resolved in her vision and she stroked his eyebrows. He promptly sat to receive more, his head drifting to her knee.

Dr. Greg's trick had bonded Mara and Griffin more than any walk or special treat had.

She and Griffin had passed the thirty-day challenge last week, but Daisy was in heat and Connor had asked her to keep Griffin away for a few more days. Mara suspected Connor had contrived an excuse to extend her time with Griffin, but she gave him the benefit of the doubt.

She and Griffin simultaneously picked up the slam of a vehicle door, and they stood.

Jack and Bridget straightened. "What? Is he here?" Jack glanced to the front living room window, even though they were curtained at his request. "I want us to look right into each other's eye at the same time," he'd said.

"I think it's game time," Mara said. Sure enough, her doorbell chimed. Griffin whined, his snout pressed to the door crack. Griffin probably knew his occasional caregiver waited on the other side.

Dr. Greg stepped into the narrow hallway and gave her a hushed greeting and Griffin a quick pat, likely aware that Jack and Bridget were straining to hear. He'd had a haircut since she'd last seen him, and he smoothed his silver hair now. He was a handsome man.

Now that the relationship had been declared, she could see the resemblance between father and son. How her aunt had kept such a profound family secret still astounded Mara.

Griffin led them into the living room, Mara ahead of Dr. Greg. "Jack, Bridget. I'd like you to meet our mystery guest."

They stood and Jack grasped Bridget's hand hard enough for her to wince. "Holy," Jack said. "My father is our old dentist."

Jack stared at Dr. Greg, who silently absorbed the inspection. "Just so there's no confusion, you're my biological father, right?"

"I am convinced, yes." He still spoke in a near whisper.

Jack couldn't seem to tear his eyes from Dr. Greg. "You did my teeth when I was a kid in middle school, high school. You knew then?"

"Yes," Dr. Greg said. He seemed to be practicing Mara's suggestion of minimal speech. The less said the easier it would be for Jack to recover from the inescapable shock.

"Holy," Jack repeated.

Mara thought it best to let Jack have a moment. "Dr. Greg, you remember my sister Bridget?" After they shook hands, Jack instantly reclaimed his wife's hand, anchoring himself in her touch. Mara knew the power in that connection.

"Can I get you anything, Dr. Greg? I've got all kinds of tea. Ice water, coffee?"

"No, I'm fine." He still spoke quietly, as if his usual voice might shatter the moment.

"Jack? Bridget? Can I freshen your drinks?"

Bridget declined, but Jack placed his order. "Whiskey. Two fingers, straight up."

Mara slipped over to the liquor hutch in the dining room, relieved to give them space. "It's a single malt, twenty-five years old," Jack said to Dr. Greg. "A supplier gave me a couple of bottles at Christmas. I gave one to Mara."

"Glenfiddich?"

"Yes."

"I visited a distillery in Scotland a number of years back. More than one, in fact." He spoke so quietly that it came out like a church confession.

"Would you like whiskey, too?" Mara said to him. Consuming alcohol during an already emotionally charged situation wasn't the best idea, but the men had bonded over a shared interest. Besides, this was her home, her family.

"Don't mind if I do," Dr. Greg said. "Same as Jack, two fingers."

Only when the drink was in hand did Jack sit. The rest of them followed suit; Mara opened the curtains to the warm light of the June afternoon before sitting on a dining room chair a short distance away. Griffin took up sentry duty at the window on the lookout for more visitors. Or just Connor.

"We've been looking forward to this meeting," Bridget said.

"I'm sorry I couldn't come sooner. I had already planned a visit to my daughter in Arizona."

"You have a daughter, too?"

"Three, actually."

Mara knew that from her travels on the internet, where she'd prowled through Dr. Greg's late wife's Instagram account to learn more about their daughters.

"Leah, my second oldest, lives in Arizona. She has two girls. Seven and four." Dr. Greg tapped on his phone and presented the screen to Jack who, along with Bridget, leaned in.

"Cute," Bridget said. "What are their names?"

"Aiden and Cara."

Dr. Greg turned the phone to Mara. She could only see a blur. Jack and Bridget froze, recognizing her difficulty. It didn't matter. Dr. Greg's voice had risen to normal levels, a sign of a growing ease. Besides, Mara had already viewed posts of Leah with her kids. In matching aprons, making a mess of the kitchen. With her husband and girls at the playground. Mara had peered closely at the image on her screen, like a kid at a toy store window. Dare she hope for that life, too?

"And your other daughters?"

"Ava is in Ottawa. She's single, no kids." Dr. Greg paused. "And there's Abigail, my eldest. She lives here with her husband and daughter."

Jack brightened. "She does? Do I know her?" At ten thousand-plus residents, Spirit Lake was large enough for people to pass by unrecognized, but the restaurant and Bridget's long history in the town meant they either knew or knew of practically every resident.

Dr. Greg hesitated and then in the same near whisper as when he'd entered said, "Shirazi. Abigail Shirazi."

"Real estate agent, Abigail Shirazi?" Jack said. "She and her husband have their pictures everywhere. Bestselling team."

"That's them."

"Do your daughters know about me?"

"Not a clue."

"Not even Abigail?"

Dr. Greg drank more of his whiskey, a sizable amount from the sound of his swallow. "Least of all her. She—she is very loyal to her mother's memory."

Jack nodded again slowly, like a patient processing critical information from his doctor. "Did Mara tell you we're expecting?"

Dr. Greg looked stunned. "No. She didn't. Congratulations."

"November. Bridget's sister is expecting the same month, too."

"My granddaughter is expecting then, too. It'll be a busy month." Dr. Greg turned to Mara. "Three new additions to our families."

What? Unless Talia had changed her mind since their session yesterday, she had not yet decided whether or not she was keeping the baby.

"She's young," Dr. Greg went on, "but I know her boyfriend's uncle. More like a dad than an uncle. He told me he'd back them up if need be."

What was Connor thinking by acting as if Talia had already ruled out adoption?

"When did he speak to you about Talia's pregnancy?"

The sharpness in Mara's voice had Dr. Greg

reply carefully. "Well now, a few weeks ago, earlier in the month."

After the family meeting in May, after she'd confronted him about not interfering in Talia's private and difficult decision, after he'd promised to keep his distance. And then he'd turned around and broken his promise.

Mara said. "He should not have made any presumptions about Talia's pregnancy."

Dr. Greg stared into his whiskey. "I didn't get the sense he meant any harm."

But harm was exactly what he was spreading by encouraging Talia's grandfather to believe that she was keeping the baby, when the matter was far from decided. She ached to set the record straight, but that would draw her into her professional realm. No. She would speak to Connor on his own. For now, she'd steer the conversation in another direction.

"I'll deal with this later," she said. Tension must've come through her voice because Griffin appeared at her side, his ears pricked to the guests. Mara touched her hand to his head, calming him—and herself. She steered the conversation back around to a different baby. "I believe we left off with Jack announcing that he and Bridget are expecting."

"Right," Jack said quickly. "Anyway, so

that's why I wanted to find my biological father. Because I want my child to have as much family as possible. And now the baby will have tons." He pivoted to Bridget. "See? Aunts, uncles, cousins."

Dr. Greg's next gulp of whiskey could be heard, Mara was sure, across the street. "That's a possibility for down the road."

Jack stilled. Bridget sneaked her hand onto Jack's thigh. "You want me kept secret?"

"I made a choice when your mother was pregnant. I chose the family I already had. It might have been the wrong decision. I will never know, but at least I built something from that. I don't want to risk it, no. Some of my children will forgive me, but—others won't."

Mara knew who he meant. "Abigail."

Dr. Greg nodded. "She has very particular ideas about the structure of a family. Her husband, too. Things with them are often… rigid. You might have noticed that."

She wondered if he knew about Abigail's abortion. Not that Mara would tell him what had been divulged in her office.

This conversation kept steering itself into her professional life, but could she expect any less from here on in? She could refuse to see

Talia based on a familial interest, but where would that leave Talia, and how could she explain her reasoning to the parents without raising their suspicions? She could think of something, but it would be a lie, and that was absolutely verboten. For her career and her own principles.

But at some point, she would have to make a decision between Talia as her client and Talia as her—what?—second, third cousin? As her family.

"And now Talia is threatening to move out. That's hit Abigail hard."

"Moving out?" she repeated. Talia hadn't mentioned that in any of their sessions.

"To Dane's place. I guess Connor had invited her, even before the family meeting."

Of course the interfering master-of-mayhem had. With no regard for its impact on Talia's family.

He had crossed so many lines.

"What are you suggesting?" Jack said. "That we carry on as before? I'm sorry, but the cat's out of the bag. And this was your idea." His face was flushed, his glass empty. Bonding over whiskey had backfired.

Dr. Greg glanced at Mara. Was he hoping

she'd get them out of the fix? She could sympathize—with both of them.

She waded in. "I don't think that we need to solve anything today. That was not the intention of this meeting. It was only so you could meet each other. That is all. That has been accomplished."

Jack threw his arms wide. "Resulting in even more secrecy."

"I am sorry for that." Dr. Greg cleared his throat. "I have…watched you over the years, and I am thankful that my absence from your life has not prevented you from becoming the good, decent, lucky, happy man you are today."

An honest declaration, but Jack grunted. "Let's hope your presence doesn't reverse my luck or my happiness."

"It won't," Mara said. For Jack's sake, she'd help them through this. She was good at reconciling differences. If she could do it for a living, then she could do it for her family.

Connor Flanagan was an entirely different matter.

CHAPTER NINE

CONNOR WAS STRUGGLING with how to best explain to Dane the impact of the Marshall Plan on globalism when Mara called.

"We need to talk."

He had hoped she would say those very words, but not with anger.

"Sure," he said, getting up from the kitchen table covered with paper, textbooks and a laptop. "Give me a moment here." Dane shot a knowing smile at his uncle. His prolonged Wednesday outings had been noted by both Dane and Kate.

With Daisy and two dogs he was boarding in tow, he hurried up the stairs into his office, converted from Dane's childhood bedroom. He and Dane had taken over the downstairs with their own separate ensuites, while Kate took the upstairs master bedroom. They all had their space, though once the baby came, the whole place might turn into a madhouse strewn with baby paraphernalia. All good, of course.

Mara lost no time. "Did you invite Talia to come live with you?"

"Not me. Dane. I happen to live in the same house."

"Splitting hairs. Was it your idea?"

He eased himself into his chair, the dogs amassing around. "Yes."

"But you knew that Talia hadn't decided what to do, right?"

"We both know that. What are you getting at, Mara?"

He heard Mara suck in a deep breath. "You are setting up an expectation in people's minds. It's indirect pressure on Talia to make the choice you want her to make."

"I have not spoken to Talia since the meeting. Out of respect for her." *And you*, he might've added.

"Can you say the same thing about Talia's grandfather?"

"Greg? How do you know about my conversation with him?"

She paused. "It's confidential. The point is, the message to him was the same. Was it not your intention to imply that she was keeping the baby?"

He could dodge the question forever, but not Mara. "Yes, I want Talia to keep the baby. That's no secret, anyway. I had not intended to create pressure for her, but I can see how it would. I guess she doesn't think very highly of me right now."

"I am fairly certain she doesn't know."

Connor did a double take on that. "So you're not calling me as her psychologist?"

Mara blew out her breath with enough energy to blast glass. "If I had to make a choice, I'd say no."

"Then, and try not to take offense, Mara, but what business is it of yours?"

"Because it—" She stopped. He could almost see her frown lines. "Because whether I say it as a professional or personally, it's the same. You are creating havoc in an already confusing situation for a teenage girl because you have failed to deal with your own issues."

Connor looked up at his wall of certificates in canine training. Proof that he could move on. "My issues are no more than anybody else's. You've seen Talia's parents."

"But it's not their issues you can do anything about, Connor. And it's not their damage you can repair."

If she was telling him to dredge up trauma

he'd dealt with years ago, forget it. Connor chose to focus on her current grievance. He had apologized for having suggested moving in to Talia, which she refused to accept. He would try again. "I can't undo what I've done, but I won't talk about the pregnancy with anyone but Dane and Kate. At least, until Talia makes up her mind because if she does decide to raise my nephew's kid, I'm telling the world, understood?"

She sighed. "I suppose that's the best I can expect."

"You're not mad at me anymore?"

He had to wait a few beats before she answered. "No. I'm rather appalled at how easily I can forgive you."

He grinned but sobered at her next words. "But even turning her private life into a public announcement should her decision go your way shows that you've not addressed your own issues."

He sat back in his chair. "Are you going to pass along advice, Mara?"

"I don't think I'm qualified to do so. As you know, I have my own issues. And between yours and mine, they are on a collision course."

But their different views on family hadn't

stopped them from holding hands. It hadn't stopped the energy pulsing between them every meeting since.

"I took your advice into account with the kids at the youth center. I played games, listened, was there for them." He hardly got to exchange a word with Mara as a result.

"I noticed, yes. I also noticed you brought two more dogs to run interference."

"I'm dog-sitting. It's temporary." He tried to keep his defense light, even as he felt his insides churn.

"There's never a problem a dog can't solve," Mara said. "Right?"

Ignoring her jab, he said, "I like it. I might make it my new logo. How's Griffin?"

"His head's on my feet. He wants to know when he can come home." Connor rubbed Daisy's head. Ideally he'd like to switch Griffin for Daisy, but it wouldn't be anytime soon.

He should really not draw this out any longer. But what if Mara's doggy conversion only needed a little more time? She was already cracking. "Daisy should be sorted in another three days."

"Griffin can hardly wait."

"And you? Will you miss him?"

"It was fine." Her casualness was the perfect sign that her time with Griffin had been meaningful. It had worked.

"Come on, admit that you made an awesome dog-mom."

Mara sighed. "Connor. I'm going to tell you a deep, deep, penetrating secret and then I'm going to end the call so you can ponder its mysteries and from it acquire untold wisdom that will transform your existence. Okay?"

He wiggled his toes. "Shoot."

"A dog," she said, "is not a person."

Then, as promised, she ended the call.

"Dog-mom?" Mara asked Griffin, slumming beside her on the couch while she'd talked to Connor. "Do you see me as your adopted mom?" Griffin flexed his round eyebrows, as if doubting the label, as well.

He dropped to the floor, sniffed the carpet and walked off. His nails clacked on the dining room floor and then he lapped from his water bowl. Soon he'd stare out the sliding doors to her ground-floor deck. One evening, Connor had found them out on the deck when he'd come over to drop off treats for Griffin, and faithful Griffin spent every evening waiting for a repeat performance.

"Miss him all you want," Mara called, "you can't have him."

Her breath caught. She'd spoken a truth about herself, not Griffin. She couldn't ever have Connor, unless she budged on her resolve not to become a mom.

Particularly a mom to a child she'd passed her disability on to. She was coping with her visual impairment just fine, but no way would she deliberately risk setting her own child on the same path.

She should take the test and find out. Krista had, with a negative result. But that was Krista, jumping into everything with both feet. Mara was…cautious. No, she was a coward. Too scared to find out because— because if it turned out she was a carrier, then the small part of her—the part that looked at Leah's photos of her girls and wondered, the part that still hoped for motherhood even as her practical mind scorned the possibility— just might be snuffed out. And she didn't know if she could bear that.

Still, test or not, she might have what it took to be a dog-mom. "As much as I hate to admit that your master's right," Mara called to Griffin, "he might have a point."

She heard Griffin stretch himself onto the

bare floor by the glass doors as he began his nightly vigil. Three more days and his dream would come true. Meanwhile, he could listen and smell through the crack in the open balcony door. *Welcome to my dark world, Griffin.*

She crossed to the spa retreat she'd set up in her second bedroom. Her sanctuary of deep pillows, a yoga mat and a sound system. From her phone she opened a playlist, pop rock from the eighties and nineties—the music played in the vehicles on trips with her parents—and slipped in one earbud. Humming, nose to her monitor, she pulled up YouTube and entered search terms. She clicked on promising ones where vloggers showed their guide dogs at work. Women handled their dogs, one just like Daisy, in shopping malls, elevators, airports, at the dentist, and told their stories about their relationships with their special canine companions.

"They are an extension of me…" Which her cane technically was, too. And didn't require feeding.

"She saves my life about once a month…" That might be useful.

"He's constantly checking in with me…" Well, even Griffin had come to her side at the meeting with Jack and Dr. Greg. Okay, a check in the "for" column.

Life with a guide dog couldn't be all sunshine and roses. She found a vlogger also with retinitis pigmentosa who had hundreds of videos on her blindness and dedicated playlists about her dogs. Mara clicked one titled "10 Bad Things about a Guide Dog."

Doggy grumpiness, other people petting your dog, refusal of access... Mara checked in with herself. Yes, yes and yes again. She could deal with these things and yes, she was willing to do them. She was even prepared, as gut-wrenching as it would be, to be there for them at their inevitable death.

And then she came to the last one: You are their mother.

She would be responsible exactly as a mother was. For the normal things like food and shelter, but for teeth cleanings, for their health, for their happiness. And in return the dog would save her life again and again.

Was that not a fair exchange? Hard percussion and the cry of a guitar from her earbud jarred her from her daydreaming. Of course. It was for her to listen to the music of life, not play it. She reached to pull out her earbud.

And then from a still core inside her filtered up another note. Courage.

She would get a guide dog. And it would be scary, but she could do it because—

Because she had Connor. He'd given her the courage. Coaxed and nudged it from her with his easy charm and refusal to accept her fears. She wasn't entirely sure if his persistence came more from his faith in his dogs than in her alone, but she was grateful. She could now see having a guide dog in her life. Another significant, living being.

She closed her computer. She laid her head on the cushioned back and let the sounds of her place drift back into her senses. Let the fireworks fill her vision. Swirl lazily about in purples, blues, greens. Was that a dog's head that appeared?

A cool draft swept over her skin.

Another sensation hit. Silence. The absence of the barest murmur, a feeling more than a sound, of Griffin's personality.

"Griffin!" She snapped to her feet, her ears straining in the darkness for signs of his presence. The whap of his tail, the scrape of nails as he pulled himself out of his doze, the pad of his feet toward her.

Nothing. He was gone. No, no, no.

She followed the draft to the wide balcony door. Sure, he could've shouldered it open, but there was a screen in place.

She stretched out her hand and encountered an empty gap. How? She stepped onto the deck and her bare soles pressed into thin screen wires. He must've pushed open the door and jumped onto the screen, knocking it flat out of its tracks.

"Griffin, come!"

She picked up the breeze in the leaves, laughter, the drip, drip, drip off the eaves from an earlier thundershower, voice rising in the dark, calling for him. But nothing from Griffin.

Her dog-son had run away.

BY MORNING, THE situation hadn't improved. Connor had come to her place the night before with the hopes that Griffin was close by and she simply couldn't see him, or that he refused to answer her call. But no. Griffin was gone.

She checked her social media to see if anyone had news when Bridget called. "First of all," she began without Mara saying a word, "that dog's smarter than most people. He's super unfriendly, so no one's going to kidnap him. He's traffic-savvy thanks to you and bush-savvy thanks to Connor. He will show up when he's good and ready."

"You're saying that to cheer me up."

"I'm saying that because I know exactly where your mind has gone. You're thinking that you lost sight of Sofia and now you lost Griffin, and doesn't this prove that you're a bad person."

"It might've crossed my mind." Every waking moment last night. Not even sinking into her inner fireworks show had induced sleep.

"Well, let it cross and walk right out. We're heading to the ranch this afternoon around two. Will that work?"

What was she— Right, Canada Day. Because the July first holiday fell on a long weekend this year, Krista had invited them out to the ranch for a giant multifamily barbecue of nearly a hundred people. Mara had not been looking forward to mingling with strangers, and now with Griffin gone...

"I can't. I need to be here in case Griffin comes back."

"Leave the back door open." It already was.

"Someone might call."

"Bring your phone."

"Bridget...I can't."

She heard Jack's voice in the background, and then Bridget. "All right, Mara. Is there anything we can do before we go?"

Another call hummed through. "It's Connor," Mara said. "No, have a good time. Bye."

She didn't wait for her sister to reply before switching over to Connor. "Nothing," she said by way of greeting. "You?"

"Nothing yet," he said. "I'll give animal control a call and see what happens." He spoke as if losing his favorite dog didn't matter.

She longed to apologize yet again, but that was pointless. What he wanted from her was Griffin back safe and sound. Or even injured. A broken leg, cuts and bruises, an infection could all be patched up. Just as long as Griffin was home.

"My posts are already getting shared," she said, aiming for Connor's optimism.

"Same here," Connor said. "It looks good."

"I was thinking of printing posters," she said. "To get the word out more, right?"

"It couldn't hurt. I can help put them up."

"That's okay. I've got it covered." She didn't, but she'd created enough of a headache for him.

"Mara—" he began.

"I do," she said, and even though she couldn't be sure, she added, "My mom will help. Keep me posted and I'll let you know if anything comes up on my end."

"Mara—" he began again. "Do you believe me when I say it's not your fault? That these things happen?"

Exactly what Bridget had said. She told him what he needed to hear. "I believe you."

Connor had tried to make her feel better but a half hour later, her mother's hug, an enveloping inside her incense-scented shawl, actually did help. "Mom," she mumbled into the folds of the shawl at her mother's neck, "I screwed up."

Her mother patted her back, quick and firm. "Rubbish. Dogs go missing all the time."

"Especially if their caregivers are blind," Mara muttered.

"You still haven't forgiven yourself for the time Sofia went missing? It was two years ago and ended happily."

"I had convinced myself of that finally, and then once again, it's happened. For who knows how much longer? Yes, it can happen to anyone, but it happens to me because I'm blind."

"Possibly. And it could've happened to a deaf person because they're deaf. And to a child because they're inexperienced, and to an old person because they're forgetful."

Her mother's psychological strategy was termed normalizing the experience. She could make every abnormality in life, every twist and turn, seem ordinary. Or wondrous. When Mara's diagnosis had come in and her future loomed dark, her mother had immediately asked the specialist, "What do the others do?" Enter devices, awareness meetings with schools, a regimen of nutritional supplements.

But her mother had also told Mara her visual impairment was her own unique and wondrous gift to the world. She could now be a role model for how to succeed despite setbacks. Now with two degrees and a thriving business, Mara knew her mother had been right. She was a role model. Just not for being a mother, even to a dog.

"I'm sorry for dragging you away from the barbecue," Mara said as they hit the congested streets of Spirit Lake, her laptop case stuffed with full-color posters, tape and thumbtacks. Canada Day was the busiest day of the year in the small town, the day when she usually hightailed it out, as visitors to the lake flooded in. But she was in the thick of it this year.

"Here," her mother said, "how about on either side of the postal box?"

"I don't think we're allowed to put posters on them," Mara said.

"Then the heartless souls can take them down. We've got a dog to find." Her mother scritched out a length of tape and set to work while Mara acted as a portable supply center.

As much as her mother—and her father, for that matter—had expected her to move on with her life, her mother had also championed Mara during the tough times. And now Mara's dog.

"Are you getting used to the idea of being a double grandma?" Mara said, as they journeyed on to commit gentle vandalism in the name of Griffin.

"I'm already a double grandma."

Sofia and Isabella, two other children she'd championed. She had shunned a sweet deal in a seniors' complex because children weren't allowed to sleep over. Instead, she boarded with a retired couple who had allowed her to convert a spare bedroom into a second home for the girls.

"Newborns are different," Mara said.

"Yes. Smaller and squishier. I'm peeking at babies all the time now to get used to how tiny they are. And so many wrinkles! As many as me."

"Does that mean you are reverse-aging, Mom?"

"I should hope not. I'm the mother of the mothers. I take precedent."

There it was. The supremacy of mothers. Save mothers and children first, the prime directive during any crisis. "I'm glad your sisters are having babies," she went on. "I must admit to having expressed my wishes more than once."

At every get-together. She'd never encouraged Mara even so much as to get married, much less have children. She'd never championed that part of her life.

"Mom, why have you never wanted me to become a mother?"

"There's the fact that you're not married," her mother said, her voice pointing away from Mara in a search for another spot for a poster along the busy lakeside avenue. "I won't pressure you to put the horse before the cart."

"There's a postal box at the end of the street," Mara said. Her cane whacked against its legs on every walk. "You haven't pressured me to marry, either."

"You will, when you find the right man."

Had she found him? Her hesitation wasn't lost on her mother. Her voice re-centered on Mara. "Or maybe you have."

"No, we had a moment. That was all." One that he'd never pressed afterward, and Connor Flanagan knew how to go after what he wanted. He must've decided that she wasn't worth it.

"I believe that was how the universe started. A single moment that got out of hand. Do I know him?"

And since their moment had imploded into nothingness, then there was no point in keeping his identity a secret. "Connor Flanagan."

"Dog Man?"

Mara ground her molars at the name. "Yes."

"I know his sister. Kate Anheim," her mother said. "She's a nurse at the senior care center. She's quiet. Her son's smart. He's picked up school awards. Graduated this year, I think. Has a girlfriend, too. A busy young man."

Her mother clearly didn't know that Dane might get a whole lot busier come November, otherwise she would've said so. No way would her mother sit on that tidbit. She'd extracted plenty of secrets from her daughters, and Mara worried she'd betray Talia's trust. Best to steer the conversation away, even if it meant to her. "At any rate, Connor seems to think I'll make an excellent guide dog handler. He persuaded me to take on a buddy dog as a starting point, despite my doubts. I've only managed to prove how right I was."

"You don't sound happy with yourself."

"I'm not. I had started to believe that he was right. I had started to believe—"

In Connor. In them. That if she could be a successful dog-mom, then their quiet moment on the couch could blossom into something more. Dog Mom meets Dog Man.

"Anyway, I think Griffin's little escapade has convinced him that I'm hardly up for the task."

"Is that what he's told you?"

"Of course not. He's like you and Bridget. Can't see how I'm to blame, thinks accidents happen."

"He's right. Others have guide dogs, so can you. A guide dog won't run off. And if it does, it'll know how to cross streets and enter shopping malls. It could be trained to turn itself into the police, probably. What's your real problem?"

Mara shook her head. She felt like one of her patients, confused and fearful. What was her problem? Other than a missing dog and a man she wanted but didn't want her and even if he did, she couldn't give him the family he wanted.

They arrived at the box and Mara pulled out a poster, and the largest word stood out starkly for her. "Missing," she said, "I'm tired of missing out, missing opportunities, feeling as if I've gone missing."

Her mother taped up the poster before she said anything. "I won't pretend to understand what it's like to lose vision. To have something so precious slowly stripped away, so that even the memory of it is gone. I would've given anything to take on that burden, you know that."

Mara nodded and waited for the "but." "But go for it, anyway." "But Connor is worth it." "But you're worth it." It didn't come.

Instead she said, "Shall we carry on?"

Not every cause should be championed.

CHAPTER TEN

BARKING, REGULAR AND HIGH, like someone repeatedly leaning on a doorbell, broke into Connor's sleep. *Griffin, give it a break.*

Griffin. Connor tore up the stairs from his lower level bedroom, Daisy running ahead, and threw open the door. In shot Griffin, and he and Daisy twisted about each other in greeting. Whoa. "Okay, you two break it up. We don't need another unexpected pregnancy around here."

He shooed Griffin outside onto the porch and followed, dropping to his knees. Now that Griffin had returned, Connor could give way to the worry that he'd kept tamped down. "Where you been? Where you been, boy?"

Griffin rammed into Connor, knocking him back onto his haunches. He wrapped his arms around the dog who furiously licked every part of Connor—face, hands, shoulder. Connor patted him down, checking for cuts. Nothing. Griffin dropped to all fours and began sniffing the porch deck.

"I bet you're hungry," he said. "Wait until Mara hears this." He called her, even though he wasn't sure she would be awake yet, confirmed by her groggy answer. But his news swept away her sleepiness.

She gasped. "Is he okay?"

"He could do with food and water. Otherwise, no worse for wear."

"Put him on, put him on."

Connor switched to speakerphone and held it close to Griffin. Both he and dog listened as Mara made smooching noises and inquired after his health. Lucky dog, maybe Connor should go missing for a few days. Then she turned to scolding. Maybe not so lucky. Griffin cast Connor a pleading look. Connor shrugged. The dog deserved it.

"—now that you're back home, I trust you will stay put."

Griffin wandered away from the phone.

Dane appeared outside in a T-shirt and boxer shorts. "You're back, you dumb dog."

Connor switched off speakerphone and brought the phone to his ear. "There you have it. All's well that ends well." He mouthed to

Dane to get Griffin food, and his nephew disappeared.

"Your challenge yielded mixed results," she said. "The subject lived but the objective was not attained."

His excitement wavered. "Repeat the experiment, adjust the variables and observe the new results."

"I think Griffin has made his point clear. Do you have any idea how he got back?"

"He's sat in the front seat often enough to know the route. Your place is close to the youth center. Maybe he found his way there, and then followed the usual route back to here. We're only seven miles out of town."

"Talented dog."

"Very." Despite Griffin's disobedience and the general upset he'd caused, Connor was proud of his stray. "Limited buddy dog potential as demonstrated."

"He's made his point. What will you do now?"

"I have an idea." But he wouldn't let her change the subject. "I'm sorry it didn't work out with Griffin. In retrospect, he wasn't the right dog to give to you. I should've known better. Let me make it up to you."

Mara sighed. "Maybe I'm not the right person for what you need. You know, it's quite possible for someone to simply not like dogs."

"Sure, but not in this case."

"I like Griffin, but I don't want to have a relationship with him. Don't take it personally."

But he was. If she backed out of dogs, then their own relationship reverted to weekly meetings starting in a distant two months. "There's a dog for you."

"You make it sound like a relationship. Soul mates."

He hesitated. They were straying into her point about how a dog wasn't a person. "I do know the difference," he said quietly. "Obviously."

"I sometimes wonder," she said. "At any rate, perhaps we should give it a break and take it up later."

Dane reappeared with food and bowl. "Look. Come on out. I have a couple of others, smaller, big hearts, a little older, heavy into snuggling."

"Now you're making it sound like a dating service." Her voice was teasing. He liked that way better than her defeatism.

"Sure," he said. "Come on out and I'll hook you up."

Dane, clattering food into the bowl, shot his uncle a sideways look. Connor turned away to avoid eye contact. "Look, I heard you on the phone with Griffin. That wasn't faked and that was with Griffin, the most antisocial dog I've got, and you still bonded with him. You took awesome care of him."

"I appreciate your kind words and I'm trying to keep my own responsibility in his escapade in perspective, but no. I'm not taking on another dog."

With anyone else, he would've accepted their answer, but he couldn't with Mara. He'd made such progress. He tried for a more indirect tack. "Fine," he said. "How about you come out and see Griffin?"

"You're holding him hostage until I pay the ransom of coming out there," Mara said.

"Maybe."

"I'll come out, but you won't change my mind."

Good enough for him. He'd convinced her once, he could do it again.

THERE WAS NO chance to experience the sweep of wind when Mara stepped from Connor's truck this time out. Griffin immediately bunted her hand for attention. "There you are, you disobedient rascal." She knelt and rubbed her cheek against the soft spot behind his right ear, felt his slobbery licks on her neck.

"Forget about you starting to like dogs," Connor said. "You're becoming one."

"Possibly," she said, drawing Griffin into a very human hug. "That's why you tolerate me. Criteria for friendship with Connor Flanagan—must display canine characteristics."

Connor's legs appeared in her line of vision. He seemed especially large today. Over his T-shirt, he wore a red plaid flannel padded shirt. Albertans called it a jackshirt, a shapeless thing he made look good. Krista said the same thing about Will. "There's a special brand of man," Krista had hypothesized, "that can totally rock the ugly."

"That might explain why the people in my life end up barking at me." He touched her arm. "You want to see the others?"

She didn't especially. It would only lead to him pressuring her to take on another dog, and she hadn't changed her mind. She was all for extending her time with him, but not in the company of dogs. "Isn't there something else we could do?"

His voice took on a special suggestive edge. "What did you have in mind?"

Was he coming on to her? Had he thought she was coming on to him? Maybe she was. She'd definitely spent a stupidly long time to make it look as if she hadn't spent a stupidly long time on her appearance. Even as she'd berated herself for the futility of it all.

"I don't know. Chess, perhaps?"

"Kate might not appreciate us in the house right now. She's cleaning. You don't want to surprise her when she's got a toilet brush."

"A walk?"

"We could, but the grass is pretty long, the rain's made it wet, and there's thistles everywhere and you…" They both looked down at her pretty sandals. Pretty useless sandals.

"You're saying you've got dogs and that's it."

"That's it. A couple dozen best friends."

Was he really that limited in his thinking?

"Dogs it is then," she said. "Lead the way."

Far from leading, he walked alongside her, his jacketed arm brushing hers, his stride matching her shorter, more tentative walk. There was something different with him today, a tension between them that felt much like whenever they touched.

If he continued to walk this close where she could feel his warmth, the length and breadth of him, she didn't trust herself not to change her mind, change her life.

And risk—no, invite—heartbreak.

It was almost with relief when they entered the renovated farm shed. Like before, dogs surrounded her.

"Down!" Connor rebuked one and all. "Sorry about that. Still working on manners. Don't worry, I've got better choices."

"Connor, I haven't changed my mind. I'm not taking on another dog."

"Even if it was the perfect dog?"

"I think I made it clear from the outset that I wasn't looking for a dog. I took on Griffin to help with his socializing, if you remember. That didn't work out as planned."

"I admit that he wasn't a complete success," he said. "He's started to balk about getting in the truck."

So that's why he didn't come with Connor to pick her up. She'd not only failed to socialize Griffin, but made him even more withdrawn. "Why are you pushing another dog on me, then?"

"Don't worry about Griffin. He's got too much of an adventurous spirit to hang on to his fears for long. In fact, this might have been a good thing in the end."

Connor's optimism was...dogged. "How so?"

"I don't know why I didn't see it earlier. He's got real search-and-rescue potential. He found his way back here after two days without a scratch on him. I bet he could've gotten back here earlier, but he took his time, smelled the roses, swam in the lake."

"He might've thumbed a ride," Mara said.

"You think I'm exaggerating his talent?"

Her point was to show how he treated his dogs as people, but of course he wouldn't make that connection. "I think Griffin is a highly capable dog."

"I'm going to train him for search-and-rescue. I've got contacts within the SR association in the province and can work with them."

"Sounds like a plan."

"See? All's well that ends well. Like I said."

"Maybe, but I'm not tempting fate by subjecting another dog to this experiment of training me to become a mother to a guide dog."

"Listen—"

Mara could feel her control fraying, like in the office during the meeting with Talia when he pushed and pushed. "No, Connor, you listen. Please don't keep denying that you had an ulterior purpose when you gave me Griffin. You used him to change my mind about guide dogs. Admit it."

He shook his head. "I admit that is what I might have made you believe, but there's more to it, I've come to realize."

He closed the distance between them. She could feel his heat, his solidness. The throaty timbre of his voice. "I've always admired you, Mara. Everyone talks about wanting to make a difference in the world. You actually do it, and you've done it on your own terms. But when you said that you didn't want another living being in your life… I dunno, I couldn't walk away from that one. The thing is, I didn't want you to be alone."

They'd had a moment, he'd said he'd wanted to be more than friends, and now this? "You told me that. So you gave me a dog. Now you discovered what I already knew. That I'm better alone."

"No, you're not better alone."

Why was he so close to her? She couldn't will herself to step away so she beat words at his chest. "Because—surprise, surprise— I don't particularly like being alone. Having

Griffin—no, losing Griffin—proved just how much I hate it."

He reached up, almost touched her arm. She could feel the warmth of his hand. "But you have to admit that it limits your options to someone who also doesn't want kids—or any more kids if he's already a father, or who has grown kids or can't have kids and doesn't want to adopt."

He'd written her off. Yes, he once stated that he'd thought about a relationship with her, but he'd always acted it out through his dogs. She should've known. Shouldn't have teased herself with imagining a relationship with him. It wasn't in the books. Her life continued to narrow, like her vision.

She'd called for honesty between them. He'd stated his position quite clearly. For the record, she should reciprocate. "I want kids, Connor. I desperately want them. I want to have what my sisters have. A husband, babies, plans. I want my vision back, but that's not going to happen."

She should leave it at that, but he hadn't moved. He seemed to have become even more cemented as she spoke. She sagged, her barrage of words falling to a trickle. "From the first time I saw you, you came with dogs."

She stared at the crisscross pattern of his jackshirt, at the glint of a metal button. She focused on it, at the swirl of purple and blue dancing on it. "But I don't want your dogs. I've only ever wanted you."

CONNOR'S FIRST INSTINCT was to crush Mara in his arms and kiss her, to seal the deal, to once and for all elevate that earlier moment, as she called it, to the next level.

He set his hands on her waist, tugged her close. Her eyes were wide-open, anticipating him. Her lips parted—

"Connor, you're not going to kiss me, are you?"

Her voice was slightly breathless, from anticipation or shock.

"That's the plan. We both want to be with each other. Seems logical."

"No, you said that you had thought about it, but all your moves since then have been on the chessboard."

Now that he knew she wanted more from him, honesty was easy. "Because I wasn't about to risk our friendship. But now that I know we're both on the same track—" He lowered his head, stopped at her next words.

"—a track off a cliff. Our relationship is problematic."

"Is there one that isn't?"

She flattened her hands on his chest. A good sign, except he could feel a slight pressing away. He eased back. "I suppose they all need a maintenance schedule, some repairs. It's just that ours has entire missing parts that I see as preventing it from running at all. You're right. I am limited. It's time I found someone who suits me and my lifestyle. The same for you."

He returned his hands to her waist, so lightly she could slip from his hold with one backward step. "I'll make you a deal. We'll talk about all our problems, but first we kiss. You never know. A good many might get solved that way."

Her lips twitched again, this time with humor and, yes, invitation. At least that was how he interpreted it. He turned her cheek to him and kissed her just below her cheekbone. He placed a matching kiss on her other cheek.

Mara looked up at him, frowning. "Is that your idea of a first kiss?"

She rose up and touched her mouth to his. Not the breezy, dry-lipped brush he expected but a deep and slow welcoming that he lost no time entering into. A dog wedged its head between them, forcing them apart.

Interfering Griffin.

"I think," Mara said, "he has just introduced a new complication. Jealousy."

Connor was riding high. He'd come off a stellar first kiss with the woman he couldn't get out of his mind or his heart. While the kiss had ended, he wasn't ready to release her from his arms, and from the way she stayed curved against him, she was in no rush, either. "Please, Mara. Don't be jealous."

"It's not—" She harrumphed, a small and cozy sound. He tightened his hold.

Lines appeared between her brow. "But it does point to the ongoing issue between us."

"I get it," he said. "I promise you that I will not let Griffin be the one to hold and kiss you."

Again her lips twitched, but the frown lines didn't completely disappear. "I'm sure there have been plenty of women for whom you took on that responsibility."

"Fewer than you might imagine. None who used 'for whom' in natural speech."

"Sometimes I find formal speech easier than conversational."

"You hide behind words, me with dogs."

"It would seem so."

"So how about we admit we have problems and help each other with them?" He pulled her closer, lining them up for a second kiss.

This time her hands did press against his chest, opening space between them. "And what about my blindness? What about children?"

"Mara, we haven't even kissed twice. I'm not sure I want to have children with you yet." He was sure, actually. He was also sure that now wasn't the time to bring it up. One step at a time with her. She had a way of plotting out entire lifetimes. "You accused me of scaring away potential partners. Now you're doing it. Not that it's scaring me away."

"Connor, there's something you need to know." Her voice dropped to a shy murmur. "Remember the first time you saw me?"

An easy one. "Yep, at the youth center. A year ago in February. I brought two dogs, both were collie mixes. Both were excellent buddy dogs, but one had the makings of a cattle dog so—" He stopped himself. "Anyway, you were there in the gym, the center in this wheel of kids."

"Which immediately burst apart," she said,

"when they saw you and the dogs. It's still that way. But I first saw you five summers ago."

He couldn't remember anything from five summers ago. "I would've remembered."

"It was so quick. My vision was better then. I was visiting from British Columbia. I was on my own down by the lake across from Penny's Restaurant. You walked past with three dogs. Your attention was on them. One sniffed my leg and looked ready to stop for a pat. But you told him to come, you said a quick 'sorry' to me and carried on."

It could've happened. He regularly took dogs down there to teach them how to deal with crowds and people of all kinds. "In all fairness it wasn't exactly a high-drama meeting."

She lowered her eyes. "For me it was."

His heart skipped a beat, shuddered to a stop.

"I didn't know your name. I didn't know what you did. I went back to Vancouver Island, a province away, thinking that if I could meet someone that made me feel the way I felt when you walked past me, I might consider marriage, kids."

She'd just handed him a real-life dream. Connor pressed her closer, but her hands stayed lodged against him. "But no sooner did I think that than my vision started deteriorating, and fast. I'd been unbelievably lucky up until then. Almost a miracle case, but I developed a moderate-to-severe case of retinitis pigmentosa.

"My thinking changed. I decided that even if I did meet someone like you, there might be marriage but no kids. Moving back here, the incident with my niece only confirmed it. When I saw you again at the youth center, I couldn't see you. I heard you, I sensed you, it wasn't until we shook hands that I saw you. Nothing had changed and everything had changed. My heart hadn't changed, but my eyes had. And my mind."

She drew breath. "I'm scared, Connor. And I have good reason to be."

No fancy words here. She was telling him that she cared for him, practically declaring her love, yet walking away from the happily-ever-after. He could say nothing to change her mind right now. He'd sound naive. And maybe he was. But there was no way he was giving up on her or giving in to her harsh decision to end what had only just started between them. He took the only route he saw open to him.

"Take Daisy."

She tensed in his arms, began to pull away.

"Listen, we both want the same thing. Each other. Logic says you will need a dog. You will need more supports than you have now. Griffin was my wrongheaded attempt to get close to you. But it worked. Now, let's make us work. Okay?"

"Connor, the reason I told you about how I've known who you are for years is to say that I've had longer to think this through."

"And still you came to the wrong conclusion because you didn't talk it out with me. You might know in your mind, but you just said that your heart is on my side, our side."

"My heart is foolish. It tore after a guy with dogs."

"Don't blame it."

"And I'm not ruling out a guide dog—"

"Then take Daisy. Another thirty-day challenge. If it doesn't work out, I'll take her back." Anticipating her next objection, he added, "Keep her and she's free."

"I can't do that."

"Consider it an investment in our future."

"That's…a big one."

"So is the potential payoff."

The frown lines remained. "I'll need to think about it."

He smoothed his thumb over the lines. "Don't think this time."

"What if it doesn't work?"

It would. Just like it would for Dane and Talia and their baby. Nobody would be left out in the cold again.

"Say yes, Mara."

And in a quiet, worried voice but also one with a breath of hope, she did. He'd changed her mind for now. It was on him to make sure neither of them regretted it.

CHAPTER ELEVEN

MARA SENSED SOMETHING was up the moment Dane and Talia entered her office. They had come together the last two appointments. Talia had insisted, and her parents had relented, now that they lived under the constant shadow of her leaving them for Dane. Talia was growing a spine as well as a baby.

Mara tugged a dining room chair close to the love seat where the teenagers sat with knees touching. This close she could catch extreme facial expressions and track body language. At first, Dane was discomfited by her proximity but today he leaned forward into their tête-à-tête.

"We've come to a decision," Talia announced. Dane's shoulders were hunched, elbows on knees. Connor had mentioned that the pregnancy question weighed on Dane, but for confidentiality reasons and because Connor was keeping his promise about not interfering, they'd skittered off to other topics. Like Daisy. A week after agreeing to his second experiment, they'd yet to set up a start date with Daisy. Connor wanted to run through another set of training exercises first.

"We've decided to put the baby up for adoption," Talia said in a rush. "You're the first we've told. We know it's our decision, but we wanted to know what you thought."

Dane fastened his gaze on Mara's, a rare move since he usually kept his head down or stared off or, at the most, glanced at Talia. Desperation radiated from the depths of his eyes. He didn't agree with Talia's decision.

Only she had not made a bad one. It was the compromise Mara had privately hoped for from the start. Yet Dane couldn't voice his opposition because he'd promised Talia to stand by her side. His position was unenviable. Perhaps she could speak to his perspective.

"You know that's not my style," Mara said. "I can review the consequences. The negative ones, since those are the ones that you need to address. First, no matter the type of adoption, you are relinquishing control over the baby's welfare. You are relinquishing part— or all—of your rights. At best, you will have to share your baby."

"But I see that as a good thing," Talia said,

scooting forward on the seat, her knee grazing Mara's. "It could be more of a partnership."

Dane raked his hand through his hair, his expression mobile as if about to speak. Talia plowed on. "And that'll free us to pursue our education, so maybe we could provide for the baby, too. Put money away for university. The baby will need some sort of higher education. My mom and dad put money into a savings plan, and now there's enough to cover my entire four years."

"So you've said," Dane muttered. Talia seemed too wrapped up in her explanation to notice his brooding.

"I don't want to give up the baby entirely. Did I tell you I can feel kicks? Like butterflies inside me or trickles of water."

Mara could only imagine the sensation, as Dane must. "My sisters say the same thing." She gave herself a mental kick. It had become tricky to erect fences between the professional and personal since discovering that Talia was family. Mara couldn't help contrasting Talia's fraught situation to her sisters' excitement. "They're expecting, too."

Talia brightened, no doubt eager to expand the conversation about her sisters. Mara searched for a way to bring the topic back.

Dane came to the rescue. "It's a boy. We went for the ultrasound last week."

"Dane!" Talia twisted to face him. "We agreed not to tell anyone."

"You agreed," Dane said, through gritted teeth.

Talia finally clued in to his mood. "What's the matter?"

Dane spoke fast as if to get it out before anyone stopped him. "The matter is you deciding to give up our baby."

Talia looked at Mara, at the room, then back at the father of her baby. "I have asked you over and over. You've heard him, Ms. M. And what do you always say? That it's up to me."

"Because I'd hoped you'd choose the way I wanted it to go."

"What do you want?"

"I want the baby," Dane said. "I want my son. With you, ideally. But if not, I'll go it alone. With the help of my mom and uncle."

Connor would approve of his nephew's stance. How much had he influenced Dane's outburst? Connor, she knew for a fact, could be very persuasive.

"There are also negative consequences to that decision," Mara reminded Dane.

Dane shrugged hard, like he was trying to dislodge a creature on his shoulders. "I've heard them all. The expense. The limitations, the constant responsibility, the worry. I have a father who thinks I'm a nuisance. I don't want my son thinking his dad doesn't want him. Believe me, that's a real negative consequence. The other stuff, that's life, so I might as well get on with living it."

Definitely his uncle's nephew. Talia was flushed, on the verge of tears. "I wish you'd told me this sooner."

"I'm telling you now," Dane said softly. "We could do exactly what Mom and Uncle Connor offered. You move in with us, now or after the baby's born. We'll work it out from there."

"My parents won't like it."

"They already don't like it. They don't like me. I hate that they're paying for us to come here, hoping Ms. Montgomery will talk us out of keeping the baby."

"I don't believe I advocated that," Mara felt compelled to interject. Though, of course, Dane might have picked up on the direction she was leaning.

"The only member of your family from around here that won't mind is your grandfather," Dane said.

Dr. Greg might very well have cast his vote for keeping the baby, though Jack said he still hadn't told Abigail about her secret brother. Talia buried her face in her hands. "Just when I thought I'd gotten it figured out."

Dane, on the other hand, straightened. Venting his feelings had energized him. He wrapped his arm around Talia's shoulders and touched his head to hers, creating an intimate circle that excluded Mara, but she could still hear his words. "Listen. We didn't plan for this baby. But we had talked about planning a life together. It might happen sooner than we thought."

Talia peeked at him from between her fingers. "Are you saying we should get— married?" The last word came out in a squeak.

Oh no. This was not the direction this session was meant to take at all. Mara cleared her throat. "Uh—"

"I think so," Dane said.

Mara hurried out words, anything to stop the flow. "I suggest we consider—"

"All right," Talia said, completely ignoring Mara. "Yes, let's do this. If we're going to have a baby, let's do this properly. Let's get married."

Dane suddenly withdrew from hugging Talia. "You're sure about this? I'm not pressuring you into this, am I?"

Good questions, since Talia had a history of trying to please others before herself. But Talia turned to Mara with a huge smile. "You're invited to the wedding."

Dane grinned, his face relaxing more than she'd seen in weeks. "You can be Uncle Connor's date."

How did— Never mind, no secrets among the Flanagans. Little did they know that she had reason to sit on either side of the wedding aisle.

THE NEXT EVENING Mara waited until her homemade strawberry-and-rhubarb pie was making the rounds of the family dinner at Jack and Bridget's house before she said, "I have a bit of news." She'd decided to inform her family of her new relationship status. Now that Dane and Talia knew, it seemed only fair that her immediate relations were informed.

"Oh?" Jack said from beside her, his attention directed on the molasses-slow progress of his favorite dessert. The process was stalled at six-year-old Sofia, who was determined to lever out her own piece.

"Connor Flanagan...from the youth center, the one with the dogs—"

"We know him," Jack said. "Amigo, remember?"

"Right. We're dating now."

"Yay!" Sofia erupted. "See, Isabella. I got the slice on my plate. No breaking it, no tipping it over. I can do it."

So much for causing a sensation.

Her mother expelled whipping cream from the can in a globby whoosh. "Dog Man? And he makes a living from that?" Not exactly encouraging.

"Apparently so."

"He lives up the road from us," Will said. "On an acreage with his sister and her son. He used to be a cop, then went to dogs."

"The son has a girlfriend, too," Krista added. "What's her name?"

Will shrugged his ignorance, so Mara supplied the answer. "Talia." Mara passed the pie to Jack and held on to the dish for a second, long enough to make him raise his eyes to hers. "Talia Shirazi." She leveled him a look, and in the slight lifting of his chin, he acknowledged her unspoken message.

He took the final wedge of pie. "You will have to invite Connor over for supper. Let him meet the family." His mild comment held a thread of insistence. A slight emphasis on the final word.

"We would love to have him," Bridget said, matching Jack's tone.

"Sure," Mara said, "we'll have to arrange a time." Beside her, Jack jabbed fiercely at his pie as if killing it. Since learning of his biological father two weeks ago, Jack had chafed under Greg's insistence on secrecy, forcing Jack to keep secrets from most of the people gathered around his table. His family.

To divert Jack, Mara decided to make another announcement. "And I'm getting a guide dog. A thirty-day trial run. Her name's Daisy." Ridiculous as it was, Mara felt a current of pride, as if making her own kind of birth announcement.

"Is it Connor's?" Bridget said, and for a second, Mara, still imagining births, was confused.

"Oh, yes. He'll do the training with me, too."

"Ah, more time to be together," Krista said. "Maybe you can stretch out the training."

Will turned to his wife. "Is that why it took you so long to learn how to ride? So you could spend more time with me?"

"Yes. Because I adore you the most when you're bossy, picky and unhelpful." Krista turned to Mara. "For your sake, I hope Connor is not like Will."

"Anything else we should know?" Jack's tension thrummed against her senses.

Perhaps she could ease the burden of his secrets by releasing one of her own without violating her professional ethics. After all, Connor knew and therefore, she could've learned it from him.

"Dane and Talia plan to get married."

"But they're so young," Krista said. "Why?"

"For the same reason young people in my generation got married young," her mother guessed. "They're having a baby."

All eyes swiveled to Mara for confirmation. The only way to maintain confidentiality now without outright lying was to obfuscate. "Connor hasn't said anything to me."

"Can we come to the wedding?" Sofia asked.

Isabella groaned. "You have to be invited. And why would they when we don't even know each other?"

"It's going to be very small," Mara said

to smooth over Isabella's condescension. "Mostly just family."

As soon as the words slipped from her mouth, Mara realized her mistake. Jack pushed away his mutilated dessert. "This keeps getting better and better," he said. "Anything else to share?"

"No, I believe I'm done," Mara said.

Jack, however, was only getting started. He followed her out onto the front porch when she was leaving. "Dr. Greg's got to own up. The families deserve to know."

Truth was always preferable, but Mara had met Talia's parents. No good could come from them knowing, at least at this juncture. "What are you hoping for? That we'll all frolic together at the beach, gather for Thanksgiving dinner? There is already enough stress in Talia's household. I can understand if Dr. Greg doesn't want to add to it."

"That stress is temporary. A flash compared to what could happen, if—when—it's discovered that secrets were kept. And now that you and Connor are seeing each other—well, we really are all family now, in this weird way. What does Connor think?"

"About Talia's grandfather being your

father?" At Jack's nod, Mara shook her head. "I haven't told him. How can I?"

Behind them, Bridget slipped out the door and stood beside Jack. Two against one.

"It's not as if there's any patient confidentiality here," Jack said.

"No, but there is such a thing as discretion. That household doesn't keep secrets. What if he should tell Dane or his sister, and it gets back to Talia?"

"You're dating a guy you don't trust to keep an important secret?" Bridget said. "That's not like you, Mara."

"I do trust him," Mara said quickly. "But the source of the secret is crucial. It should come from Talia's family first."

Jack made a grumbling noise. "But can you see the position Dr. Greg is putting us all in? I like the guy. I want to know him and his family. I want him sitting around the dinner table every week with everyone else. But he's undermining trust with my family by swearing us to silence. We can't even tell Aunt DeeDee or Krista. That's not right. He came clean with me, and he should come clean with everyone."

He opened his phone and hit a number. Bridget watched, not interfering. Jack didn't dwell on opening pleasantries with his new-found father.

"Something's come up. I just learned that Mara's dating Connor Flanagan. And it's getting pretty serious, pretty fast between them."

A lie. Mara poked her cousin in the leg with her cane, but he was on a roll. "Keeping you and me a secret isn't going to work anymore. You need to tell Talia's mom and soon. Especially now that Dane and Talia are engaged. Our families are blending together, anyway."

Jack listened, his jaw tightening. "The time will never be right. In fact, it's only getting worse. I stayed quiet because it was your family. But it's my family, too. And my family has a right to know." He didn't even look Mara's way when he next said, "Mara has agreed to set up a meeting for us all at her office."

She delivered another poke that Jack sidestepped. "Sometime in the next week or two, agreed?"

Jack listened, and this time his strict features softened. "Don't worry. This'll come out right. We'll do this together." He handed the phone to Mara. "He wants to talk to you."

"I don't know what to think," Dr. Greg said

when she had the phone. Almost the exact words his granddaughter had said when she came to Mara about her pregnancy.

She could relate to Greg's default to privacy. It had worked for him for so many years, and for her, too. It was less a habit than a philosophy by now. But good things had come from opening up—Connor, Daisy and…hope.

"It's still your choice, Dr. Greg. There's no one right answer." She paused. "I will say this. You made a choice years ago, and gave up Jack. Maybe this time you can make a choice where nobody is left behind."

"You both better be right," Bridget said, after Mara ended the call. "Or else families from here to Arizona will blow up."

GRIFFIN LOCATED DANE nineteen minutes and twenty-two seconds after Connor started the stopwatch. Dane sat braced in brush along the shared fence line with the Claverleys. A barking Griffin jumped at Dane, despite knowing better. Dane blocked with one arm and kept tapping at his tablet with his other hand.

"Off," Connor ordered. "Sit." Griffin obeyed, though it clearly pained him to do so. If there was another living being Griffin might choose to bond with, it would be Connor's younger version of himself. He and Dane were often mistaken for father and son, and half the time, neither bothered to correct the impression.

Connor unhooked Griffin's long line and handed over a doggy treat. "Good boy. Play." He turned to Dane. "Didn't expect to find you so soon. I'll have to step up his game. What are you doing?"

Dane glanced up, looked right through Connor and returned to pecking away at his tablet. "Job application."

"Don't you already have two jobs?" He worked at a car wash and delivered pizzas.

"It's not enough. Especially if I'm going to college this fall. Talia won't be able to. I mean I can barely afford the marriage commissioner for the wedding. I actually have to save up for a stroller."

"The wedding will be simple and it's only a month away. There won't be time for costs to run up," Connor said. "As for the stroller, your mom and I got that covered."

"Have you seen how much they cost? You could buy a secondhand car for the same price. But if I want to get married and be a father, I should be the one paying for this stuff."

"This is the way family works. At least the way this one works. When your mom and I moved out here, we helped each other out. We didn't think that because we were adults, we couldn't buy groceries for us both, or cover the utility bill during a slow month for the other one. Besides, you're still a minor."

"A minor with major problems." Dane looked up at Connor again, this time focused. "Have you ever decided on something, then when you started going after it, you wondered if that's what you should've done?"

Connor was about to give a confident "no" when he remembered his previous career. He'd harbored doubts from the start about being a cop but had pushed on, and in the end, it had all collapsed. But that was a career, not a person you wanted to marry. Like Mara. He had no doubts about them. But he wasn't about to discuss this tender new thing between them with Dane. "Getting cold feet?"

Dane swept his hand at a mosquito. "Yes. I know you and Mom will help out, but neither of you signed up for this. And you, you'll want to do more yourself, now that you and Ms. M are finally getting serious."

Dane's own situation must've made him finely attuned to anyone in the same position. Connor had begun idle calculations. He'd never earned a great deal, but neither had he spent much. He figured he could hold his own, if there should ever be a second wedding after Dane's. Not that he could rush Mara. She might have had a five-year crush on him but she was taking her time now that it was really happening. True, they'd only shared their first kiss two weeks ago, but her natural reserve felt more like a withdrawal. Any prodding resulted in a change of topic, usually back to Daisy. And here she'd accused him of hiding behind dogs. "Serious or not, I'm not pulling out on you and my great-nephew. Who knows, if things go well between Mara and me, your kid might have cousins to play with."

"You two already talking about having kids?"

More like about *not* having kids. Connor's face must've conveyed something of this conflict because Dane sighed. "Look, even I know about you rushing things too early in relationships. Don't scare Ms. M off."

"I'm not."

"She wants kids, too?"

Connor hesitated too long and Dane pounced. "You're pressuring her just as you pressured Talia. You gotta back off. Especially given she's kinda blind."

Connor felt his hackles go up. "Visually impaired. Her vision has nothing to do with her capability as a mother."

"All I'm saying it's a consideration. Like being too young to be a parent for me and Talia."

His nephew was projecting his own worries onto Mara and him.

"If life could be figured out from the start, we wouldn't have to live it," Connor said. "I could train a dog to help. It's in their instincts to care for the young. Basic stuff. Check for dirty diapers, block stairs." He intended it as a joke, but why not a nanny dog?

"That's a step away from having them raised by wolves. You're not serious."

More serious than he probably should be.

"She always seems happy with the way her life is," Dane said. "Just enjoy each other for now."

"Don't you have your own problems to worry about?"

"Didn't you just say that we're all family? What you two do affects us all. I just think you're taking advantage of her. Especially if you know she's into you."

Connor started. He'd always thought he was encouraging Mara to open up to life's other possibilities, to acting on her dreams. But was he on some level manipulating her feelings for him into creating the life he wanted?

Dane snapped shut the cover of his tablet and pushed to his feet. "Anyway, I gotta head back. Pizzas don't deliver themselves. Yet."

Griffin turned with Dane, then stopped and looked back. "Go," Connor ordered. He wanted time alone to do some hard thinking about his future. And Mara's.

CHAPTER TWELVE

AT THE AUTOMATIC doors of the grocery store, Mara took a firm grip on Daisy's harness, her empty wire shopping dolly trailing along in her right hand.

Farther to her right, out of Daisy's direct line of sight, Connor said quietly, "You're good to go." He was trying to keep a low profile for her inaugural trip with Daisy to one of her favorite places.

She could order the items and have them delivered, but she'd clung to this outing as her vision deteriorated. The store's familiar layout had allowed her to navigate the aisles easily enough, but displays changed and the shoppers with their carts provided moving pieces that had gradually stripped the joy from gathering food for herself and the meals she made for her family. Connor had promised her Daisy would make things easier, and had trained her in this specific store. Just for Mara.

She hoped for his sake as much as her own

that she and Daisy passed the test. Added to the level of difficulty was that it was Civic Monday, on the first weekend in August when it was crowded with tourists and locals. Connor had offered for her to go at another time but so long as he was close, she'd give it a shot.

"Forward," she ordered Daisy, and felt a tug in her shoulder as Daisy obeyed. The doors whooshed open and they passed through, her dolly rattling behind. Step and repeat through the interior doors and they were inside. Mara paused to allow her senses to absorb the light and sounds, and for Daisy to adjust her own canine antennae. Mara had no certain idea where Connor was. For the first week, Connor had hung close in her home training, but in this second week, he'd pulled back. With this visit, they'd agreed he'd only intervene for safety concerns.

The customer service desk was situated to their left. She gave Daisy one of Connor's custom commands. "Counter."

Daisy didn't move but the harness did as Daisy looked from side to side. "Good girl. Counter." Daisy started them forward a dozen steps and then stopped. Mara encountered heat and the smell of barbecued chickens.

"I don't blame you," Mara said, "but no. Counter." Again, she felt Daisy look about for this so-called counter. Mara knew where it was in relation to the chicken stand, but Connor had emphasized making sure that Daisy experienced her own success. It built confidence. Perhaps a dog was a bit like a person.

"Daisy," Mara said. "Left." Daisy made the turn. "Counter."

Daisy headed straight to the customer service desk. "Good girl! Good girl," Mara gushed, ridiculously proud. Had Connor seen how well their dog had performed?

"Hey there, I saw you come in." It was Sheri. Mara had taken to bringing her purchases to this desk to avoid congestion and not to hold up the lines, and the two of them had struck up a store friendship based on cooking.

"I'd introduce you," Mara said, "but she's working right now, so I can't let her be distracted."

"Oh yeah," Sheri said. "Connor came to our staff meeting last week. He gave us a full rundown on the dos and don'ts."

He hadn't told her that. She'd have to find a way to thank him. Sheri's voice dropped.

"Do you know he's over by the barbecued chicken?"

"He's trying to keep out of Daisy's sight," Mara whispered back. "But if you ask me, I think she knows and is trying to ignore him."

Sheri gave a loud laugh, one that Mara hadn't heard before in all the times they'd chatted.

Mara had deliberately shortened her grocery list and crafted it to cover all parts of the store. A slow process at the best of times, Mara scanned signs with her app but even then, when it came to meat and produce, she had to rely on touch to determine exactly which she wanted. Today, she was at the Granny Smith apples.

"Can I help you?"

The voice was young, male. Like Dane's. No one had ever asked her that question before. She generally rolled apples in her hands to check for bruises and sizes. On the cusp of declining his offer, she heard Sheri's laughter echo in her mind. "Yes. A half dozen apples. Not too large and bruise-free. If you pass them to me, I will put them into a bag."

The faint tear of a plastic bag ripped from a spool. She held out her hand, took it and the operation began. She'd long ago learned that it was on her to set people at ease around her vision loss, and so she asked how he stacked fruit to keep them from rolling off, which led to a discussion about laws of motion, at the end of which her bag was full, and she and Daisy continued on their merry way to the bright display cases for the meat. Connor, she supposed, was sneaking about the potatoes.

"How can I do you for today?"

The mashed-up grammar belonged to a man-sized block of white. The butcher in his apron. What was this? Even with her white cane, no one paid her the least attention, unless she solicited it. "I'm looking for steaks. Your best. Largish. Two."

"I set out some nice cuts an hour ago. Let's see, excuse me." Daisy pressed against her leg as the man passed by.

"Turn. Left." Daisy got them facing the butcher.

"You like it marbled or not?"

"A little. I'd like a half-inch trim."

"You, too? You ever caramelized onions in the fat?"

Mara felt a flash of camaraderie. "Is there any other way?" Which led to a discussion of the best combination of spices and side dishes to serve—long green beans and asparagus ranking high, which precipitated a return trip to the produce section since asparagus was on sale this week. Connor was still incognito. It didn't matter. She and Daisy were doing just fine. She was actually having fun.

"Let's go get ice cream," Mara said. She tried out the second store word Connor had trained Daisy for. "Aisle. Find me aisle. Good girl."

Daisy jumped into action, walking to a spot where Mara felt a sense of space. An aisle straight off the frozen meats. "Forward." As they moved on, Mara heard a customer request a hundred grams of Havarti. The deli. Ice cream was clear across the store. At the top of the aisle, Mara picked up on the beeps of the checkout. "Daisy. Turn right. Right." Daisy complied. Mara could make out aisles to her right, a flower display off to her left. They'd done it! "Good girl, good girl." Again, pride burst through her, and she resisted calling out to Connor.

At the hum of fridges, Mara ordered Daisy to turn right. The ice cream was close. She opened a fridge door and the scanner app reported that indeed she'd reached the ice cream.

For the fun of it, she said to Daisy in a carrying voice, "I wonder what Connor's favorite ice cream is."

A cart and tap of heels stopped beside them. Someone waiting for her to hurry up. "Are you aware that he's behind you?"

Talia's mom. Through email, she had canceled the sessions after Talia had announced her decision to keep the baby and to marry. Mara had sent a neutrally worded reply that Abigail had not responded to, but it was probably safe to assume that Talia's parents were disappointed with the results of the counseling.

"Uh, I was aware he was close by."

"I see."

Mara could detect Abigail's general appearance. Some kind of Mondrian-like patterned dress, with thick bracelets clicking about her wrists. She became acutely aware of her shorts and off-shoulder tunic, her hair back in a loose ponytail. Connor favored that look, but she couldn't help feeling a little underdone next to Talia's mother. Not that it should matter.

"I expect we'll meet next week," Abigail said. "At my father's behest, no less." Imagine Abigail's shock when she learned that she was related to the blind ragamuffin before her. "Has he indicated the nature of the discussion?"

Sarcasm underpinned the question and Mara felt herself flush. Daisy's fur brushed against Mara's bare leg, and it was as if she'd been injected with the dog's quiet support. "He has," Mara replied coolly, "but I'm not at liberty to say."

"Naturally. You are a model of discretion. I'll leave you to your confections." The heels tapped on, stopped. "All men like French vanilla."

Mara waited until the steps faded, reached in and took out salty caramel.

Outside with Daisy and her loaded dolly, a wave of euphoria hit Mara. She'd done it, but more than that, she felt connected, her run-in with Abigail notwithstanding. Daisy's very presence had opened her to people in a way her cane never had. No one had interfered with Daisy or violated the golden rule of not touching her, but Connor was right in that there was something about a dog that changed people. She'd taken on Daisy to increase her independence but it had also brought her closer to people.

Connor clamped his arm around her waist

in a sideways hug. "You two were amazing. Good job, Daisy."

"We were, weren't we?" Mara said, her heart full with the excitement of her success, of Connor pressed next to her, of Daisy's warmth against her leg.

"Does this mean that you and Daisy are partners?"

The one month was still a few weeks away, but here was Connor tugging for an early answer. "Yes. If she'll have me."

Connor's grin flashed white. "She'll have you all right. Just remember, she's mine for a few days in a bit when I take her to the vet to get spayed. She just cycled, so she'll be okay for a few months, but she can't be both a guide dog and a mom."

Mara hadn't thought of that consequence to her decision. She was stripping Daisy of the chance to have her own offspring. "Oh. I didn't think—I'm sorry."

Connor kissed her temple, held his lips there as he spoke, his every word like a feather stroke. "Don't overthink this, Mara. You're giving her love and purpose. Nothing more a dog wants." He paused. "Or a guy."

Mara twisted to get a better look at him, but he turned away to ease the pull cart from her hand. Huh. Even as he told her not to overthink, he left her to mull over that little plea for love. As for purpose—"Tell me the truth, Connor. How many times did you almost rush in?"

"The only time I was tempted was with Talia's mom. I wasn't sure if it was her or the fridges keeping the ice cream frozen."

"It's…her way."

"What's this meeting next week with Greg?"

He'd overheard, but it wasn't for her to say. "You'll find out soon enough."

Stiffness entered his arm. He didn't withdraw but he was clearly waiting for more. She touched his face and kissed him. "What I can say is that I don't think I've felt happier than right now."

As the simple honesty behind her words broke through her, she realized what she had to do. As much as she'd been annoyed at Jack for declaring that she and Connor were moving fast, they were. And if they were to have the kind of future they'd both dreamed of, she needed to face the truth. And that meant undergoing one more test.

But she'd say nothing to Connor until the results were in. For now, she would live in the moment, enjoy the promise of tomorrow the same as other couples. "Come on," she said. "There's an apple crumble for me to make and you to eat."

Connor looped his arm around her waist. "Deal. And did I tell you I like my steaks medium rare?"

She gave his tummy a playful pinch. "And did I tell you that I have a lawn for you to mow?"

She'd feed him his steak, lawn or no lawn. She loved cooking for this man, loved the life he was creating with her.

Please, please, let this next test go well, too.

MARA'S SEAT BELT JERKED tight as her mother brought them to a hard stop in the parking garage of the city high-rise. Daisy's nails scraped the back seat to gain purchase. Mara was the only one in the family who submitted to riding with her mother at full highway speed. Bridget allowed her mother to drive the girls so long as they were buckled into the back seat and her mother didn't leave Spirit Lake on the theory that an impact at forty kilometers per hour would not be fatal. As for Mara and her mother: "You two shouldn't be alone in the same car. One's blind and the other drives as if she is."

But Mara wanted only her mother on this particular trip. Coupled with her regular eye specialist appointment, Mara was also going to a private genetics clinic, having obtained a booking a mere four days after resolving to get the test. Destiny seemed eager for this test to get done.

Her mother's finger drummed on the steering wheel. "I'll ask one last time. Are you sure you want to do this?"

"Yes," Mara said quickly, ahead of her inner voice who begged her not to subject herself to this particular genetic test. "I've put this off for far too long.

"The truth is," Mara said as much to herself as her mother, "this test will be routine. There hasn't been a specialist who remotely thinks that I will pass on the genes."

"It'll be stressful enough. You shouldn't have brought Daisy when she's still in training," her mother said as Mara opened the back door for Daisy to spring out.

Mara held the harness at the ready, and Daisy fitted into it. "I depend on her, and you're with me if we get into a jam. Besides,

Connor said I should work her as much as possible."

"Who am I to argue with Dog Man?"

The name had stuck, largely due to Connor himself. At Jack and Bridget's house, he'd introduced himself to the girls with that dreadful label. Among the Montgomerys it was now his username.

The visit to the genetics clinic was predictably understated. The greatest adventure was getting from the parking garage to the office itself, as her mother misread the signs, and it was Daisy who led them to the bank of elevators. She wished she could tell Connor of Daisy's smarts. She hated keeping secrets from him, and they were fast piling up.

After being told the results would be sent in four to six weeks, the three of them careered over to her ophthalmologist appointment. Her vision continued to deteriorate, as Mara already knew. She merely had her gray haze and tunnel vision translated into numbers.

"I'm glad you've got yourself a guide dog," her ophthalmologist said.

"It was from a private business. I know the owner." She felt herself flush. Lovely, she was betraying exactly how she knew him. "Tell me, we both agree that I'm nearly legally blind. When will I go completely blind?"

In his light shirt and dark tie, the contrast likely in consideration to his visually impaired clients, he shifted on his leather chair, the wheels rolling on the bare floor. "I can't say for sure that you will, but it is accelerating. I am classifying your case as advanced."

Mara nodded, forced her mind to gloss over the verdict. It was what she'd expected.

"Are you still taking supplements?"

"I am. But there's really little point anymore, is there?"

Another squeak of the chair, clearing of throat. "Therapies are limited right now."

The various advocacy groups for the blind occasionally imparted chipper news about this or that breakthrough therapy but most of their energies were devoted to assistive strategies. Dogs and devices. The doors had closed for her but maybe he could provide hope for the next generation. "Are you aware of any other upcoming treatments?"

Squeak, hum. "Only with related eye diseases. Research and experiments are happening, but RP is far more...complicated."

Whereas some retinal diseases were linked to a handful of genes, retinitis pigmentosa spread its mutations to more than sixty-four genes. "I understand."

In other words, there was nothing out there for her or her children, if she proved to be a carrier. At her feet, Daisy stood, her subtle ask for them to get a move on. She had a point. There was nothing new under the sun here. She would have to trust that the genetic test would allow her world of Connor and Daisy to continue to widen.

MARA WAS GRATING ginger when her front doorbell rang. Not expecting anyone this evening, she assumed it was someone trying to sell candles or socks or cookbooks. Or perhaps Connor paying an unexpected visit. Well, if it was him, good thing he liked casual, because tonight she was wearing shorts covered with an apron.

It was Talia, also in shorts and a loose halter top. Despite being six months into her pregnancy, she covered up well. Then again, Mara's abysmal depth perception routinely flattened curves.

Talia followed Mara into the kitchen and accepted a glass of iced tea, once Mara assured her that the low sugar and caffeine-free state of the homemade brew made it a prenatal alternative.

"Good for you making healthy choices for you and baby," Mara said as she resumed grating ginger.

"At this stage, it's totally on me," Talia said, peering inside a bowl. "What are you making?"

"A marinade for kebabs."

"I love making kebabs. Can I help?"

"Uh…sure." Had Talia, bored on a hot August evening, just come over to visit? Mara was tempted to ask if her parents knew where she was. Word from Connor via Dane was that tensions ran high in the Shirazi household. They'd flood the banks come the meeting with Greg, scheduled for the day after tomorrow.

As Talia loaded kebab sticks with chunks of meat and vegetables, Mara asked, "How are you and your bump doing?"

Talia wiped her hands dry and pulled her top tight across her middle. "Getting bumpier." Mara nodded, faking that she could differentiate the contrast. "Do you want to feel?"

Mara's first impulse was to decline that intimate a connection. Both Bridget and Krista had set her hand on their solid, extra-warm bumps so the experience wasn't novel. Yet there was a stiff hopefulness to Talia's voice. Her parents certainly wouldn't be looking to do baby rubs.

"I'd love to," Mara said, and let Talia set her hand on the baby bulge. It felt much the same as her sisters' and Mara was set to withdraw her hand when she felt a heave and a roll under her hand.

Mara gasped. "Was that—?"

"Yes," Talia said, a smile breaking across her young face. "It's the baby. He pushes and prods during the day, but really starts his workout from now to bedtime."

If the results from last Friday's test came back as they should, she might experience the same for herself—and Connor—one day. Mara slipped her hand away. "That was… special."

"You're the only other one to have felt it outside of Dane."

"None of your friends?"

"No. They're supportive, but I think they're a little weirded out, too. And our futures are so different now…it's hard for us to relate to each other."

"I bet. And your parents? They haven't warmed to the baby?"

Talia impaled a beef chunk with a skewer. "No. I'm thinking I should move out. Less embarrassment on their part, less guilt on mine."

"Is it that bad?"

"Mom isn't so bad. She actually left some prenatal vitamins on my dresser and asked if I was seeing a doctor. But my dad—he's not talking to me, barely looks at me."

"That must be tough."

"Dad used to ask me every day about school. We would talk about what I was learning and he'd give his opinion and we'd watch documentaries on YouTube that argued against what the teachers were saying. Now it's as if I'm not there. It's…it's as if I no longer exist."

Habit more than hope forced Mara to ask when she could've predicted the answer. "Have you tried to talk to him?"

Talia scoffed. "You've met him. Try having a heart-to-heart with him—and he's always like that. Always intense, always right. I eat and hide out in my room upstairs. He eats and goes to his office downstairs. Mom stays in the kitchen. Maybe he and Mom talk when I'm with Dane, I don't know."

"What does Dane think?"

"He keeps inviting me to stay at his place. And Grandpa is still good to me. He just nods and listens, and takes me out for a burger and shake like he has since I was six. But he must be thinking about what's happening if he called a meeting. Wednesday at four, right? At your office?"

If Talia was angling for a reveal, like her mother, Mara didn't fall for it. "Yes, Wednesday at four."

Daisy came and sat between them. Talia squeaked. "She's going to jump for the meat."

"No, no," Mara said. "She just wants to hang out, and this is where the action is." My, she sounded like a real dog-mom.

"Sorry," Talia said, laying a third kebab beside Mara's one. Sight made work faster. "I'm not used to any kind of dog. But I guess I'll have to learn if I move out there."

"You don't want to move?"

"It's as good a place as any. Dane and I will have a couple of rooms downstairs to ourselves and the thing is, I guess I feel that me and the baby don't belong anywhere right now. I know that Dane and his family will take me in. But there's a difference between them making room for me and me belonging there."

Oh, Mara could relate. She'd spent almost her entire life minimizing her impairment to avoid imposing on her family. Family hikes had to be shortened because Mara couldn't navigate the terrain or shopping trips modified because she continually got turned around in department stores. "Believe me, I get that."

Talia stopped. "Oh, yeah, I forgot. Except you're not to blame for your condition. I am."

"It wasn't you alone."

"I kinda carry the consequences."

"True, but your consequences will give you joy. I don't get to say the same." Mara winced at her self-pitying words.

Talia didn't appear to take it that way. "How do you keep from being depressed?"

"You mean how do I become more than what I'm seen as?" In the occasional motivational speech she'd given, Mara had addressed that question with answers she recognized as rock-solid. Every challenge was an opportunity to grow. A knife gets sharp against a rock. You have to lose to understand what it takes to win. They were the same lines she'd trotted out for her clients, even for her sisters on occasion.

Talia needed something different. She

needed something she could whisper to her baby and believe. Mara had received her diagnosis at Talia's age. She'd persevered through university but her personal life had suffered. Romantic relationships were broken off before there could be talk of marriage, much less babies. Until Connor. He made her believe.

Except there was only one unstoppable Connor, and Dane might not have his uncle's singular capacity to ignite faith. Talia might have to depend on herself.

"Can I tell you a secret?" Mara said.

"Will it be one I can keep?"

"I hope so."

"Try me."

"I envy you," Mara said. "I would love to have a baby."

Talia pointed a half-made kebab at Mara. "At sixteen? With two hundred and fifty bucks to your name?"

"If that's how it happened. Because the circumstances for becoming a mother rank far below the fact of motherhood itself. Four months ago, when you first came to me, I didn't think I had it in me to be a mother. But now I'm reconsidering." Thanks to Connor.

Talia laid a hand over her bump. "I get what

you're saying, Ms. M. I should be thankful that I have the basics to raise a baby. And I am excited, a little. And if you and Dog Man work out, you'll be an auntie again."

If she and Connor worked out, if the test results were as expected, she could be an auntie—and mother.

CHAPTER THIRTEEN

"AND I SUPPOSE that's all there is to tell," Greg said to the assembled in the living room area of Mara's office. To emphasize her nonprofessional status, Mara had deliberately tucked herself into the far corner of the couch with Bridget sitting between her and Jack, who sat to the left of Greg. Talia, her parents and Krista formed the rest of the circle.

Mara strained her ears, especially toward Talia's parents. Nothing. If she hadn't known for a fact that they formed a largely gray mass before her, she might think they were absent. From Talia had come fidgets and tiny noises of disbelief.

Krista had vocalized the most, even though Mara had asked everyone to remain silent during Dr. Greg's testimonial. Her sister had gasped, said "wow" softly and clapped once.

Not surprisingly, Krista was the first to speak from her perch on the couch arm next to Mara. "Basically, we're all related in this room, one way or another."

"That's about the size of it," Jack said. He sounded ready to pop the cork and toast the glorious occasion.

"Wow. Wow. So…you're my cousin's father. Which makes you my uncle. You knew that I was your niece when you were my dentist?"

Krista's question mirrored Jack's. There was something about the invasion of the mouth that made Dr. Greg's secret more unnerving.

"Yes," he said, clearly opting again for minimal response.

"So all of you—" Krista gestured to Jack, Bridget, Mara "—have known for two whole months and not told me or Mom?" Their mom had agreed to take care of Isabella and Sofia, declaring she'd heard enough secrets in her lifetime.

"We wanted to," Bridget said, "but Dr. Greg preferred to wait for a bit." She didn't give the reason, leaving him an opening.

Their old dentist cleared his throat, stayed silent. If he was waiting for his ice-princess daughter to speak first, he might as well leave. Next to Krista, Talia said, "Ms. M said you guys are having babies in November."

"That's right," Krista said. "Two weeks apart." Krista cited their due dates and Talia gave an excited squawk. Talia smoothed her baggy top over her middle as she'd done with Mara. "My due date's right between yours."

Krista turned on Mara, her mouth in a perfect O. "You said at dinner that Connor hadn't mentioned any pregnancy. But you've seen her. You must've known."

Krista addressed the room. "Am I the only one in the room not to know this?"

"Yep," Bridget said.

"Is there anything else I should know? Mara? Any more secret babies?" Krista sounded half-serious.

"I am most definitely not pregnant."

"We'll have to get together," Krista said to Talia, "since we're—I don't know, cousins of some kind. Hey, I should order new T-shirts. Something about triplets, maybe—"

"Did Mom know about this?" Abigail's question tore across Krista's chatter.

Dr. Greg jerked. "I don't think so. If she did, she never let on."

"Of course she wouldn't," Mr. Shirazi said, speaking for the first time since his father-in-law had revealed his connection to Jack. "She had class and dignity."

"Yes," Dr. Greg said to his son-in-law. "I suspect that if she did know about…Jack's mother, she would've said nothing."

"Because she was a cold fish," Talia said.

"Talia," Abigail said sharply.

"She was, and you know it. I remember as a kid I wasn't allowed to touch anything. Remember the basket of toys? I had to play in one corner of the living room behind the couch. Or go outside. But only in the backyard, not the front in case I wrecked her flowers."

The dead opposite of Mara's mom and Auntie Penny. Toys were strewn from one end of the property to the other, girls shrieking from dawn to dusk. They'd gotten better with the toys when Mara had tripped over a croquet hoop and gashed her forehead on a nearby bat. "Even you were only tolerated, Mom. Remember how we couldn't visit for more than two hours?"

"Enough," Mr. Shirazi cut in. "You need to remember that she did nothing to dishonor you or our family."

"You mean like me, Dad?"

Talia was poking at her father, trying to

goad him into speaking. As much as Mara wanted to keep a low profile, she'd better say something before matters escalated. "I understand your frustration, Talia, but this might be a conversation for another time."

"You understand because I can talk to you," Talia said. "I can't talk to my parents because they won't talk to me. Isn't it usually teenagers who have trouble communicating?"

"This isn't you communicating," her father snapped. "This is you acting out. Indulging yourself as—" he stopped, then said in a firm voice, a judge passing verdict "—as you did in the past, Mr. Rasmussen. You've insulted us all by not keeping the matter to yourself."

"The matter? You talking about me?" Jack cut in, face-to-face with Mr. Shirazi. "For the record, I forced him to have this meeting. Our families are growing. Come November, we'll all be connected—Montgomerys, Holdstroms, Claverleys, Anheims, Rasmussens, Shirazis—"

"Don't lump my name with yours," Mr. Shirazi said.

"Too late," Jack said, just as sharply.

Mara realized she was content not to be here in her official capacity. She quite liked that Jack was tearing into Mr. Shirazi. Someone ought to take him on.

"You mean," Abigail said faintly, "this won't be kept secret? Among us?"

"I don't plan an announcement across social media, if that's what you're wondering," Jack said. "But it defeats the purpose of discovering my biological father to keep him a secret. If Talia enjoyed her grandfather, then why can't my children?"

"Because," Abigail said in a cold voice, "Talia is the real granddaughter. I am the real daughter. As are my sisters."

Bridget's hand dug into Jack's thigh "The fact I'm sitting here tells a different story," he ground out. "Sis." Beneath the surface harshness, Mara detected a questioning edge. It was the first time he would've called anyone that.

Abigail sucked in her breath. "Dad, do Leah and Ava know?"

"No," he said.

"Good. They don't need to," she said. "One of my sisters lives in another province, the other in a different country. It won't make any difference to them."

"Isn't it for them to decide if they want to meet their own brother?" Jack said.

"If Grandfather doesn't tell them," Talia said, "I will."

Mr. Shirazi stood. "Where has all the dignity gone in our culture? A secret is a secret for a reason. So that we can make a mistake, fix it and carry on without our lives being destroyed. So we have a chance to do better next time. You are the psychologist here, Ms. Montgomery. Is what I say not true?"

This was not about her. "I suppose it would depend on the secret," she hedged. Certainly, she didn't have any regrets about keeping the secret of her test from Connor.

"Your job is to keep secrets, isn't it? You help people with them and they go on to better lives. Is that not right?"

"I also coach them on the best way to open up about their secrets." How exactly would she open up to Connor on the off chance the results were not what she'd hoped?

"Like me and the baby," Talia said.

"You couldn't have kept that secret, anyway," her father said.

"You wished I'd chosen a way to keep it a secret," she answered, and turned away to say coolly to her newfound uncle, "I'm with you. It's always best to let go of secrets."

Mr. Shirazi grunted. "To what end?" To

his father-in-law, he said, "You have brought betrayal and disappointment and chaos to our family. I once respected you."

"I am truly sorry." Dr. Greg's voice was barely louder than the overhead fan.

"Too late now," Mr. Shirazi said. "This mistake cannot be fixed. Come, Abigail. We'll leave them to their little family reunion."

When Abigail reached the door, Mara wished again for sight because she thought Abigail turned to look back. With regret or disdain?

From the way Dr. Greg suddenly bowed his head, Mara assumed the latter.

"Wow," Krista said. "What now?"

Talia had an answer. "Would you like to come to my wedding?"

Daisy, off harness, greeted Connor at Mara's door, her tail brushing both sides of the entry hallway. "Hey, girl. Where's Mommy?"

Daisy made for the living room where Connor expected Mara to be. He didn't expect to catch her napping. He thought she'd be too keyed up from the day's events as related to him by Dane via Talia.

Earbuds in and eyes fluttering open, she lay curled on the couch under a throw. Connor couldn't resist. He drew her warm, sleep-heavy softness into his arms. Perfect.

He kissed the top of her head. "Hard day?"

Mara sighed. "As you probably heard. And then I had a tricky client afterwards. I'm beat."

"Too beat to lock the door?"

"I can listen to music and meditate for a bit, and you can come in without me moving an inch."

"Works for me." He could sit for the rest of his days here. In dog fashion, Daisy jumped onto the couch and draped her head and front paws across their laps, making it uncomfortable for everybody except her.

"Connor," Mara murmured, "are you ever without a dog?"

"Ha. Are you?"

"Thanks to you, not anymore." She cuddled tighter against him. Daisy butted her hand and Mara complied with petting. "But I might like to give it a try for a few days."

"Dog Man turns into Mara Man?"

Her hand, nails done in petal pink, stopped petting. "I really like the sound of that."

"I'll draw up new business cards."

She giggled, a delicious trickle. "Are you suggesting we go away for a few days?"

Alone together? Yes. There was Talia and Dane's wedding coming up in a couple of weeks, but after he could pay Dane to take care of the dogs, with Greg as backup. That would help Dane's financial crunch. But where could he safely take Mara?

"Wouldn't we bring Daisy, anyway?" Connor said.

"I can use my cane for a few days, and Daisy could stay at your place. Give her a few days off." She lifted her face to his, her blue eyes zipping back and forth as she planned.

He couldn't resist a kiss, and when her fingertips touched his cheek, it lasted for longer than he'd planned. They drew their mouths apart. "I thought you might be a mess. Dane said that the coming-out was pretty intense."

Her animated expression, so close he could see the details of the single small freckle on her left cheek, quieted. "It was. But I wasn't in the eye of the storm, so to speak. And I already knew Dr. Greg was Jack's father."

Yes, her secret and a professional one she had a right to keep, but it was one that involved him. "How long have you known?" he asked casually.

Inside his arms, she shrugged and said,

every bit as casually, "A couple of months, give or take."

Months? "I didn't have a clue."

"No. Do...do you feel I should've told you?"

Yes! "It's a professional confidentiality thing, isn't it? You couldn't have told me, right?"

"Right." She spoke carefully, like a witness in court.

Now was the time to act on the resolution he'd made after his conversation with Dane. No crowding, no pressuring, give her space, play it safe. "Then I guess you shouldn't have. I suppose we are pretty new in our relationship, so no, I guess I have no right to expect that you should. But just so you know, the wedding list has quadrupled."

"You're not angry with me?"

"No."

"Disappointed? Annoyed?"

"No and no."

"But you are feeling something?"

He was, and he had no right to feel it. She had done nothing wrong. "It's just that you're really good at keeping secrets, of keeping to yourself. I first called it independence but it's more than that. More than privacy. You burrow away from everyone." He tugged on the throw in playful demonstration. "I bet you've been doing that since you were a kid."

"What do you mean?"

Connor touched beside her right eye. "You kept your bad vision a secret for as long as you could. Am I right?"

"Yeah. Part of it wasn't intentional. I didn't even know what I was supposed to see. I remember playing catch with Krista and Bridget. I didn't know I was supposed to see the ball from the time it left their hand to it landing in my glove and not a split second before it beaned me on the head. Sometimes I don't say something because it's a secret. And sometimes I say nothing because I don't know that it matters."

"How about we make a deal? If it concerns you and me and how we operate, you tell me. Otherwise, it's at your discretion."

"Deal. Do you have secrets concerning us?"

Lots of teasing ones. Like how he pictured them six months from now, a year from now. Ten, twenty. But the fact that he was snuggling with her right now pretty much communicated how he'd framed their future. "I do find your talent at keeping secrets a little scary but since I just told you that, it's not a secret."

"Why do you find that scary?" Her expression was suddenly guarded, ready to duck into her old private world.

He squeezed her hard. "Because I like you this way, Mara. A lot. I like it when you're soft and open with me and there's nothing between us except this dog."

"I…I like us this way, too."

"So you don't like keeping secrets from me?"

"No."

"Are you keeping secrets now?"

"No."

"Are you lying to me?"

"No."

"But since I'll never know, I'll just have to trust you, right?"

"Yes."

Every answer quick and to his liking. Maybe his dog instincts were in overdrive, sensing reserve and tension that on the human level, didn't exist. Heel, Dog Man.

"I LIED TO HIM," Mara said to Daisy, raising her voice a notch. She was preparing salad in the kitchen while Daisy lounged on the living room sofa. "Straight to his face. You were there. And do you know the thing that worries me?" She started slicing the cucumber, gauging the thickness with her finger. She'd sliced so many this way that she could do it without thinking, which was a good thing, given her buzzing emotions. "I was good at it. He swallowed it. What does that say about me?"

Mara went to the shiny bulk of the stainless-steel fridge for the feta cheese. "What it says is exactly what he fears. I'm good at secrets, too good."

Back at her salad, Mara wondered if she'd remembered to put in the pecans. Forgetfulness had happened regularly in the days since Connor's evening visit. This was not the first self-chastisement Daisy had been subjected to.

Fingering through her salad in search of nuts, Mara pursued her monologue along a new line. "I feel that I have no choice but to play it out. If the results are negative, I can fudge the timelines. If they're positive, well, then I… I guess I'll…" She couldn't even voice to Daisy what that would mean.

"Hello?"

The female voice rose from the hallway. Daisy barked and scrambled to the front entrance. There was a muted groan from the visitor. "Mara? Hello? It's—"

Abigail. Mara mouthed the name as her visitor spoke it. Mara hurried from the kitchen to the hallway, Daisy between them. Abigail wore a light-colored top and matching pants. She held a dark gym bag.

"I'm sorry if I surprised you," Abigail said. "Your door was open and I heard…voices."

Mara had accidently not only left her front door unlocked, but open. Thankfully, Daisy had not wandered off. How much had Abigail heard Mara ramble on about her lies?

Daisy had not moved from between them, expecting a pat from the new arrival—the petting toll, as Connor said. Abigail didn't seem the type to pay up, studiously ignoring the wags of encouragement. "Come, Daisy," Mara said. "Away." And to Abigail, "Would you like something to drink?"

"I can't stay," Abigail said, though she entered anyway and followed Mara to the living room, likely surveying the place with her interior designer eye. Was the throw folded, the chip bag tossed? "I came to drop off a few of Talia's things. She said to bring them here."

Oh. Talia had moved out to Dane's place the day after the meeting. What must it have been like for Abigail to come home to find her daughter gone? She might be a stern mom, but she cared. She would not have sought help from Mara in the first place if she didn't.

But now Talia and her mom had taken Mara's helpfulness a step further and turned her home into a transfer station for the Shirazi family. Then again, they were technically family now in a weird, tangled way. Thank heavens Abigail had fired her, removing any professional conflict of interest. "I'll make sure she gets them. Please leave the bag on the coffee table."

Abigail hesitated and Mara stared hard at the table. Something must be on it she couldn't see. Abigail set the bag on the floor. The woman could demean without a single word. "I also added vitamins, though they weren't on her list."

"I'm sure she'll appreciate them."

Abigail seemed fixated by the metal-and-glass installation above her fireplace, so her next words sounded removed. "How are you so sure she appreciates anything I do for her?"

Talia's chief disagreement was with her father, not Abigail. Though really it seemed like picking your poison. "I think she knows she can count on you, which is its own kind of appreciation."

Abigail tilted her head, probably tracking the shifting light, as Mara liked to do. "It is difficult to be a good wife and a good mother."

Especially if your husband was Mr. Shirazi.

"How…how is she doing?" Abigail asked.

"I haven't seen her in a week. Connor says that she's adjusting well enough. Busy with wedding plans."

Abigail touched her temple. "Yes…the wedding. She hasn't asked…for help?"

Meaning had she asked for Abigail's help. It was hard enough being a mother. How much harder when denied the chance to act like one? "I am sorry about the state of things," Mara said, not sure if she was referring to her messy coffee table or their family. "I'm…trying out a salad for the wedding. Do you mind joining me in the kitchen?"

"It won't be catered?" She said it as if they planned to serve up popcorn and gumballs.

"Since it's relatively small and informal, the plan was for everyone to bring something."

"I see. Is the…new family attending?"

"Meaning me, my sisters and your brother?"

"Yes. My family," she said the last word dryly. Poor Abigail. Her daughter had moved out, her father was an adulterer, her newfound brother was quick-tempered, and one of her cousins was blind. She was not having a good week. Then again, neither was Jack, stung by the Shirazis' snobbery.

Mara tested the frying bacon with a fork. "Does Jack threaten who you are?"

"Of course not," Abigail said, her heels clicking on the tiled kitchen floor as she entered, but then she contradicted herself. "What does he want from me?"

Mara thought she best not root through the salad for pecans with Abigail watching. She didn't put it past her to send out health inspectors. She flipped the sizzling bacon instead. Mara said, "When Jack discovered he was related to Krista and me, he acted more like a brother than a cousin to us. I imagine Jack was thinking he could enjoy the same closeness with you and your sisters as he does with me and Krista."

"I don't want a brother," Abigail said.

"That's your business. If you change your mind, I can't recommend him highly enough." If she were sighted, she could stare down Abigail. As it was, she performed her own small act of rebellion and returned to hunting for pecans.

"I suppose it is…good," Abigail said, "for Talia that she can go through the same experience as your sisters together."

"Talia's cousins, I believe."

"The familial connections are rather convoluted. They will only get more so if your relationship with Dane's uncle proceeds."

If Abigail had considered that, probably every family member had. Whatever the future had in store for her and Connor, Talia's baby ensured that they'd always be part of one another's lives to some degree. "Quite possibly."

The bacon was plenty crisp. Mara slid the pan from the burner onto her wood cooling block…but it wasn't on the counter. She patted around for it. "Here," Abigail said, the familiar corner butting under her hand.

How humiliating. "Thanks. I could've moved it back onto a cold burner."

"Of course," Abigail said flatly. Mara felt the same snobbery Jack had experienced.

Daisy came into the kitchen, her nails clicking on the tiles. "No, you're not getting bacon," Mara said automatically. Connor had read both of them the riot act about not feeding Daisy human food, otherwise she'd be too distracted in grocery stores, restaurants, at events where food trucks parked, by debris on sidewalks—the list went on until Mara had interrupted him and promised. But it wasn't food Daisy wanted. She pressed past Mara and up to Abigail again for a pat. Abigail folded her hands behind her back. Mara finally clued in.

"When she's off harness, you can treat her like a normal dog," Mara said. "You can pet her. In fact, if you do, she'll go away."

"Well then." Abigail patted Daisy's head. Short, almost shy pets. "I should go. Thanks for getting the bag to Talia."

At the door, Mara said, "Hopefully I'll see you at the wedding."

Abigail made a stifled noise in her throat. "I'm afraid we won't be attending. My husband—" Abigail fluttered her fingers, her rings sparkling and shooting off rays of light.

"I see," Mara said.

"The dress…before Talia…went, she and I picked one out. It's getting altered. If I were to drop it off…"

"I will see that she gets it."

"I'll bring along the shoes and veil, a little one. She said she wasn't going to bother with bridesmaids, so I don't know if she can manage it all."

"She'll have lots of help," Mara said. "My sister is doing her hair and makeup. She's a professional."

Abigail nodded and left, her heels clipping along the walk, as if late for a business appointment. Mara leaned against the inside of the very firmly closed door.

"Daisy," Mara said, "you're part of one very mixed-up family."

CHAPTER FOURTEEN

"You'll be okay?" Connor said to Mara at the door to his house.

She could tell he was distracted, focused on returning to his truck to run errands ahead of the afternoon wedding ceremony.

"I'll be fine. In the kitchen the whole time. And I have Daisy." His goodbye kiss hadn't cooled on her lips before his truck tires were crunching over gravel.

The entire kitchen table had been prearranged with all the makings for the three different salads Mara had agreed to prepare. There was hardly room for the bottles of her homemade dressings.

It took a while to figure out where everything was, to sort the ingredients, to resist the temptation to sniff fresh cilantro and basil, by which time Daisy had flopped down and stood a dozen times, clearly unhappy about the lack of action.

Mara removed Daisy's harness. "Go." She

called out a warning against letting Daisy out, which was bounced from person to person, room to room, upstairs and down. Talk bubbled about her, popped up and floated overhead. Dane's school buddies messed with a computer and speakers, outbursts of music mashing with their boyish disagreements about what constituted romantic songs. Mara normally shrank from these kind of gatherings but this time it felt…doable. Maybe it was because she could help without feeling in the way. Maybe it was because Connor would be with her.

And maybe it was because it was a wedding.

Mara was stirring pecans into the first salad when two teenage girls, pencil thin in tight dresses, popped into her circle of vision. Light reflected off their glasses, their eyes wide and anxious. "You're Ms. M, right? It's Talia. Your sister has done her hair but she's crying. And we can't make her stop. Could you talk to her? Before your sister does her makeup?"

A block of window light cut through the room, setting off sparks among Mara's inner fireworks as she followed Talia's friends into the room. There was a shape of whiteness on the bed, and the chemical scent of hair spray and other lingering fruity smells. On a chair before the glint of the mirror sat Talia, breathing heavily, hiccuping.

"I'll be down in the kitchen," Krista said, shooing Talia's friends out ahead of her.

"Don't touch the pecans—or the chocolate," Mara said in automatic response to her sister's tendency to pick and lick at edibles.

Once they were alone, Talia said through hiccups, "Krista stuck her tongue out at you when she left."

"She did that because I knew that was exactly what she would do. I'll have to warn all those on cake duty. Otherwise you'll end up with a big finger swipe through the wedding cake."

Talia ejected a laugh, but the force dislodged more tears and her crying resumed. Without cane or Daisy, Mara managed the cluttered floor over to Talia, who was a clash in style between her T-shirt and shorts, and her hair abloom with curls. Mara touched Krista's creation, sticky and hard from the spray. Bright pins were arranged in a halo and her bangs swept softly across her temples.

"Your hair is gorgeous," Mara said.

"It's—it's straight out of a magazine Mom

showed me. She said it would suit me and—Mom's right." Fresh tears flowed.

Talia was missing her mom. Her management, her taste, her expertise. Abigail certainly had a knack for presenting the right face to the world.

Well, she wasn't Talia's mother, but she could be the best possible some kind of cousin. Mara thumbed away Talia's tears. "I am so sorry your mom isn't here."

"It's because of Dad. He won't forgive me. And Mom had to choose, and it wasn't me. I don't blame her. Dad isn't a bad person, despite…everything. I don't know what I'd do if I had to choose between Dane and the baby."

"I would hope that Dane would never put you in that position."

"I didn't think it was ever possible that Dad would do this. I knew he'd be angry and disappointed, but he's taking it out on Mom, too. It's not right."

It wasn't. If they were in her office, Mara could give Talia the space to shed tears and they could stitch together a way forward. But it was three hours from her wedding, and barring a last-minute miracle, her mother wouldn't appear.

"What would your mom say if she was here right now?" Mara said.

"She'd tell me to stop crying." Talia swiped at her face. "She'd lecture me about how it'll make my face puffy and my eyes bloodshot and my skin blotchy. And think of the pictures. I'd see myself like this for the rest of my life. But I wouldn't be crying if she were here."

"True," Mara said, "but she isn't."

"So you're telling me to suck it up?"

"No, I'm saying I'm here. And I'd be honored if you'd let me help any way I can. We are also backed by my very talented sister who is a professional at weddings, if you can keep her out of the kitchen. And your friends are here, too. That's quite a few people who want to give you your best day."

"My friends want to be biochemists. They've got no idea what to do with me and this." She gestured to her baby bump.

"So they came to me and found help for you. That's also what friends do."

Talia pressed her hands to her cheeks. "I'm such a mess."

Mara drew her arm around Talia's shoulders. "Here's a fact. Your mom is not here right now. But do you believe that she is thinking of you?"

"Yes, she must be. We bought the dress together, and she planned on being here."

"So you two are joined in thoughts and hopes for the future. This is an important day in your life, but there will be many more to come. We don't know that she won't be part of those."

Talia drew a deep, teary breath. "All right. Let's figure this out, then."

Mara called for Krista to return to the room to do makeup, while Mara made her way back to the kitchen to finish the salads.

As she passed the front door, she felt a breeze from outside. The front door was open. Daisy.

Mara called her name. Nothing. She hurried to the kitchen. "Has anyone seen Daisy?"

Answers flocked to her, nothing definitive. She stepped onto the front porch with the harness. "Daisy! Harness!"

Daisy wouldn't run off, not like Griffin. *Please, please not like Griffin.* On this of all days.

A scrabble of nails on the steps and Daisy was there, shoving her head into the harness opening, reporting for duty. Mara dropped to her knees in relief. "Good girl, good girl. Where were you?"

Daisy licked Mara's face and divulged nothing. Mara picked up a whiff of wood and fresh air and dog shampoo from Daisy's fur. Smells that could've come from all kinds of places. "Whatever. Don't worry your mommy like that again. And I won't tell Dog Man what happened."

Some things about your children, even your canine ones, both parents didn't need to know.

CONNOR WOULDN'T CHANGE his life for anything right now. The chatter and laughter of family and guests around him, a wedding successfully pulled off and now alone with Mara on the dark porch with its strings of lantern lights, slow dancing. She'd worn a light green dress of a material that was so airy he could feel the warmth of her skin, the curve of her ribs like his hands were on bare skin.

"Just you and me," he said. "No dogs."

"Daisy will give me a guilt trip when I get home," Mara said.

When he'd come back from his errands, Mara said she'd asked Greg to take Daisy back to her place. "I'm not putting her to good use," she'd said, and with ordered chaos spreading through house and yard, Connor didn't blame her. Besides, he then had the perfect excuse to stick close to her throughout the event. Which turned out to be a good thing for his own sake. Seeing Dane, awkward in his suit that had doubled for his graduation earlier in the summer, take on the responsibility of husband and father...well, Connor needed that tissue Mara had pressed into his suit pocket minutes before. "These things hit hard," she said. "Believe me."

She had brought her own tissues. Turned out that all the Montgomerys cried at weddings. Even Jack had swiped at his eyes.

Would they do the same at Mara's wedding?

He grazed his thumb across her bare ring finger. "Have you thought about your wedding?"

She tipped her head up to him. "Why do you ask?"

"Curiosity. Every girl dreams about their wedding, right? You must have some idea."

She hesitated. "Yellow. My sisters had yellow at their weddings. It was our favorite color when we were little, and we all agreed on yellow at our weddings."

He hadn't expected colors to be much of a priority. "Can you see... I mean you said that colors...?"

"No, I can't see yellow," she said. "The brain only keeps a visual memory of colors for seven years. Yellow slipped off my color palette about five years ago. Now I just have the memory of its warmth, its brightness."

"You'll have to get married before it fades altogether. To give new life to the memory."

"I require someone to marry first. Any suggestions?"

Oh man, she was flirting. He really, really didn't want to be anywhere else in the world. "I might have a few. When you were a girl, how did you picture the groom?"

"Back then, I continually swapped him out. My parents traveled a lot. Mexican, Puerto Rican, French, Romanian. He had many faces."

"Ever Irish?"

"Never."

"Were any into dogs?"

"Oh, yes. Dogs bounded about on vast estates. There was a vineyard, white sandy beaches and a private amusement park."

"I'm up against stiff competition."

"I didn't know I was going blind then. I'm not so particular anymore."

He didn't like what that implied about how she viewed herself or her potential grooms. "Are you saying your standards have dropped?"

"I'm just saying that I don't need vast estates, if I can't trust myself to hike them."

"A few acres will do?"

She pressed herself closer. "I have modified my dreams."

Modified always meant reducing. "You—you still have that crush on me?"

"It hasn't entirely gone away."

She made it sound as if it were a nagging rash, but the flirty edge was still there. It spurred him on. "I'm adopting Griffin out."

Her soft body tightened. "Griffin? But why?"

He trotted out the reasons he'd given to his sister. "His training couldn't be going better. The search-and-rescue organization wants him. They have a handler right in the mountains who can finish their training, and they're really short on dogs. They can secure funding to buy him. I'll take part in his backwoods and water rescue training, just a bit of upgrading there, and he's launched."

For the second time today, Mara looked ready to cry. "But he loves you."

Trust Mara to cut to the heart of his own misgivings. Connor was going to miss Griffin, more than all his other dogs put together. "He's grown on me, too. But I need to face facts."

"Facts?"

"That I run a business. That I need to make money."

"Don't you already make money?"

"I do…but not enough. Not for what I've got in mind."

"Upgrades to the kennels?"

"And family."

He hoped that one word would be enough of a hint to open Mara up, but she took it in a different direction.

"I've met with Abigail. My impression is that no matter how estranged they are with their daughter, they won't let her or their grandchild go without, if only from a sense of pride."

"And it might be Talia's pride that'll prevent her from taking it."

"Hopefully, her good sense as a mother will come before her pride. Griffin is your family, too."

"Part of what I like about Griffin is the reason I can't keep him. He's quick, stubborn,

independent...disobedient. He'll become unhappy if I don't let him realize his purpose."

"You'll break his heart."

"Mara, you're breaking mine with your
guilt trip. You know he's not happy unless
he's working. I think he ran from your place,
not to get back to me but to prove to all of us
that he's meant for bigger things."

Mara's eyes rose to the lantern lights. "You
might have a point."

"Anyway, it's not for a while yet. I'll make
sure you can say goodbye to him. But if I can
train more like him, it'll open up another rev-
enue stream."

"What has brought this on? You always
seemed content with where you are in life,
Dog Man."

"I was content. Now circumstances have
changed."

"Oh?"

How to express his feelings for her without coming across as pushy? "Well, I've got
a vacation to finance."

"We agreed to split expenses."

She had him there. "Well, I'm taking stock
of where I am and where I want to go."

She nibbled her bottom lip. Something he'd
like to do for her. "That's a fine ambition,

Connor. I admit that I'm also taking stock of my…assets. Testing myself."

"Testing? What do you mean?"

She played with his collar, her fingers skimming the opening at his throat. "I once said that I wouldn't have children. But lately, I've been wondering if…well, I have it in me. I'm thinking of testing out the theory."

He stepped back, rounded his hands on her slim shoulders. "Did you decide this on your own or because you felt I pressured you into it?"

She stroked a finger down his cheek. "Connor Flanagan, are you actually letting others make up their own minds?"

Her voice was teasing, but he answered her seriously. "I am."

She met his gaze. "Yes, I want this. I already told you that." Her blue eyes widened. "Don't you?"

A million times, yes. Connor felt his chest swell just like when the waterworks went off at the wedding. He couldn't say silent, as if he didn't care about her change of heart. He bit back a whoop of victory and went with calmer feedback. "I'd be happy to help with any testing."

She snuggled against him and his arms

wrapped automatically around her. "You'll be the first to know."

Connor let the music and noise drift them away. It wouldn't be much longer before the guests here would be assembling again, for another wedding, if he had anything to say about it. A yellow one.

THE ENVELOPE FROM the genetics clinic lay on the coffee table, next to the chess set; Krista and Bridget pressed on either side of Mara, her mother in the adjacent chair. Daisy paced, her nails clacking on the dining room floor. She was off harness but she'd picked up on the tension among the women and hung close to Mara, coming over to bump against her every so often.

Mara hadn't moved the envelope since its arrival the Monday after Talia's wedding. Her hands had shaken too much for her to open it. If the document inside was in Braille she couldn't have stilled her hands to read it.

She'd very nearly told Connor about the test at the wedding, even planted hints, but now she thanked her old instincts for secrets. The ordinariness of their relationship had been preserved, no looming question to trouble their time together. At least, for Connor.

"Ready when you are," Bridget said, their shoulders brushing, and Krista leaned in on the other side. Mara had expected them to chew her out for not telling them about the test, but their mother must've warned them not to. Or else one look at her and they'd decided that she was already about to dissolve.

Mara reached for the envelope, and her stomach heaved. She swallowed and passed it to Bridget. "Could you open it?"

"It seems a rather impersonal way to pass on the news," Bridget said, taking it. "Don't they do it face-to-face, like doctor results?"

"This is the way it's done," Mara said. "You can do what you want with the information."

"Bridget," Krista said through clamped teeth. "Do it."

The splitting open of the envelope by Bridget burst on her ears like fireworks. "There are two letters," Bridget reported. "One's in print. The other's in Braille."

"You read it," Mara said, her throat thick, courage utterly failing her. Bridget pressed against Mara. Her mother's face disappeared as she lowered her head, her hands clamped tightly between her knees. Krista was yogic deep breathing. They were like anxious family members in an emergency waiting room.

Bridget flipped through the enclosed sheets. "It's long. Lots of letters and numbers."

"No kidding," Krista snapped. "Did you think it would be in emojis? Get on with it."

"I'm trying to find the executive summary or something. Oh, wait here's the conclusion. 'Based on the current literature and well-established role of—' and then there's a list of a bunch of genes here, letters and numbers '—the clinical presentation of the genes—' okay, there's another long list of them '—is inherited in an autosomal recessive manner.'"

"What does that mean?"

"It means," their mom said in a muffled voice, her head still lowered, "that she inherited it because of mutated recessive genes on her parents' part. It doesn't tell us Mara's likelihood of passing it on."

"'The clinical presentation of the genes—' another list '—most likely explains compound homogeneity of the variants. The pattern of inheritance for children born to the patient is X-linked.'"

Their mother exhaled, a pained gasp, as if she'd broken a bone.

Krista clutched Mara's hand. "What? What?"

Their mother's head remained lowered. "It

means that Mara's sons would be affected and her daughters would run a fifty-fifty chance. At any rate, all the daughters will be carriers."

As if in mocking celebration of the news, sparks and swirls erupted in her vision. Her mind floated toward them, detaching from her sisters, mother, the white sheets of paper. *Take me away. Make me forget for a little while.*

She listened to their conversation as if from a distance. As if her soul had departed. Lights blazed and scribbled, spiraled and collided.

"But," Krista said, "how come I'm not a carrier? I'm female. And you are a carrier, Mom, but Dad didn't carry it. I don't get it."

"I've done a bit of research since Mara went for her test," their mother said. "I thought— I'd hoped it would be a recessive gene that wouldn't be inherited. There would only be a slim chance of X-linked. But your father's gene mutated in Mara."

"So I got the good genes and by horrible luck, Mara got Dad's bad ones."

"Yes, and because of the way she inherited them, she will pass them on to all of her children."

"But wouldn't Con—or whoever the father was—not have the gene, so their kids wouldn't get it?"

A dandelion rose, a round puffball of purple and blue lights. Held there. Perfect. A present to her alone.

"That's not the way the inherited genes work in this case. It's…it's just mean, horrible luck."

The puffball crumbled. Mara's hand tightened painfully in Krista's grasp. Bridget banded her arm around Mara's shoulders. "We can do a retest. They could be wrong."

Wrong? No. This festival of lights in her vision was wrong, yet they were real. Wrong, real, unlucky.

Daisy's collar rattled, the faint flapping of her ears as she shook her head. Her classic signal that she would like a movement break. Connor's gift and hope to her was right. Time to move on. Mara looked beyond the scattering remnants of her dandelion to the solid, dull shapes of her family. "No," Mara said. "No retest."

Her voice came out creaky and thick, as if she hadn't spoken in months. "Even if the results were different, they might also be wrong. No, it is done. I'm done."

Krista's grip eased but the pain lingered. "What—what will you do?"

Do? It was like the map of inherited genes, the clinical family tree, over which there was laid the flowchart of her life possibilities. If yes, the arrow points to Connor and family. If no, it points to—a different option. Nothing left to do but play it out.

"I do nothing," Mara said. "Nothing changes. I will be an aunt. I will not be a mother."

Through the whirling lights, she caught Bridget and her mother exchanging looks. "You think I'm selfish, that I could adopt."

Bridget hooked her dark hair behind her ear and looked squarely at Mara, her dark brown eyes inches from Mara's blues ones. "It's never selfish to want your own baby." She cupped her hand over her pregnancy bulge. "I'm a case in point."

Their mom leaned over and stroked her finger down Mara's cheek. "Adoption is its own path. You shouldn't feel forced to take it." She paused. "Are you going to tell Connor?"

Lights danced into vague forms. Perhaps they'd blaze his name across her vision. Shape into his face smiling onto hers at the wedding, just before his lips touched hers. "Yes," she said.

The lights configured into balls, like the lantern lights at the wedding. She could frame Connor's face below them, relive it all, when the possibility of a life together included blindness, but at least she could offer him a future with children of their own. But she had failed him and herself. Through no fault of her own, yet somehow that made the situation all the worse because she could do nothing to change the hard, hard truth.

"Thanks for coming," she said. "I'd like to be left alone now."

CHAPTER FIFTEEN

"I DON'T CARE. It doesn't matter."

Connor heard the little-boy petulance in his voice, but he couldn't help himself. Mara was the stubborn one. She wore a pale green shirt and pink denim shorts, the same pastel colors of that hard candy that showed up around Halloween wrapped in a clear plastic roll. Not a chocolate fan, he'd happily crunch through the sweet bits. Mara had the colors today, but nothing was sugarcoated.

"Of course it matters. I will never be a mother. This disease dies with me."

Connor turned away to the silver-blue glitter of the lake. He'd asked her to go fishing with him. During the summer, he kept his father's canoe roped in bushes along the bank and he'd pictured them together on the water, sunning themselves, laughing and talking, maybe even catching a fish. But she'd pulled back and asked instead to go on a Sunday walk. He'd agreed and the Labor Day crush of beachgoers had provided the perfect opportunity to still get her out to his own private beach.

It was within walking distance of the town but across a patch of rocky terrain, so he'd driven the few minutes there. A good thing, too. Even the descent from the parking spot at the adjacent campground had white-knuckled Mara, a couple-minute walk stretching into ten. He should've let her bring Daisy but he had assumed he could look after Mara well enough.

To think Mara's balance had been his only concern. Now that she'd delivered the news about her test, fear banged around inside him, hope chasing after it, like a father trying to catch hold of his tantrum-throwing kid. "Isn't that a bit melodramatic?"

Her face reddened around her sunglasses, but she answered coolly. "Are you saying I'm exaggerating my condition?"

Her calmness grated on his frustration. "I'm not. But look at yourself. You've taken your—your challenge and made the most of it. It's what we all do."

She scowled, her smooth forehead chopping into squiggly lines. "What we all do?"

"I realize your challenge is greater than

others. I admire you because you've over-come what would knock others down."

Her forehead lines fractured more. "Over-come? You overcome a mountain when you reach the top. You overcome a leaky roof by patching it. There's no fixing my blindness. It's deteriorating fast. I have overcome noth-ing."

She believed this. Worse, he was starting to believe her, too. The snake of her lies, con-ning him into accepting her pronouncement. "If you could see yourself—"

"But I can't, can I? I look in the mirror and I see the light off the mirror but my face is a blur, like the smudge from an eraser. I only know from memory that my shorts are mauve."

"Pink. Your shorts are pink." He squeezed his eyes shut at his involuntary correction.

She crossed her arms. "Well then," she said softly. "You've only proved my point. I haven't even overcome the challenge of dress-ing myself. Imagine the sartorial disaster I'd make of our infant."

A what kind of disaster? Never mind. "There are supports out there and more will come. And you'd have family around you."

"My family has made enough accommodations for me over the years. They shouldn't have to bend their lives even more out of shape to support my whim to have children."

"Daughters wouldn't be affected."

"Fifty-fifty aren't good odds when it comes to healthy children. Connor, listen. There is nothing you can say or do that'll change my mind. I will not pass my genes down."

At his feet, a ripple of water, brought on perhaps by a powerboat far out or wind or a twelve-pound whitefish, lapped over a rock at his feet, darkening it. The sun would soon dry it back to its original paleness. Dark, light. Action, reaction. Bad genes, no kids. "Would you consider adoption? If we were married?"

"Would you?"

He couldn't stand it if a single cold lab test broke them apart, broke her. "Yes! If we got together, we could still adopt. Or implant a donor egg or…something."

He could hear the insincerity in his words, and Mara sighed. "My limitations are mine alone. You are free to—" She turned away, to the glitter of the lake. "You are free."

"You're breaking up with me? Because you don't want to have children?"

"Because I don't want us to have blind children, and that's all I can give you. Blind or with the genetic power to make their off-spring so."

"You haven't answered my question about other options."

"Neither have you. And this is where you'd have to decide. Beyond jumping through hoops to permit a severely visually impaired parent to adopt or carry a baby, is that what you really want, Connor? Don't you in your heart want to father children of your own blood?"

He did. He'd ridden on her belief that her children would escape her disease. He had pictured their future with sighted kids. His challenge had been to convince Mara that she could mother them. But the kids themselves?

"Connor. If I were one of your dogs, would you allow me to mate?"

No way was she trapping him into an answer. "If my kids were blind, I'd care for them."

"Of course you would. But if you had the choice?"

He wasn't ready to answer that question. "Aren't we getting ahead of ourselves?" He sounded like a few of his old girlfriends scared off by his talk of children early on. He understood now how important it was to focus on the partner first.

Mara, too, looked out across the water in the direction of Griffin wading in the water. She would see him as a 3D shadow. "Isn't that what we're supposed to do? Right from the start, my disease placed our relationship out of the ordinary. We have to look ahead."

She was definitely doing that. Like the kicker in football who starts running from far back in order to send the ball forward the farthest distance.

From far back.

"Mara. When did you get the results?"

She slipped her hands into her front pockets, toed a rock. "Monday, but I didn't open the envelope until Thursday."

"But the test itself. You must've taken that before."

She turned to him, her eyes hidden behind her sunglasses. "I got in on a last-minute cancellation, a few days after my first trip to the grocery store with Daisy. I saw…a future for us, and I wanted it confirmed."

"So at the wedding, the test you mentioned…you already knew how things might work out."

"Yes. There was the possibility, but I'd honestly expected the results to go the other way. I didn't lie to you when I said that in the majority of cases of RP the children aren't affected. At the most, they are carriers."

He scanned the rocks at his feet for a flat, smooth one, good for skipping. Out of superstition, he launched one every time he came out here. The number of skips correlated to the general success of the day. He could really do with something to throw right about now. "So that would be after you swore you weren't keeping secrets that affected us?"

She licked her lips. "Yes."

Warm and cozy in his arms, she'd lied to him.

She took a small, tentative step toward him. "It was about us. But we're a new couple, so it was more about me. I needed to know first, to process the results whatever they were." She spoke so softly he could barely hear her above the slap of water on the rocks and Griffin's splashing. "And I also felt I was correcting a lie. Remember when I told you that it wasn't likely I'd pass it on? Then when we started dating, I felt responsible for having got your hopes up without verifying it first. And I didn't want to alarm you until I knew for certain."

"You hadn't wanted to get your hopes up, Mara. Mine were always up."

"I'm sorry," she said. "For not telling you. For the way things have turned out."

Even aware of her deception, he believed her. He always would believe in her. Except that the whole point of the exercise, of why he'd convinced her to take on Griffin and then Daisy, was to also make her believe in them. Maybe that had been his only purpose.

And he had made her believe in a future together. That was why she'd taken the test. Its results were disappointing, but they were more than genes. She must know this, and if she didn't, then time for him to tell her. He closed the distance between them, cupped her face with his hands. "I love you, Mara. All of you."

Her breath hitched and for a moment, he thought he'd won. She turned and kissed his palm, her lips staying there, so he felt as much as heard her next words. "I love you, too. That's why it won't work."

"I don't want to give up on us."

"But eventually, you'll have to," she said. "You need to find somebody else."

No. He pulled her to him, pillowed his cheek on her soft, vanilla-scented hair. "That's not possible."

"You've got a big heart, Connor." Her voice

was muffled against his chest. "You expect Griffin to attach himself to someone else. I'm sure you can, too."

"Gee, you keep telling me I'm not a dog. Now you're telling me to behave like one."

She breathed so deeply he felt her shoulders rise. "It's all my fault. I wanted that dream of us to become a reality so much that I denied the reality of my genes. I indulged myself, dragged you into it."

"If you have to lie, at least tell yourself the truth. There was no dragging. I bullied my way in."

"Okay, we'll say it was mutual." She pulled back. Her sunglasses were tilted from contact with his front, and she righted them. "Shall we say that it ends mutually, too?"

There had to be a way through this.

"But I love you." The repeated declaration sounded pathetic, like the condemned insisting on a different outcome when the ruling had already been made.

Mara, who could see straight into his soul, said, "And I love you. But that's not the problem, is it?"

He couldn't answer; he couldn't give in. He just needed time to think up a solution. "I'll take you home, but this isn't over."

She stepped back and gave a small, sad, knowing smile. "It is, but take the time to figure that out."

Turning to take her back home, he found the perfect skipping stone. He let loose with it. It must've hit the water wrong, because it sank straightaway.

"WHERE'S DOG MAN?" Sofia peeked around Mara's hug to look behind her.

So much for hoping that she wouldn't have to face her family about her breakup. She'd hoped that the fuss over Greg's official announcement party at the house might mask Connor's absence.

"He couldn't make it tonight, sweet pea," she said. "But I brought Daisy and homemade ice cream." She nodded at the wheeled cooler by her feet.

"Oh," Sofia said politely. "That's nice."

She was not so easily bought.

"I hear there are balloons."

That worked. Sofia herself trundled the cooler first over to the freezer to deposit the ice cream and then out to Jack at the barbecue to deliver the kebabs, before dragging Mara farther into the backyard to the finished gazebo where Bridget was stringing up balloons.

"It's covered in decorations. I wanted pink and purple but Isabella said those aren't man colors, and Auntie Krista said we could just ask him, and so now we have royal blue and silver and orange. See? These are the blue balloons and this is the blue streamer." Sofia did the effective but not subtle technique of placing Mara's hand directly on the objects.

Both girls had accepted Mara's vision loss as ordinary. If you could survive being orphaned in ruined Venezuela, then you could survive not being sighted in a rich country surrounded by family.

"Go get the napkins," Bridget ordered Sofia. "I left them on the kitchen counter. And you can bring out the flowers, too. Get Isabella's help." Sofia's feet pounded across the gazebo.

"Amigo, get out. You and Daisy can play later."

"I'll unharness Daisy," Mara said. "I can manage without her." She actually wasn't sure if she could. She'd begun to count on Connor to help her transition from one place to another in social settings.

"Where's Dog Man?" Bridget said to Mara when Sofia was gone.

"Connor couldn't make it tonight," Mara said. "What flowers did you go with?"

Bridget wasn't so easy to distract. "What do you mean he couldn't make it? This is the Montgomery family event of the year. When Jack's other father is officially welcomed into the family. Bigger than Christmas."

Mara pulled out a chair to sit, Daisy shuffling to make room. "I don't think it'll outdo this year's Christmas. Two new family members then."

"Three, remember? Anyway, quit trying to change the subject. There's nothing more tiresome right now than baby talk to someone seven months into the process. What was his lousy excuse?"

Mara ordered Daisy to sit to buy herself a moment to compose her reply. "We decided to take a break for now."

The ladder rattled and Mara pictured Bridget falling. "Bridge!"

"I'm fine. But Dog Man won't be. What do you mean by 'a break'? Is this because of the genetic test?"

"Yes and no. It was my idea, Bridge. He wants kids, and I don't. It's…nobody's fault."

"So…you two are done. Just like that?"

Harsh, unbelievable but—"Yes. There's no way around it."

"I'm sure there is, but here come the girls and oh geez, they're trying to carry all the flowers. Give me a moment."

Mara was rescued from any more Bridget moments by the man of the hour, Dr.—Uncle Greg followed by Krista and Will pulling in minutes later. Then their mother arrived. And Dane and Talia. The lull of the party broke into an excited storm, and questions about Dog Man were trumped by food and games. Dane and Talia would already know about the week-old breakup, anyway.

No one else asked about Connor's whereabouts. Bridget had probably spread the word, and Mara remembered to laugh in all the right places, participate in the conversation and always appear as if she'd rather not be anywhere else.

At some point after too much food, the empty lawn chair next to her creaked under a weight and there was a male groan. Uncle Greg. Daisy rose for a pat, Mara having taken her off harness.

Daisy's collar tags jingled as Uncle Greg

scratched her neck. "Taking good care of our Mara? Not letting her play in traffic?"

"She's amazing," Mara said. "I don't know why I worried about being her mother when it's her that takes care of me."

"Connor did a good job with her."

"Yes, he did." Mara didn't dare say anything more, afraid to gush about the man she no longer dated.

"I'm glad you two are together. Connor went through a rough patch a few years back."

It would seem Uncle Greg had not heard from Bridget, and Mara didn't have the heart to tell him herself. This was his night, when he shouldn't have to feel uncomfortable about what he said. "Yes, he told me. When he was with the RCMP."

"That's right, Connor told me a bit, here and there when we were working the dogs. I'm glad he started his business, but he got so attached to them, you never saw him without one." Uncle Greg's voice lowered. "Now that you're in his life, I think he won't need the dogs so much anymore."

Mara felt like a small bird had released in her chest, its wings beating around inside. She forced out a lie of omission.

"Thank you. Unfortunately, my disease means I will be the one always around a dog."

"I imagine that'll suit Connor."

She murmured a neutral reply.

"Greg-pa!" Jack called from where he stood on the lawn. "You up for croquet?"

Greg sighed. "Are they always on the move?"

"Always."

The chair creaked as Greg rose. "You know I live just a few blocks from you. You need anything, you be sure to call me. You're family now."

"I will," Mara said.

He still didn't move. "I mean it. I couldn't have had this—" Mara imagined that he was indicating the noisy backyard "—without you putting it all together."

"I will, I promise."

Greg moved off and Mara wondered if it was too early to leave. "Where are Krista and Will?" Jack called. "It's going to be dark in another hour. We need to do this."

"At the front," Mara said. "I'll go get them." Because if Krista and Will were playing in the back, she could rest on the front porch and not have to pretend for a little while.

She was coming up along the side of the

house with Daisy in harness, the same side where the ladder had leaned the long ago day Sofia had escaped on her, when she heard Krista and Will arguing. Those two never argued. Krista would bring something up and Will would say a word or two, or just smile, and all was well again.

But this time it was Will, not shouting but not staying quiet, either. "Because asking Mara to be godmother is rubbing it in, that's why."

"How can you possibly think that?"

"You said it yourself. After the test, she doesn't want to be a mother. Asking her to be godmother to our baby is like giving her a consolation prize."

"Did we feel that way when Keith and Dana asked us to be godparents to their baby girls? No. The same thing applies here. It's saying that we hold her in such high regard that we would give her the care of our child, if horses trampled us to death."

"But would we? We really going to call her to babysit? Leave her alone with the baby? If she doesn't trust herself, why should we?"

"Not when the baby's a baby. But there'll be a lot of years where Mara's blindness won't matter where they can walk and talk and play games and—and do normal stuff."

"I don't think she wants the responsibility is all I'm saying. Why can't we let her just be an aunt without added pressure?"

"Mara wouldn't see it as added pressure. It'll make her feel more like part of the family."

There was a pause, and Mara sensed exactly what was happening. Will was studying his wife, her unrestrained sister. "She already is part of the family," he said. "I don't know that we need to make her feel more."

She could pretend she hadn't heard. Shout out their names, or tiptoe back. Except the last thing she wanted was for Krista and Will to argue over her, especially when they were both right and both wrong.

She stepped into view of the front porch. "My ears are burning."

Krista gasped. "I didn't—"

"I know," Mara said. "Daisy, stairs. Stairs."

As Mara climbed the few stairs onto the porch, Will pulled a deck chair out for her. "Four steps or so ahead, Mara. One o'clock."

Will had been so nervous around her when they'd first met. She'd given him pointers and he adhered to them, as if any deviation might result in her immediate demise. She settled herself into the chair. A second chair scraped and Will sat across from her. Krista was already seated.

They were waiting for her to speak. To set them straight, to restore order. It had always been her role. Everyone turned to her for insight. A regular King Lear she was, who only when blinded could finally set his kingdom aright. Her family had cast her in a similar role, and she'd done nothing to dissuade them. She had trained to be a psychologist, compiling wisdom for the confused. "I hear you two can't decide whether or not to make me godmother."

"It's settled. Will has arguments that don't make sense. He says—well, you heard."

"His points are fair, Krista."

"They're based on fear."

"And what are yours based on?"

"Greed. I want you to have everything you can."

"Sounds more like love to me. Thank you, but I don't know that it's possible. Or even desirable."

"You should get something. You lose your sight. Which is rare. You can't have children that aren't affected some way. Which is rare.

You can't be in a good relationship because you can't give him the baby he wants, so he dumps you. Which is—okay, maybe not so rare. But it all stinks."

"Connor didn't dump me," Mara said. "If anything, I suggested it might be best."

"You broke up with him? Why would you let him get off so easy?"

"Krista," Will said warningly. "None of our business."

"Krista! Will! Mara!" Jack's voice ripped up the side of the house. "Get over here. We're waiting."

Right. "I forgot," Mara said. "Time for a courtly game of croquet."

Will snorted. "There'll only be peace if I let Jack win." His chair shot back. "Which isn't happening."

The deck floor vibrated through Mara's chair as he jogged down the stairs. Mara heard faint grit on the cement walk as he turned his heel back to her. "Mara, listen, about what you overheard me say—"

"You said in private to your wife and I eavesdropped. Your heart is always in the right place, Will. But that means it can't be everywhere, right?"

She sensed his smile and then he rounded

to the back. Krista reached over and hugged Mara. Krista had magical hands…and for those who got her hugs—well, Mara felt her entire body go to mush.

"I'm sorry I came on strong. It's just that you and Dog Man are good together. You two are the cutest couple out there."

"More than cuteness is required."

"You guys have that, too."

They did, but they also had an intractable problem.

"Look, do you want to be godmother to our child?"

Leave it to Krista to bite the bullet. "You both know that I will love your child—" Mara stopped, unable to go on. Not because tears clogged her throat or she lacked the word power to frame the rest of her thoughts. But there was love, and that, in all its inadequacies, was all she could give. She pulled herself together to finish, "As if she were my own."

Krista pressed Mara's hand between her own. "Okay," she said. "Here's what's going to happen. We need godparents, so you can't be godmother unless you're with Dog Man. When you two are back together, I'll ask both of you then."

Mara nodded, knowing full well that Krista

would never have reason to ask her again. But at least this way, she could let her hopelessly romantic little sister discover that for herself.

CHAPTER SIXTEEN

THREE TIMES CONNOR had picked up a pen to sign the sales contract for Griffin. Each time he'd made the mistake of looking down at his favorite, resting with his head on his paws, dozing, oblivious that his owner was set to ship him off for extra bucks.

Connor could justify his decision when his plans included building a family with Mara. What was the point now? He might as well not disrupt Griffin's life.

Or was it his own he didn't want to disrupt? He preferred to pretend that nothing had changed. Hope and delusion spoke the same lines.

He must find the strength to let go of Griffin—and Mara. He reached for his pen again.

"There you are," Kate said, stepping into the airy building. Griffin perked up, pushed open the pen gate to receive pats from Kate.

"You're all set up, I see." To make room for a nursery, Connor had moved his office out here, his desk now occupying the whelp-ing pen.

He had no intentions of breeding yet. If ever. Another dream for the trash heap. "It'll do. You coming or going?"

"Coming. I took longer than I planned. I finished at work but met Deidre Montgomery. She's pretty hyped about the new addition to the family. Dr. Greg. I guess there was a fam-ily dinner at Jack and Bridget's last week."

Mara's kebabs would've probably been there, too. He could taste the ginger and gar-lic marinade. She might've invited him—if they were still together.

"Deidre flat-out asked how you were bear-ing up without Mara."

"Why is it assumed that I'm the one suf-fering here, and not her?"

"I asked Deidre that myself, and she said her sympathies were with you, since she couldn't imagine life without Mara."

So at least one member of Mara's family was on his side. Not that there were sides. Leave it to Mara to break his heart with no one to blame. "Is what it is," Connor said.

"You've said that about twenty times this week. Your new motto?"

"It's a good one. You've used it yourself."

"Exactly. It's mine. I'm the pessimist. You're the ray of sunshine. That's how we play it. You can't have my role."

"Not a question of optimism or pessimism. I want kids, she doesn't. What's Dane's physics say? Two equal and opposite forces create balance. That's what is happening here. Balance."

"In your relationship? Or in you?"

Connor sat back in his chair, an old captain's chair of their dad's he couldn't bring himself to toss. "I don't see the difference. I can't picture life without kids. And I can't picture a life without her."

Kate angled through the gate. She pushed aside his contract and perched on his desk. Griffin moved off, ears perked to a distant sound. "All right, one time only. I'll be the optimist. First, do you love her?"

He knew where she was heading. "Yes, I love her and she loves me. But that doesn't solve our problem. In a way, it makes it worse because it's so hard to walk away."

"Maybe, maybe not. Love is a good start."

"Yes, but it doesn't end well."

Kate poked him in the shoulder. "You really got this pessimist shtick down."

"Learned from the master. You'll have to dig deeper."

She crossed her arms, stared him down the way two siblings barely a year apart could. For the first decade of his life, she beat the snot out of him, and a quarter century later, his muscles still involuntarily flexed when she gave him the stink eye. "How about you take stock of what you don't have?"

"All right, you got me. Shoot."

"You don't have an office indoors."

"This works fine. In fact, it's better because I'm literally closer to my business."

"You don't have a business with easy hours and a predictable income."

"At least it has an income, and a growing one, too."

"You don't have a brother or a dad to help you with the heavy lifting."

He could see her game. He couldn't help but turn everything into a positive. He was an obsessive optimist. "I've got Dane and Dad's old skid steer loader."

"You don't have any other animals besides dogs."

"I only want dogs."

"You don't have a house of your own."

"I prefer sharing a place, anyway."

"Last one. You don't have a woman who wants to have children with you."

A kick square in the gut. He couldn't find a way out of this one, but his cursed habit hunted for the silver lining.

"Yes, but—" He stopped. She raised her eyebrows, waiting. "Yes, but—" Nothing. He had nothing.

She shook her head. "Let me tell you something as your sister. Once in my life, I fell in love. Within months I was out of it. The lesson I learned was to understand what real love is. I learned by not having it. It's a crummy way to learn. I think Dane and Talia have what Jackson and I couldn't manage. I think you and Mara have it, too. Love doesn't solve problems. In your case, it might even complicate them. I have no idea how you and Mara will solve them. You two are backed into a real tight corner. But I can tell you one thing. When there's no love, there's no digging your way out."

"You're telling me to count myself lucky."

"Lucky. Blessed. Lightning-strikes-twice, lottery-win kind of lucky."

Kate hopped off the desk, the contract slipping to the floor. She picked it up, scanned it. "This about selling Griffin?"

"It is. I'd planned to use the money for—I don't know, to make plans with Mara."

"Sign it because there's another thing you don't have."

"What?"

"Time to waste."

MARA REGRETFULLY SPOONED the last of the mint cheesecake into her mouth. She couldn't justify staying for much longer at Penny's Restaurant, her whipped mocha coffee already nothing more than a sticky ring on the mug rim. She could order another dessert, but in the past couple of weeks she'd eaten far too many desserts at Jack and Bridget's restaurant. She couldn't stand the emptiness of her town house.

Daisy didn't mind coming, either. She happily lay at Mara's feet for the entire time, not once rising to ask for a change. Probably depressed about not seeing Connor. Extra pounds had gathered on the dog's stomach, and Mara suspected it wouldn't be long before padding appeared on hers as well.

"Daisy. I'm done here. Let's head for home." Silent, ordered, Connor-less home.

The restaurant door opened. A cool evening lake breeze drifted across to Mara and then the click of heels and the gliding of bracelets.

"Abigail." Daisy rose to her feet. "Sit, Daisy."

"You recognize me?"

Mara indicated her own wrist. "They're distinctive."

"Oh. I—I didn't realize they were so noisy."

"I don't think they are. My ears have become wired to pick up any noise. My sisters have called me Batwoman because I have developed echolocation." Why share these private details? Abigail probably already thought her batty enough. Except nervousness was rolling off Abigail, and Mara couldn't deny her instincts to set anxious people at ease.

"Oh. I see." A clatter of bracelets. "I mean, I understand. Do you mind if I sit for a bit?"

Had Jack spotted Abigail? He was working the front tonight, while the regular waiter took the evening off. Abigail had wandered into enemy territory. "Sure, but the place is about to close."

The chair opposite scraped on the floor as Abigail sat. "I won't stay long. I saw you through the window. I was out walking."

Out walking in heels? No, more likely she was driving by when she'd seen Mara enter. An hour ago. Had Abigail Shirazi sat in her vehicle for all that time before mustering the courage to enter?

"Can I get you anything?" Jack. None of his usual friendliness.

"A coffee, please. A decaf."

"We're out. We have decaf tea."

"Oh. Tea, then."

"Is that it?"

"Yes. No. I'll also have a dessert."

"Here's the dessert list. Do you need time to think?"

"Yes. No." The laminated list flapped back and forth in Abigail's hands. "I'll have the—the—"

Mara couldn't bear it anymore. "The mint cheesecake is delicious."

"Mint? I'm not—" Abigail sighed. "That sounds fine."

"I'll be right back," Jack said. "We close in forty minutes."

Jack left and Abigail swallowed loud enough for Mara to hear. "He's angry with me."

Livid, furious, enraged. "He's disappointed. He had hoped that when he discovered this whole other family we'd happily coexist. I reminded him that he'd gone in wanting to know his father, and he did gain that."

"You told him to ignore me." Abigail sounded defeated.

"No—I—" But she had. *Be glad for what you got, and leave it at that.* She wouldn't have blown off his emotions as a professional, yet she hadn't blinked an eye when it came to her own family. "I'm sorry. Was I wrong?"

"Not based on our last meeting. Talia told my sisters. They both plan to come out with their families for Christmas. To meet the—the baby. And Jack."

"That's good news, isn't it?"

Another audible swallow. "Not entirely. They have both made it clear—" Abigail's voice was distanced; perhaps she'd turned to the window "—that they are not coming to see me or Reza."

"Oh." If Abigail was half as close to her sisters as Mara was to hers, their rejection must be crushing.

"Unless I make peace with Jack. More than that. Make him feel welcome. And fix my relationship with my father."

"Except that will go against your husband's wishes."

Abigail's bracelets clunked against the tabletop. "I don't know what to do. What can I do?"

First Talia, then Dr. Greg and now Abigail, three generations voicing the same plea for answers. She'd told Talia to choose, accept that loss is built into it, and don't look back. She'd told Dr. Greg to try to have it all, but that was when she was riding the wave of a bright, shiny future with Connor. That advice hadn't worked out so well. What should she tell Abigail? She was certainly no expert. She'd made her choice with Connor and while she didn't regret it, her world had shrunk in the past two weeks. Her choices now lay between mint and praline. Her loss measured in sagging willpower and tightening waistbands. Not for her to send slim, trim Abigail down the same calorie-laden path.

Jack returned with the tea and cheesecake, and amid the quiet rattle of saucers and cups, Mara's mind raced.

"Jack," she said, "perhaps you'd like to sit with us for a moment?"

"Sorry, I'm closing up."

Mara reached out and caught the thick cotton of his apron. "Please, it's important."

Jack made a growling noise, spun a chair so its back faced the table and sat, arms across the top. The position looked friendly enough, but it kept him at a distance, one it was up to Mara to bridge.

"Abigail has something to say, Jack."

His half sister stammered the news about the Christmas visit and its conditions.

"That's pretty harsh," Jack said flatly.

"It could be said that I was likewise harsh with you," Abigail said. "I apologize for my behavior."

"Are you apologizing because you're sorry or because you're trying to make it up to your sisters?"

Abigail's teacup clattered in its saucer. "It's true I wouldn't be here if they hadn't given their ultimatum."

"Because you agree with your pigheaded husband."

"Jack," Mara said, "her husband is off-limits."

"Fine," he said. "I don't know what you want me to do, Abigail. I was open to getting to know you. But I don't particularly want to be around someone who doesn't like me. Because I have plenty of people who do." He stood, his shape looming over them. "That's my position, do with it what you will." The chair thudded back into place. "Drinks and desserts are on the house. For both of you."

So much for her effectiveness as a go-between. Abigail zipped opened her purse and there was the distinct snap of a crisp money bill. "As generous as his offer is, I'm not about to become indebted to him. I'll leave. I'm making everyone uncomfortable."

Mara couldn't let her go like this. "Abigail. Could I make an offer you might like? It's about your daughter."

Mara sensed the tension spike even more in Talia's mother. "Yes?"

"She missed having you at her wedding. If you two want, you can use my place to meet. Neutral and private, but homey."

Mara's hand was caught in a sudden squeeze. "Thank you," Abigail said, her voice choked. Was the Ice Queen about to cry? She turned her face away and released Mara's hand, and clicked her way out of the restaurant. If she was going to succumb to her emotions, it wouldn't be in front of her.

"Okay," Mara said to Daisy, "now we're definitely leaving."

"She didn't touch the cheesecake," Jack said, pulling into Abigail's vacant spot.

"Sorry, Daisy. I was wrong. Lie down." Daisy immediately dropped to the floor. She was really depressed. Mara decided to let

Abigail's dessert go to waist, and set it in the center of the table. "Abigail insisted on paying. You can put her fork to use, too."

They silently absorbed bites of cheesecake before Jack asked, "Do you know what she's going to do?"

"If I know anything about her, go home and not whisper a word of this conversation to her husband."

"More secrets, you mean?"

"Less conflict. In her mind."

"But in reality that's not the way it works." His voice had taken on a challenging edge.

"This is no longer about Abigail, is it?"

"We missed Dog Man at Greg-pa's get-together."

The cheesecake turned to chalk in her mouth. Perhaps there was such a thing as too much of a good thing. "What would you suggest I do?"

"I don't know," Jack said. "That's usually a question I ask myself. What would Mara do? If you don't know, I'm no help. All I know is that you've done a terrific job with the girls. I'd be the last to criticize you for not wanting kids considering you've put in time with them."

"You mistake me for your wife."

Jack's fork clattered to his plate. "Do you remember the first night I came to the house with the girls?"

"Not easy to forget." On the day of Auntie Penny's funeral, Jack had arrived unexpectedly on the doorstep of the house, his two adopted daughters in tow.

"You settled us in, found new toothbrushes for the girls, brushed their hair with your brush, made me feel at home when you didn't even know yet I was family."

"I did it for Bridget. She was too shell-shocked."

"The point is you kept us from becoming unglued. You still do. It's no small thing."

The glue, the go-between, the conciliator. All important roles, but not the one she'd played with dolls for. "I just wanted to be a mother to Connor's kids so badly," she whispered. The eternal fireworks in her vision became watery. She blinked furiously and the lights tumbled. Tines of a fork poked her skin. Jack.

"Hey," he said, "you mother us all. That's the truth. I hope you'll one day see how much it means to all of us. You're the Montgomery matriarch, even Auntie DeeDee knows that."

"It's not the same."

"No, it's not. But if you want me to throw in dirty diapers and two a.m. crying jags, I can arrange for that starting November."

Trust Jack to find a way to make her feel grateful for her miserable state. Abigail didn't know what she was missing out on.

But as she walked home in the crisp fall air, Daisy at her side, loneliness crept in again. Where did the matriarch, the fixer in the family, go when she was becoming unglued?

To an empty home to watch light she couldn't share with anyone.

CONNOR'S VOICE ON the phone jarred Mara, even though she was the one calling him. It was a disconnect between what it meant not quite three weeks ago and what it now signified.

"Mara? What's the matter?"

He had correctly read her silence as impending doom. "It's Daisy. She's not fat."

"Okay."

"She's pregnant."

The phone thudded and crackled, as if it had momentarily slipped from his hand. "You sure?"

"I took her to the vet. She hasn't been herself. Lethargic and putting on weight. I thought at first she was...was missing you."

"You could've called me as soon as she seemed off."

She should've, but to say what? *Come see my dog because I'm lonely for you.* "I didn't know, and she is my responsibility now."

"That doesn't mean—" He sighed. "Did the vet give a due date?"

"About a month from now, the third week in October."

"Which means that it happened a month or so ago." He groaned. "The wedding. We took her back to your place. She must've gotten out then. Can you remember if the door to the deck was left open?"

Mara wished she didn't have to say this next part. "No, it wasn't then. It was earlier in the day, when you were in town with Dane. Daisy wandered off on me. But she was back at the house not a half hour later. I didn't think anything had happened. She didn't seem different." What a stupid thing to say. Had she expected Daisy to return with her fur disheveled, the smell of Griffin on her collar?

"She wasn't due to cycle for another three months at the earliest. She must've gone into it fast. Shoot. I should've taken her as soon as you agreed to keep her, because what—three weeks or so later—she gets into trouble."

"With Griffin, right?"

"He's the only non-neutered male here," he clarified. "The two were inseparable."

"It's kind of sweet."

Connor grunted. "Say that when puppies are overrunning the place."

"Speaking of which, I had an ultrasound done."

"And?"

"Seven, maybe eight."

His breath came out with a hiss and a gasp, like she'd ripped off an adhesive.

"I thought you liked babies."

Silence. "I think we both know what I meant."

She did. "I'm sorry, Connor." Sorry about Daisy, about her silly joke, about her and her stupid genes. Sorry over and over again.

"Is what it is. Can I come by? To see Daisy?"

Very specifically not mentioning her. "Of course."

Twenty minutes later Mara was opening her door to him, Daisy barking her welcome, tail wagging. "This is the most animated she's been all week." The most animated she'd felt, too. She surreptitiously breathed the air around him. The fresh scent of soap and shaving cream, and damp hair. Had he taken a shower before coming?

She'd changed and touched up her makeup after all. The issue had never been their lack of attraction for each other but that she couldn't give him what he most wanted.

Connor had Daisy stand, and he felt her lower belly, his fingers gently prodding. "Definitely preggers. We need a plan."

We need a plan. The two of them together. "We're going to be puppy parents," she said. She meant to sound lighthearted, but it came out a little breathless.

"Technically, they're yours," Connor said.

Mara tried again for lightheartedness. "You and Griffin plan to be deadbeat dads?"

Connor laughed, and Mara's heart soared. "No. I was thinking about their care and training, and their sale."

Of course, of course they'd have to sell the puppies. Eventually. "Couldn't we just enjoy them?"

"We're going to be parents, time to prepare ourselves. Find homes for the puppies ahead of time. I have interested people and I'll put it on social media."

"Don't you want them? Given Griffin and

Daisy, the puppies will make great guide dogs or search-and-rescue. You had planned to breed them, anyway."

"Not to each other. There might be one or two at the most that would qualify for some kind of training. Even then, most of the dogs don't make the cut later on. Daisy is one of a kind. Griffin, too."

He was right. Anyway, there was no way she could care for Daisy's puppies. "I'll take her," Connor said. "Give her prenatal care. Part of my dad duty."

He might as well have said he was taking one of her vital organs. "But what will I do? I depend on her." She impulsively kissed Daisy's temple.

Daisy casually licked Mara's chin in return.

"Mara from four months ago would've never imagined saying that."

"Yes, well, a lot has happened since then."

She could feel him withdraw, his humor swept away from her like a forbidden toy into a drawer. "Yes. A lot has happened. And nothing at all, too."

He was still disappointed in her. And what of it? It was selfish of her to expect anything else.

"I suppose she's fine here for now," he said. "We could even set up some sort of whelping pen, if you don't mind your living room or office turned into a nursery. Then we can move her after. But there would be two, three months where she wouldn't be available. And then she'll need retraining before going back to you." He clicked his tongue against the roof of his mouth, not his usual one of thought but of self-disgust. "I really messed this up, Mara. I figured I had time. I should've been more cautious."

"And if you had been, I would not get to be Dog Mom." He snorted a soft laugh, and she took that as her cue to press on. "It might be good—for Daisy's sake—if I was still part of her life after the birth. I could put her in the harness for a few minutes, take her through the paces, so she doesn't lose her edge. I could socialize the puppies."

"You could. You'd have to visit my place a few times a week." Connor's voice had gone flat. "Weekends, too. To do a proper job."

"That's fine," Mara said. How she'd get out there, she'd no idea. Beg Jack. Ask Uncle Greg. He'd said to call him if she needed help. She could pay him back in desserts.

"I'll drive you in and out."

"You don't—" She stopped. What was she thinking? Time alone with Connor. Not as a couple, but for a little while longer, she could still breathe him in.

"Thank you. I'm looking forward to it," she said politely, her heart bouncing and tumbling like a puppy.

CHAPTER SEVENTEEN

"DAISY, YOU'VE NO idea how soft these are," Mara said, stroking the tiny sleeves of a onesie. "They're like your undercoat."

Driven in by her mom, Mara had brought Daisy with her into the large baby store in Red Deer where Talia and Dane had registered. Her mother had gone off to shop for scarves and shawls and outlandish hats at the secondhand store down the avenue. She said she'd be back in an hour or so. They'd entered the "or so" part forty minutes ago, but Mara didn't care. She could've wandered for hours. The good thing about baby stores was how much of the stuff was multisensory.

Still, she had to gauge from the tones what the different colors might be, and the indoor fluorescent lighting was no help. She'd ask at checkout. In the meantime, she folded all possible colors into her already stuffed dolly and aimed for the section with strollers. Connor and Kate had agreed to buy the car seat and stroller, but there was plenty more to cover. Perhaps she could pick up those fidget rings that clipped onto the stroller.

Acting on the directions the sales assistant had earlier breezed through, she and Daisy negotiated their way to where the strollers were parked in a squared-off space on the floor. The stroller accessories should be to the side somewhere. Hmm…she might have to go back to customer service.

She could make out a figure ahead, a man, she supposed from his height. She hoped he'd take the hint from her hold on Daisy's harness and give way. Instead, he remained unmoved.

"Ms. Montgomery."

Mr. Shirazi. What was he doing here? She felt herself coloring. While she was here, Abigail and Talia were having a clandestine meeting at Mara's place. Mr. Shirazi was supposed to be in Calgary at a convention. Secrets, secrets, secrets.

"Hello there." Mara didn't trust herself to say anything more until she'd sorted out who knew what.

He seemed at a loss for words, too. He was likely in the same boat, wondering what might reveal his hand, not realizing she already knew.

"I'm shopping for a few November arrivals. Hard to believe it's only a month away now," she said, leaving it open for him to comment.

Instead he altered his stance into a resting pose, as if expecting her to continue talking. "I understand the fidget rings are down this aisle." She meant for that to be a hint to let her, Daisy and the cart bump past him.

"Fidget rings?"

"You know, things for them to play with when they're in the stroller or car seat."

"Ah, yes. I saw them about halfway down. Here, let me show you."

Mara and her ensemble bumped and shuffled past protruding strollers, following the much more light-footed Mr. Shirazi. He stopped before a display of objects. "Here they are." Triumph marked his voice.

He liked to help, she realized. No, not quite. He liked to solve problems. He must miss doing math with Talia, discussing world crises. "Thank you," Mara said. "I'll let you get back to your shopping."

"I'm not shopping," he said quickly. "I'm only looking."

"Then back to your looking."

"Ah," he said and then again, lower and longer, like practicing notes. "Ah." She caught the glint of his wedding ring and a watch below his long sleeve. He wore a dark shirt and darker pants. Blue or brown, likely not gray. Maybe even green. Talia once joked her parents dressed like the queen might visit at any moment. "You've caught me out," he said. "I am shopping. Abigail mentioned that Talia had registered at this store."

"Is Abigail with you?" Mara said innocently, just to see what he would say.

"Ah. Ah. *Ah*." He rattled his keys in his pocket. "She thinks I'm in Calgary. I was supposed to be. But I got as far as Red Deer and I decided that…well, Abigail said that Dane's mother and uncle were buying some of the big items, but they are doing enough. I thought I'd do my fair share."

"I am sure it will be appreciated. Make sure that you have the items checked off the register, or they'll end up with two."

"Ah. Yes. Thank you." More rattling. "Since you are here, could I ask for your opinion?"

Now he wanted her opinion, but not when they were in her office. "Sure." She turned to follow Mr. Shirazi back. Daisy audibly sighed. She was missing her pregnant mom nap.

"Talia has requested this one," Mr. Shirazi

said, pointing to one of several strollers with a car seat, "but wouldn't this one suit their purposes more?"

He pulled out what she managed to catch in her vision was a three-wheeled stroller, ideal for all-terrain duty. Krista had crowed about its merits, using it to off-road her in-laws' newborns around the pastures. "In the snow, if she's in town or out...out there, it'll be more useful and easier for her."

It would be, but it was also pricier. Neither Talia nor Dane wanted to burden Connor and Kate with any more expenses, which was why they'd gone for the lower-priced model. And—"I don't believe the three-wheeler comes with a car seat."

"I could get both, no problem. Only, do I get them what they say they need or what I think they need?"

Mara lost her breath. Mr. Shirazi had worked out the essential difference for himself. "Abigail and I normally would make these decisions together. Only I've made things...difficult for her. And I hoped..." His voice trailed off. "I'd hoped to surprise her with this gift."

"You have to buy for two is what you're saying?"

"Yes."

"And you have two choices?"

"Ah! I see what you mean. I could get both. The grandparents will need a car seat, too."

"Yes," Mara said. "There needs to be a registry for grandparents."

Mr. Shirazi laughed. He had a rich, baritone laugh. Not as infectious as Connor's, but nice nonetheless. "And aunts."

"Especially triple aunties."

"Three? You are expecting three?"

"My sisters and Talia. She's family, too."

"Which makes us—"

She had no idea what that now made them in their relationship that had started months ago as the father paying the bill for his troubled daughter to talk to her. But it was interesting that he had acknowledged that there was a relationship. "Have you changed your mind about Talia's choice?"

"No." The thick rubber on the stroller wheels hummed on the linoleum as Mr. Shirazi rolled it back and forth, back and forth. "But she is my only child, and Abigail, she is my one and only, too. They were my choices, and I have not changed my mind about them. It follows that I must stand by them—and their choices."

Mr. Shirazi had worked through his problem then, in no small part due to the stubbornness of his wife and daughter. She left Mr. Shirazi instructing a store clerk to bring him this stroller and that one with the car seat—and could he perhaps look at the list to see what else was on there? His wife and daughter visiting in her home would be well pleased. Not that she would whisper a word. Let Mr. Shirazi surprise them.

Neither would she tell him that his wife and daughter were presently online shopping for a crib and bedding. Oh well, that's why return policies existed.

What were the chances she'd meet him here? Perhaps Jack was right. Perhaps she had the God-given talent for bringing families together. Aunt. Adviser to the Department of Gifts. Minister of Internal Montgomery and Related Affairs. Even Overseer of Dog Families. What was the saying? It takes an entire village to raise a child. In this case, it would take Mara in all her entirety to take care of her little family village.

Connor walked Griffin down to the same hidden spot he'd come with Mara when he'd imagined a romantic outing. Instead, they'd declared their love for each other and broken up. How ironic was that? Some people were just not meant to be together no matter how much they cared for each other, despite what Kate said.

Still, before coming out here, he'd stopped in at her place to check on Daisy. It wasn't necessary. Mara had already taken her to a prenatal visit at the vet two days earlier, but Connor felt responsible, as he'd told Mara. She'd tilted her cheek to him, listening, and he'd only barely resisted from kissing the soft curves, a temptation he'd indulged six weeks ago. She promised she'd relax with Daisy, hoped he had a great day enjoying this unseasonably warm weather in mid-October and would he give her best to Talia and Dane? She had him out the door before he could think of any way to delay his departure.

It was almost as if she knew that he had planned to ask her if she wanted to go fishing, a sport that depended on touch as much as anything. It wouldn't be a date, just two people hanging out with their dogs. Mara was right to hustle him away, though. They were nothing more than puppy parents.

He'd left his truck at Mara's. An excuse to see her again? The meetings at the youth center had restarted, but their stilted weekly contact wasn't cutting it. He didn't even get to drive her home now that she had Daisy.

"Heel," he ordered Griffin, who reluctantly complied. His dog for one more week. Then the search-and-rescue organization would take Griffin and finish training him. Today's session wasn't necessary, but Connor was struggling to let his bullheaded buddy go. And yet he had to. Of Griffin and Mara.

The instant Connor unclipped the leash at the secluded beach, Griffin tore in and out of the frigid water, shaking himself and plunging right back in. Griffin loved water. The outdoors, adventure, the next thing. He would thrive at being a hero.

"Come on, Griffin. Ready to work?"

Griffin whined and barked and twisted in paroxysms of anticipation. The plan was simple enough. He and Griffin would row out in the canoe, and Griffin would "rescue" a life jacket a few times, mostly to get him used to jumping in and out of a boat. He might also do a bit of endurance training, hooking Griffin to a line and having him drag Connor to shore. Maybe. Connor didn't have a neoprene suit to protect himself against the perpetually cold waters of Spirit Lake. Maybe they'd call it a day and go fishing after all. He had rods and tackle box already under the canoe.

Griffin balked at getting in the boat, and it was only because Connor was in there along with a treat that Griffin clambered aboard, only too happy to obey Connor's command to stay.

But he got his water legs soon enough. On his own he maneuvered to the prow of the boat, sniffing the air. Connor hoped for Griffin's sake that the day went well. Nothing made Griffin happier than getting what he came for.

Like dog, like owner. He'd come for Mara, wanted to rescue her and in the end, all she'd needed was a dog. The lake was an expanse of silvery glints, always changing. Yes, Mara would love fishing, if only to watch the play of light on water. He'd be temporarily blinded; she, stimulated.

When they were about fifty yards offshore, Connor tossed in the life jacket. "Help," he ordered Griffin. "Go get it. Go."

Griffin tensed and sprang, his body an arc, the long line unspooling through Connor's fingers. The life jacket was in Griffin's jaws a dozen doggy paddles later. He was a natural. Connor had him perform the task twice more. "Good enough, boy. Let's go fishing."

Maybe if he landed a good-sized whitefish, he could clean it and take it over to Mara's. She'd prepare something special, maybe invite him for supper.

And maybe he should get in his truck and go home.

Connor paddled farther out, a soaked, panting Griffin at the prow. He left Griffin's vest and the line on to get him used to the equipment.

Griffin tensed, his body rigid with attention. He barked and scrambled to Connor, swaying the boat. He bounded back to the prow, ears pricked, homing in on something.

"What do you see, Griffin-boy? What do you see?" Connor pulled in the oars and took Griffin's place at the prow. Twenty feet out, he spotted what had caught Griffin's attention. His blood went cold. As cold as the night his light had shone on the frozen baby.

Connor jumped into the water, swimming fast. Griffin barked and barked from the boat. Seven, six more strokes. Three, two.

He took hold of the baby, flipped the body over.

Glassy blue eyes stared up at him. Tiny painted lips. A doll.

He was an idiot. Of course it would be a

doll. A missing baby and every emergency re-
sponder would've been alerted. He would've
likely been one of the first.

Instead, his mind had fallen through time
to the baby he'd failed to rescue. Could never
have rescued. That baby was gone. Less sub-
stance than the waterlogged doll in his hand.
And yet he'd kept chasing the baby girl ever
since then.

He said to everyone, to Mara, that he
wanted his own babies. But now, treading
the cold waters of Spirit Lake, he understood
that what he had really wanted was the dead
baby back. Someone else's dead baby. He'd
carried a burden that had never been his.

His mind had understood that enough to
pull himself out of the bottle and launch a
business that gave his life purpose. But his
soul had still wanted a second chance to make
things right. And Mara had become that second chance. His love had come with expec-
tations that she couldn't fulfill. He had made
their love impossible and lost her.

On a wave of recrimination and sorrow,
he released the doll. Unexpectedly another
wave of emotion struck him. Peace. It flowed
through him, washing all away until it alone

filled him. As the doll drifted off farther, Connor turned and swam back to the canoe. He'd find the words to explain to Mara what had just happened. Let her know that all was well.

Griffin was beside himself with worry, the boat rocking from his pacing. A hand on the side of the canoe, Connor said, "Easy, boy. We're good."

Not good enough for Griffin, who launched himself into the water. The sudden sideways tilt combined with Connor's holding weight overturned the boat. At the same time that darkness fell around him, Connor heard the scrape of the fishing tackle box before it struck the back of his head.

Dizziness engulfed him. He flailed for the edge of the boat, his hand entangling Griffin's long line. Fighting unconsciousness, he ducked and swam out from under the capsized canoe and surfaced.

Griffin was right there, licking and licking, his long tongue flicking inside Connor's mouth.

Connor tried to focus, but his thoughts rippled away. Cold clenched around him. Okay, flip over the canoe, get in it. He fumbled for the curved edge, blinking. He couldn't see straight. And he was cold.

Griffin bumped around him, the line tightening around his fingers. More by touch than sight, water and sky and dog fur blurring, he gripped the line. "Back to land." It was a command he'd never practiced with Griffin.

Griffin wouldn't stop licking Connor's face. It helped to keep him conscious but that wouldn't last. They needed to get back to shore. He pushed Griffin's head in the direction of what he hoped was the shore. "Back. Back, Griffin. Go. Go."

Griffin finally understood and swam. "Good boy, good boy." Connor kicked his legs to ease Griffin's chore, but it was a poor effort. He concentrated on holding on to the line, his consciousness.

Nothing felt sweeter than the harsh scrape of his hands and chest on the shore rocks. Griffin didn't let up but dragged on, forcing Connor onto his knees. He crawled to the shore and collapsed. He couldn't go any farther.

Neither could he just lie here. Or could he? The warm sun penetrated his wet back. He could lie here and dry off, sleep a bit and carry on.

Griffin whined and licked Connor's cheek, nose, eyelids. "Griffin, stop."

Griffin didn't. His head swam. Sunlight sparked across his vison. Was this what Mara saw? Mara. He'd call her. Tell her everything was okay. His phone. Where was his phone? He needed to call her. Set things right.

He fell onto his back, stones pressing into his skull. Mara would come soon. She knew this was his special place. She loved him, had told him so right here. He pushed himself onto his elbow, Griffin still licking away. How much slobber could one dog have?

"Listen, Griffin. Listen." He grabbed hold of Griffin's ruff, their eyes inches apart. "You want to do this? Want to work? Work?" Griffin's body quivered with emotion. "You ready? Ready?"

Griffin's body bucked but Connor held on. Griffin tensed for the work order.

"Go home. Home."

Griffin was off like a bullet, streaking away. Connor gathered himself together and said one final time, "Home."

Home was a good seven miles away, but Griffin made it once before on his own. Connor just hoped it wouldn't take him two days.

CHAPTER EIGHTEEN

DAISY'S LETHARGY IN her last week of pregnancy had infected Mara. The two of them had retired to their small backyard, where Mara stretched out on the single lounge chair and Daisy occupied a shaded strip of deck.

Barking erupted from the front yard. Griffin. She sat up and slipped her feet into her sandals. Daisy barked once and scrambled down the narrow walkway between the town house and the fence, ornamental rock dislodging under her paws. She had no qualms about meeting her former beau.

Mara opted to approach through the balcony door, giving her time to retie her messy bun, tidy her shorts and T-shirt. She opened the door, her senses honed to take in the scent and shape of Connor. It was just Daisy and Griffin, twisting around each other in greeting.

"Griffin? Where's Connor?"

Griffin broke from Daisy and barked.

Barked and barked. As if calling for Connor to appear.

"Connor?" Mara called, listening. But it was just Griffin barking. His barking distanced as he ran to the public sidewalk. Mara followed. No Connor.

But his truck was there. He couldn't be far.

"Griffin, did you run away?" No, that didn't make sense. Connor was the one person he would run to.

Griffin did not let up on his barking, just as Connor had trained him during high alert situations. What was going on? She reached down to pet Griffin. His fur was damp. She barely touched his head before he bounced away with a bark, her fingers brushing against some sort of jacket he was wearing. She reached for him again and found his nylon long line. Also wet.

Dread prickled over her skin.

She made her way back to her lounger to her phone, Griffin barking away in the front yard.

She called Connor. It went immediately to voice mail. She called Talia, the only other person in Connor's household that she had a number for.

"Talia? Griffin has shown up on my doorstep without Connor. And I can't reach him on his phone. Do you know what's going on?"

"No. Dane and I, we're out for the day hiking. He hasn't called us, but we've been out of cell range. You only caught us because we stopped at Nordegg."

"This isn't normal, is it?" Mara said. "Do you think Connor's in trouble?"

"I don't know."

"Connor dropped by earlier. He had Griffin with him then. He said—" What had he said? She deliberately hadn't asked what he was doing, otherwise she'd obsess about him. She'd hurried him out the door because she couldn't handle being with him and not having him. And now she had no idea where he was. "Griffin's wet. He's wearing a vest and his leash is tied to it. It's all wet, too."

"The vest is used in water training and so is the line, but this doesn't sound right. Do you want me to call Kate and ask?"

But Kate, it turned out, wasn't picking up. "Do you want us to come back?" Talia asked.

Nordegg was a hamlet at least two hours away. By then, another plan of action needed to be in play. "No, stay there. It could be part of some training exercise, for all we know. Connor could show up any second."

Except she knew Griffin's bark. She had listened to it for months now. Today it held an extra stridency. Suddenly he jumped on her, barked in her face and then ran off a few paces.

He wanted her to follow him. Daisy was agitated, too, pushing between Griffin and Mara. Wanting attention, a walk, to do something. "I can't follow you, Griffin. Daisy already pulls enough."

Who to call? All her family was either working or busy or underage, and none of them could handle Griffin. Her phone rang. "Talia just called. She said you might need help."

The man she'd forgotten was family. "Uncle Greg. I could really use someone with dog-handling skills right about now."

A quarter of an hour later, he was gripping Griffin's long line, fully updated. "I'll go with Griffin." Griffin's claws were scraping the sidewalk as he strained on the line.

"Go. I'll call the police." Connor Flanagan's name would still mean something at the police department, despite his seven-year hiatus from the force.

She couldn't swear to the officer that this unusual situation meant Connor was in trouble, especially since this was not the first time Griffin had run away. And all officers had been called out to a multi-vehicle highway accident outside of town. They would follow up as soon as they could. What was the best number they could contact her at?

Which meant it might be minutes—or hours—before they might respond. Meanwhile, Connor could be lying injured, bleeding...in the water...alone. Mara gasped in fear. The fireworks in her vision exploded and she fought to see through them.

Mara ached to follow, only Uncle Greg and Griffin could cover ground faster if she stayed put. They were both sighted and if Connor really was in trouble, then every minute counted.

She needed to think, think! Where could he be?

"Connor Flanagan, you had better not be worrying me for nothing. You had better be on your very last breath."

What if he was?

She couldn't think like that. She loved him. He loved her. Out there on his private beach, he'd told her so.

His private beach. Connor had driven for only a few minutes from town to get there.

Griffin could've traveled that same distance if he'd gone by way of the lake, instead of taking the road. It would explain why he was wet.

She called Greg. The first time he didn't pick up and it rang five times on her second try before his voice came on the line. His breath came heavy, labored.

"It could be," he said, when she told him her idea. "Griffin has taken me to the far east end of the lake, and he's pulling me through water and brush. I got stuck in the mud. I'm not dressed for this, but—but Griffin's onto something."

"Can you take him back around to the road? And go from there?"

"I'm trying to, but he's dragging me this way. You know what he's like. I don't know the commands. I'll see what I can do."

And what could she do, other than wait alone, fear eating her up? She reached for Daisy's harness. "Girl, we've got to do something." At the door, she stopped. What could she possibly do?

She needed someone to drive there. Her phone rang.

"This is Abigail. I understand from Talia that Connor Flanagan might be in trouble."

It didn't matter she'd only called to allay Talia's fears. "Yes, he is. Could you give me a ride to where I think he might be? It's around the lake, the east side. I'm not sure where the exit is, exactly. There's a campground close by."

"We'll be there right away."

Mara was on the front step when a vehicle pulled up. She listened for the click of heels and bracelets, but instead she heard the footfall of a man's stride.

"Ms. Montgomery, would you follow me?" Mr. Shirazi. "Abigail is with me."

They had an SUV with wide leather seats in the back and a sunroof. "Thank you for coming. Your dad is already searching with Griffin."

Abigail must've turned in her seat because her voice shot straight at Mara. "Dad's out there?"

"Yes, he's coming along the lakeside but it's tough going. It's muddy…and Griffin's pulling him."

"I know the area you are talking about," Mr. Shirazi said. "A campground, right?"

"Yes."

"Then let's go find your Dog Man."

Her Dog Man.

If the Shirazis cringed to have dog hair or claw marks on their leather seats, they didn't let on. Instead they were largely silent as Mara told the story of Connor's disappearance in fits and bursts, Mr. Shirazi inserting pointed questions to straighten out Mara's muddled chronology.

At the campground parking lot, Mr. Shirazi asked, "Where to?"

"I'll check." Mara brought Daisy out of the SUV. And sniffed. The breeze was stronger today, but there was still the right kind of airiness from when Connor had parked here with her.

"He took me downhill, along a path. North of here. Do you see anything?"

"Not from here," Mr. Shirazi said. "I'll go down the hill and check."

"We need one that ends with a pile of rocks," Mara said. "I remember Connor tried to scare me by saying there were snakes."

"I'll ask at the camp station," Abigail said, moving off, her retreating step light and firm. Mara waited, Daisy pressed to her side. Abigail returned before her husband.

"They said there are a half dozen trails that lead off."

Lovely.

"I'm sure Reza will find the right one," Abigail said.

He returned to say he'd found a possible path, and should he take it?

Mara tightened her hold on the harness. "Yes, we're all going. Daisy and me, too." She wasn't going to be left behind when they were this close. "We'll keep up."

Mara sensed their hesitation but then Abigail sighed. "Lead the way, Reza."

Mr. Shirazi had picked the right path. It fit perfectly into Mara's memory and when they reached the rocks, she gave a small hoot. "From here Connor took me along a deer trail, through prickly grass."

"Ah yes. Here it is. Please follow."

"It turns down to the lake, and the beach is there."

"We are close then?" Abigail said from behind her.

"Yes. Within shouting distance."

At the same time, they both called.

"Connor!"

"Dad!"

They waited. And then from behind them and closer to the lake: "Abby-girl?"

Abigail gasped. "Dad! I'm here. We're here. Are you okay?"

"Yes! I've got Griffin."

The shouting had set Griffin off, the silence splintered by his barking. If Connor was close, he'd be calling out to them, too. If he could.

"Mr. Shirazi, please hurry."

They broke out onto the beach minutes later, the open lake breeze sweeping against Mara's face. Mr. Shirazi gave a sudden shout and began running from her. Abigail clutched Mara's arm. "It's Connor. He's here. On the ground."

Mara pulled away. "Follow!" she commanded Daisy, but her empathetic companion was already on the move to her fallen former owner.

Daisy halted and Mara registered licking. She heard a groan of annoyance. And pain.

"Mara?" Connor's voice was a whisper.

She dropped to her knees and shouldered Daisy away, her hand coming to rest on his chest. She felt for his face. Wetness.

"Connor. Is this water or blood? Are you okay? Are you hurt?"

Connor's hand took hold of her fluttering hand. "Mara," he whispered again, his brow pinching in pain.

"Yes, what? What?"

"Mara," he said again. "The doll...isn't coming back. And that's...okay."

He wasn't making sense. She dropped her head to his chest. Breathed him in, like when she told him she loved him. He smelled like his usual self...except wet. Shivers ran through him.

"Sure," she straightened, Abigail's worried face across from her. "That's okay."

"All's good," he slurred. "Going to nap now."

Then he turned his head and vomited onto Mara's lap.

ABIGAIL TOOK CHARGE of the situation. She ordered her husband to return to the campground and ask any camper he came across for sleeping bags, blankets, anything warm. Uncle Greg hovered close by with the dogs and called 911.

"I can call," Connor mumbled. "Where's my phone?"

Likely at the bottom of the lake.

"We need to get him out of these clothes," Abigail said from Connor's other side. She reached for Connor's shirt buttons but he weakly pushed against Abigail's hands. "I'm not having my niece's mother take off my clothes. Do it myself," he mumbled, his speech slurring. "I can't see is all. Got water in my eyes."

Abigail probed his head. "There's a bump on the back of his skull. He's got more than hypothermia, he's concussed. Connor, listen. Can you remember what happened?"

Connor's eyes drifted to Mara. "The baby died. 'S'okay. Nobody's fault."

She needed him rooted in the present. "I'll undress him," Mara said to Abigail, "and try to figure out what happened."

Connor groaned as she unbuttoned his shirt, exposing his bare chest to the mid-afternoon sun.

"I'm getting you out of your wet clothes, get you warmed up. Did you fall into the water?"

He looked to the lake as she unbuckled his jeans. "I guess so. I was with Griffin. Where's Griffin? Griffin?"

Connor hadn't shown this level of concern when Griffin really had gone missing. This anxiety wasn't Connor. "He's right there," Mara said, pointing to the blobby shapes of Uncle Greg and the dogs. "You were on the water with Griffin. And then you hit your head?"

She peeled his jeans past his hips, not easy given his deadweight.

"I don't know. I don't remember. Where's my phone? Where's my canoe?"

Uncle Greg appeared at his side. "It's okay, Connor. I can see it from here. We'll get it pulled in. You take it easy."

"Check for my phone."

He wouldn't let go of his fixation on the phone. He was disoriented. Mr. Shirazi and another camper arrived weighted down with blankets and sleeping bags.

Connor was slow-cooking under the layers when the emergency crews arrived. The fire department first and then the paramedics under police escort. She stepped to the side, and then her own shivering started. Shock.

Mara had never experienced this level of fear. Even when she'd first been diagnosed, she'd managed to work her way through the grief, the loss.

But again and again, as the paramedics plied Connor with questions that he fumbled, always circling back to his phone and boat, the same thought ran over and over through her head: *if I lose Connor, I don't know how I'll carry on.*

As the paramedics gave it their best shot to

get a straight chronology of events, Connor's anxiety darted into new territory. "Where's Mara?" Panic sharpened Connor's slurring.

"She's right here, Connor. She hasn't gone anywhere. You come with us and we'll check out that bump on your head." The other paramedic rose and spoke to a suited member of the fire department. Something about a backboard.

"I can't see her."

Mara took a few steps closer. "I'm right over here, Connor. We'll talk later. You go get yourself checked out, okay?"

"I can hear you," he said. "But the sun's in my eyes. I can't see you."

Mara wrapped her arms tight around herself to prevent herself from shoving her way to his side. "I'm here."

Two firefighters appeared alongside with the long shape of what Mara took to be the backboard. "Connor," she said, "you go with them, okay?"

Connor frowned. "Okay. Call me. I need to explain about the baby. I saw it in the water."

"A baby? What's he talking about?" The firefighters looked to the water.

"No, no," Mara said. "It's not a real one. I know what he's talking about."

A police officer stepped forward. "I know him from years back when he was with the force. She's right, it's something else."

"Connor, listen. I'll call you," Mara said, forcing herself to steady her shaking voice. "You go get yourself checked out, and I'll call you later."

"But I need my phone."

"There are phones at the hospital you can use," the paramedic said.

Connor frowned. "Okay, okay. Make sure. She'll wonder where I am."

When they got him secured into the back of the ambulance and then departed, sirens from all units blistering through the campground, panic surged through Mara.

Was that the last time she'd see him?

Abigail's arms came around her. "Come, let's get you home. You won't want to miss his call."

RETURNING FROM THEIR morning walk five days later, Mara released Daisy from her harness and went for a shower. She had two clients this morning and then an afternoon break before two more clients in the early evening.

She'd call Connor during her break. Make

sure he was resting according to the doctor's orders. He'd suffered a concussion, and was told not to move for a full week to ensure a complete recovery. Five days in, Connor's usual good humor had evaporated under his current confinement. Talia complained that if her baby inherited any of Connor's genes she and Dane were in for a traumatic parenthood.

Every bit of Mara wanted to see Connor, but not while he was recovering. She needed to talk to him, and she didn't want to rupture his bruised brain with what she had to say. She came out of the shower and rubbed her wet hair before wrapping it in a towel.

Through the open door, she heard faint panting. Daisy? She pulled on her housecoat as she made for the living room. Panting from the whelping pen, a technical term for what was in fact a plastic kid's wading pool.

Was she—

Mara carefully stepped into the pool. She'd laid down an old blanket and dog pee training pads already and Daisy was stretched out on them, her chest heaving. Mara skimmed her hand down to Daisy's lower belly. It was contracting.

Yes, she was.

Mara felt down Daisy's length to her hindquarters and past that. There was a warm wet bulge. The bulge swelled, wiggled and fully emerged. Daisy butted Mara out of the way in her eagerness to get to her firstborn. Loud, sloppy, vigorous licking ensued. Mara reached to see what was going on. The sac was disappearing and the umbilical cord—she needed to cut it. She retrieved the fully equipped diaper bag from under the coffee table, and took out the scissors, dipped them in alcohol.

Mara followed the mewling of the puppy, but couldn't locate the umbilical cord. Connor had said some bitches took care of the entire process themselves. Daisy was nudging the puppy to her belly. Right, latching. Mara managed to lift the damp, wriggling anxious arrival to one of Daisy's nipples and with a snuffle and a lap, the puppy was latched.

Mara collapsed back on her haunches.

This was happening. The vet had said to call if there were problems, which there didn't appear to be. Dane had already offered to help if Daisy went into labor before Connor was well enough to come. His phone went to voice mail. She called Talia.

"Is Dane there?"

"He's working. What's up?"

"It's Daisy. She's giving birth. One puppy has just come."

A shriek from Talia's end drilled into Mara's ear. "I'll be right over. No, wait. I have a doctor's appointment and I already canceled once. Grandpa will know what to do. No, wait, he's in Calgary with Mom." Her voice moved away from the phone. "Nothing! Nobody. Go lie down."

Connor's voice rumbled something about how he was not a dog, and could she answer his simple question.

"It's Mara, okay? Daisy's having her puppies and—wait! How did you know where I hid the keys?"

More rumbling.

"You're not allowed to drive. Here, talk to Mara at least."

Mara supposed Talia wanted her to talk sense into Connor but when he came on the line and said, "I'm coming, hold on," she replied, "Drive carefully."

She canceled her appointments for the day. Her last one of the day, a brand-new client, warned her that if she didn't get her priorities straight and show up as promised, she could forget ever seeing his business. She wished him luck and ended the call.

Connor would arrive in minutes, and she'd had no time to do her makeup and hair. Not that he was coming for her. Still, the occasion deserved celebrating.

So it was that when she opened her door to Connor, his attention went directly to her shirt. "'Double Auntie premiering November.'" He raised his gaze to her, smiling softly. "Seems appropriate somehow."

From behind her came a soft whine. Connor set his hands around her shoulders and turned her aside as he strode to the living room. His voice softened. "Hello, Mama. How you doing? You got yourself a little…a little…boy! Congratulations. Getting ready to have another one, I see."

Mara didn't know the effect his tender prattling had on Daisy, but it massaged her nerves.

"I've got the collars all ready," she said, reaching for the diaper bag. "Here, the darker ones are for the boys."

A collar slipped from her hand, his fingers brushing hers. It was their first contact since his accident. "How…how should we do this?"

Mara heard the brush of the collar as Connor wrapped it around the puppy's neck, then the plastic-y protest of the pool ring as Connor stumbled against it.

"Connor, you okay?"

"Uh...yeah. Just a little...dizzy."

She didn't need to tell him to lie down. He flopped onto her sofa. "I think," he said slowly, "the way we're going to do this is I'm going to lie here and tell you what to do. And yes, I'm okay. You got this, Mara."

His presence helped her to believe the lie. She set the scale on the coffee table so Connor need only turn his head to read the digital display, and weighed the firstborn.

"The number might be a little inflated," Connor said. "From the milk already in his tummy."

Right, she needed to be better prepared. The second puppy came and Daisy rose to lick the new arrival while Mara held the first against her chest for warmth and because she couldn't resist its damp, helpless cuteness. The licking done and Daisy resting again, Mara probed the lower parts of the latest arrival. "Uh, another boy," she called over her shoulder.

"Get me the collar bag," Connor said. "I'll weigh and band from the couch."

And that became their routine. As each

puppy arrived every thirty to forty minutes, Daisy licked them clean while Mara kept the other puppies warm. Once licked, the puppy was taken to Connor for weighing and a collar. Mara returned the newest arrival to one of Daisy's teats and relatched the others, and fed a treat of vitamins and minerals to Daisy.

"The first puppy is dry," Mara remarked after the fourth, the first female, had arrived. "What color is it?"

"Darker than most Labs, but still golden."

"And its eyes?"

"No idea," Connor said. "They're shut. They will be for the next week or two."

Mara hugged the little guy to her chest. "'S'okay. I'm blind, too."

She felt its ears. "I think they're going to be upright like Griffin's. What do you think?" She settled the puppy on Connor's chest, steadying it with her hand.

His hand covered hers, and his thumbs brushed the stubs that formed the puppy's ears. "You could be right. They'll have dark tips."

"Like Griffin's. And his tail? Does it have dark tips?"

"Yup. Not much there, but it's definitely darker than his body."

"He's perfect," she said.

"You saying the others aren't?" His voice was soft and teasing.

"I don't know," she said. "Tell me about them."

The others were just as perfect as the first. One had the trademark saddleback markings of a German shepherd, another was golden with floppy ears and another was patchy with an uncertain direction to its ears.

"Should we name them?" Mara said, propping herself against the couch seat, Connor stretched out above. The puppies were all nursing. Daisy was lightly panting in preparation for the fifth.

"Seems a little early to do that. We should wait until they're all born."

"Okay," Mara said. "We'll name the girls with a *D* and we'll name the boys with a *G*."

"We will, will we?" His voice was still deep and teasing, but inviting, too.

Mara's training had taught her how to broach difficult subjects and since his accident, she'd rehearsed entire conversations with him, always driving to the heart of the problem. Somehow the start had never occurred to her. She'd assumed a situation would arise where she could tell him and they'd go from there.

The middle of Daisy's whelping didn't at all seem like the right time. "We will, but you're right. Later. Sounds like her contractions are beginning again. I'd better get back to my station."

She began to move but Connor's hand caught her shoulder. His fingers glided down the bare skin of her throat. Then up to her ear, tracing its outer curve. She listened to his touch, the watery echo of skin against skin amplified.

"We need to talk. Soon." His words floated about her.

"Yes."

His hand slipped away, and she moved off to help Daisy.

The fifth was a female, the lightest so far at thirteen point eleven ounces. She even felt less substantial, her heart ready to burst through her chicken-bone chest. Mara lined her up with the teat. "C'mon, little one. Drink."

But she didn't latch, her jaws lying limp around Daisy's full teat. "Connor. She won't drink. Or she can't drink. What should I do?"

Connor didn't bother with instructions. He

rose and knelt beside her and worked on the puppy, while she stroked Daisy's head, telling her over and over again that everything was all right, what an awesome mother she was, to rest and not to worry.

"She wants to do it," Connor said. "That's not the problem. It's like she doesn't have the strength. I'm squirting milk straight in and stroking her throat to get her to swallow."

"Is there anything I can do?"

"You're doing it. Keep Daisy calm. She knows something's up."

Daisy's head kept lifting to Connor, and Mara had to bring it back down, the effectiveness of her reassurances lessening the longer her latest arrival took to start suckling.

"There!" Connor said. "She's on. Making a mess of it, but she's doing it."

"You hear that?" Mara said to Daisy. "Your little girl is fine."

Daisy must've felt the singular pull of her puppy on her teat because her eyes closed in relaxation. Connor shifted up onto one knee and rested his cheek there as he stroked the puppy. He looked completely at peace.

Whatever they weren't or couldn't be outside of this whelping pool, she, too, was at peace with who they were inside it. Caregivers and lifesavers. She inched over and laid her head against his shoulder.

"Something happened on the lake. Before the accident." Connor's warm voice trickled into Mara's thoughts. "The baby that died when I was a cop, the one I told you about. I realized she was never coming back. I could have one, five, eight babies and she would've still been left to freeze to death."

He kept petting the tiny puppy, the ripple of his movement rising up to his shoulder where her cheek lay. "Sounds obvious, doesn't it?"

"It's pretty normal to hope our actions now will make up for what happened in the past. To do better."

"But giving up the woman I love isn't doing better, is it?"

"I haven't changed. At least, not medically. But there's something I have to tell you, too. I pegged you as a family man, Connor Flanagan. Defined you according to the one thing I feared I couldn't deliver on, and guess what? The test results proved me right. At least, that's what I thought.

"The day you called from the hospital, you tried to talk and I wouldn't let you, because I wasn't ready. Me, the psychologist, devoid of words. I reread the letter from the lab. All these letters and numbers to tell me what I wasn't. And I thought that meant I'm a lesser person."

She rushed on, her rehearsed lines scattering under the onslaught of her emotions. "But here's the thing, Connor. I've dealt with loss. I've lost people I loved, I've lost most of my vision and everything that vision brings. And I've handled it all fairly well. Until the day at the lake when I nearly lost you." Mara blinked against the morning light. "I figured out then what I should've known all along. There are things that you lose because they are taken from you and there are things you lose because you give them away. My vision was taken from me but I gave you away, Connor. And now, I'm taking you back and I'm not ever, ever letting you go because as good as Daisy is, there's no guide dog that can get me through a life without you in it, Connor Flanagan."

Connor's arm banded tight around her shoulder and he whispered against her temple. "Okay."

She turned to him, and his face filled her vision, nothing and nobody intruding. "That's it?"

He framed her face with his hands. She

could still feel the warmth of the tiny puppy on his palms, the scent of new, damp fur, and hear the mewling, snuffling grunts of the litter searching for warmth from one another, the comfort that they were not alone. "That's it."

They kissed, hands warming each other. Mara soaked in Connor—his muscles, his whispered words into her open mouth, his arms wrapped around her middle, pulling her flush to him. Her legs hooked around his middle, her hands raked through his hair, her breath came short and hard. His, too. They were panting.

They pulled apart at the same time and glanced down at Daisy. She was also panting, her chest heaving.

"Back to parenthood," Mara whispered.

His lips brushed hers one more time. "Back to us."

EPILOGUE

DAISY HAD ABSORBED her handler's excitement all morning. From the light of the spring morning when she'd awoken to their quiet breakfast, and then when she'd left to come back with the sister called Krista. Krista had not brought her baby which was a relief to Daisy's ears but a little sad, too, because a baby meant life and life was good.

It was Krista who dressed Mara. It was nothing like she'd ever worn before—long and filmy, and Daisy had to watch carefully to avoid stepping on it. Onto the harness, Krista attached a garland of flowers with a delicate scent. Bridget arrived and the sisters also dressed with skirts that cascaded down their legs but showed off glinty shoes with spikes. The voices of the three sisters rose and rebounded about the town house.

"Hard to believe how much our lives have changed in two years," Bridget said.

"Tell me about it," Krista said. "I've opened

a business, gotten married and am a mother to a seven-and-a-half month old."

"Almost the same here," Bridget said. "I managed to hold on to Auntie Penny's place with Jack, got married and, yep, a mother to a seven-month-old."

In the living room, Mara gazed at the giant metal-and-glass fixture. Daisy had often caught her looking there in quiet moments. She herself found the reflecting shine and patterns of light to be absorbing.

"I am not the same," Mara said, smoothing a hand down her dress. It had lots of glinty bits on the top part and then spirals of glints fell down the skirt and the sleeves. It matched the glint on the ring she'd worn for months now, since soon after they'd found Connor down at the beach with Griffin.

Daisy missed Griffin. As, now and again, she missed her puppies. Two still remained at Connor's place, and the others she'd see now and again on walks or the dog park.

Mara reached down and touched Daisy's head. "I'm not the same," she repeated. "I opened a business, yes. I am not married for a few more hours yet, and I didn't become a mother."

The sisters exchanged worried looks but

Mara smiled proudly. "Instead I became an insta-aunt to two girls and then a VIP aunt to three babies."

"A feat I've not pulled off yet," Bridget said. "Unless Krista has something to report."

Krista shook her curls. "Nothing yet, though Will has broached the subject. I said I suppose we need to start thinking about it and do you know what he says?"

Mara and Bridget shook their heads.

"That he'd talk to Jack and see what they could line up."

Bridget growled. She often did that but nothing ever came of it.

"Perhaps Connor and I should join the discussion," Mara said. "We are already quite busy as godparents to all three babies. This next rollout needs to be carefully paced."

That was true. On more than one occasion, all three babies had been dropped off for a short time with Mara and Connor. If napping happened, all was well. If it didn't… well, Daisy had taken refuge in the bathtub more than once to escape the mayhem. The boy baby was a regular howler and ear-puller.

"Are you sure?" Bridget said. "We appreciate all the help you give us. But don't let us take advantage of you."

Mara stretched her hands to them. "Please do. I just wanted to say how much I love—"

"Don't," Krista said. "You say it and I will cry, and then we all will. And my makeup has to last at least through the ceremony. C'mon, let's get you married."

That involved a car ride in the same vehicle that they'd gotten into when searching for Connor, except today the woman was driving. She smelled different, though she still wore clicking bracelets. They arrived at a building Daisy recognized from a few recent visits. Today, she and Mara stood at the entrance to a large room with an aisle like at the grocery store. People were seated in rows. Daisy caught glimpses of faces she knew. She forced herself to concentrate.

She had a job. Mara needed her.

The sisters proceeded in a line and reached the far end where Connor stood. It all fell into place. That was where she would take Mara. Always to Connor.

"Forward," Mara whispered, and Daisy obeyed.

It was terribly distracting. Most everybody that had ever patted her was gathered here. Now and again, she heard her name mentioned, but she maintained an even pace, not stepping on the dress.

Daisy brought Mara right to Connor, who stepped forward to stand before Mara.

"Sit," Mara said, releasing her harness. The command that Mara was, for the moment, safe.

Mara and Connor turned to each other. Their expressions held a tenderness reserved only for each other. Daisy had seen it loads of times.

It meant that they were at peace with themselves and each other.

From this day forth.

* * * * *

Get 4 FREE REWARDS!

We'll send you 2 FREE Books plus 2 FREE Mystery Gifts.

FREE
Value Over
$20

Both the **Love Inspired®** and **Love Inspired® Suspense** series feature compelling novels filled with inspirational romance, faith, forgiveness, and hope.

YES! Please send me 2 FREE novels from the Love Inspired or Love Inspired Suspense series and my 2 FREE gifts (gifts are worth about $10 retail). After receiving them, if I don't wish to receive any more books, I can return the shipping statement marked "cancel." If I don't cancel, I will receive 6 brand-new Love Inspired Larger-Print books or Love Inspired Suspense Larger-Print books every month and be billed just $5.99 each in the U.S. or $6.24 each in Canada. That is a savings of at least 17% off the cover price. It's quite a bargain! Shipping and handling is just 50¢ per book in the U.S. and $1.25 per book in Canada.* I understand that accepting the 2 free books and gifts places me under no obligation to buy anything. I can always return a shipment and cancel at any time. The free books and gifts are mine to keep no matter what I decide.

Choose one: ☐ **Love Inspired**
Larger-Print
(122/322 IDN GNWC)

☐ **Love Inspired Suspense**
Larger-Print
(107/307 IDN GNWN)

Name (please print)

Address   Apt. #

City   State/Province   Zip/Postal Code

Email: Please check this box ☐ if you would like to receive newsletters and promotional emails from Harlequin Enterprises ULC and its affiliates. You can unsubscribe anytime.

Mail to the **Harlequin Reader Service:**
IN U.S.A.: P.O. Box 1341, Buffalo, NY 14240-8531
IN CANADA: P.O. Box 603, Fort Erie, Ontario L2A 5X3

Want to try 2 free books from another series? Call 1-800-873-8635 or visit www.ReaderService.com.

LIRLIS22

Get 4 FREE REWARDS!

We'll send you 2 FREE Books plus 2 FREE Mystery Gifts.

FREE Value Over **$20**

Both the **Harlequin® Special Edition** and **Harlequin® Heartwarming™** series feature compelling novels filled with stories of love and strength where the bonds of friendship, family and community unite.

COUNTRY LEGACY COLLECTION

19 FREE BOOKS IN ALL!

Cowboys, adventure and romance await you in this new collection! Enjoy superb reading all year long with books by bestselling authors like Diana Palmer, Sasha Summers and Marie Ferrarella!

#419 RECLAIMING THE RANCHER'S SON
Jade Valley, Wyoming • by Trish Milburn

Rancher Evan Olsen lost everything, including his son, in his divorce. Now he wants to be left alone. But when a snowstorm traps him with cheerful Maya Pine, he might discover she's just what he needs.

#420 HILL COUNTRY PROMISE
Truly Texas • by Kit Hawthorne

Eliana Ramirez is optimistic but unlucky in love. So is her best friend, Luke Mahan. Single and turning twenty-seven, they follow through on a marriage pact. Could their friendship be the perfect foundation for true love?

#421 THE MAYOR'S BABY SURPRISE
Butterfly Harbor Stories • by Anna J. Stewart

Mayor Gil Hamilton gets the surprise of his life...twice. When a baby is left at his door and when his political opponent, Leah Ellis, jumps in to help! Can a man driven by duty learn to value family above all?

#422 HER VETERINARIAN HERO
Little Lake Roseley • by Elizabeth Mowers

Veterinarian Tyler Elderman has all the companionship he needs in his German shepherd, Ranger. But when he meets widow Olivia Howard and her son, Micah, this closed-off vet might discover room in his heart for family.

HWCNM0322

Visit ReaderService.com Today!

As a valued member of the Harlequin Reader Service, you'll find these benefits and more at ReaderService.com:

- Try 2 free books from any series
- Access risk-free special offers
- View your account history & manage payments
- Browse the latest Bonus Bucks catalog